THE HOME-MAKER

THE
HOME-MAKER

BY
DOROTHY CANFIELD

Academy Chicago Publishers

©1924 by Harcourt Brace Jovanovich
Copyright renewed 1952 by Dorothy Canfield Fisher

Introduction ©1983 by Academy Chicago Publishers

Published in 1983 by arrangement with
Harcourt Brace Jovanovich

Reprinted in 1996 by
Academy Chicago Publishers
363 West Erie Street
Chicago, Illinois 60610

Printed and bound in the U.S.A.

Library of Congress Cataloging-in-Publication Data

Fisher, Dorothy Canfield, 1879–1958.
        The home-maker.
        Reprint. Originally published: New York:
Harcourt-Brace & Co., ©1924
        I. Title.
PS3511.I7416H6   1983   813'.52   83-6326

ISBN 0-89733-069-2 (pbk.)

Introduction

Although "role playing" may be a contemporary term, the ideas it encompasses are far from new.

When *The Home-Maker*, Dorothy Canfield's thirteenth novel, was first published in 1924 it evoked a mixed response, but very little of the criticism was harsh or outraged. American reviewers seemed to think Miss Canfield had attempted something unusual and ambitious; most of them thought she succeeded in what she tried to do. The *London Times*, on the other hand, advised Miss Canfield to return "to the thoughtful style of her earlier books. It would be better," the review exhorted, "for her to take to fairy tales, and let the lives of salesmen go unrecorded."

In the same year the novel appeared, Miss Canfield wrote an article for the *Los Angeles Examiner* on the subject of marital relations. It is written with the same feeling and common sense that the reader finds in the novel itself and we have reprinted it here in its entirety.

Dorothy Canfield was born in Lawrence, Kansas in 1879 and was graduated from Ohio State University; she earned a doctoral degree in Romance Languages at Columbia University.

She was married in 1907 to John Redwood Fisher and they divided their time between the Canfield farms in Vermont and travel abroad. They both grew so strongly attached to France that they took up active relief work there in 1916 and remained at it through the end of the war.

She published 22 works of fiction under the name Dorothy Canfield, and 18 works of non-fiction under the name Dorothy Canfield Fisher. She died in 1958.

For further information about her see *Dorothy Canfield Fisher, A Biography* by Ida H. Washington (Shelbourne VT: New England Press, 1982).

* * *

"Marital Relations"
by Dorothy Canfield

When people ask me (they will keep asking anyone and everyone) such questions as, "Should a girl marry young or wait till her character is formed?" "Should a married woman have a profession?" "When there is friction at home should married couples divorce, or try to rub along together?" I reply seriously, "I'll try to answer your question, if you'll first answer one of mine—How big is a house?"

This always brings an outraged or amused stare and the answer, "How foolish! What kind of a house?" Then I come back at them triumphantly, "What kind of a girl? What kind of a wife? What kind of a profession? Above all, what kind of a marriage?"

Any little girl would laugh in the face of a giver of good advice who told her solemnly that "Brown is the most becoming color for tailor-mades, and pale pink for evening dresses." Yet, grown-up little girls are expected to listen respectfully to aphorisms of exactly the same value, such as: "Wives should keep close track of their husbands' business so that they can give intelligent advice and sympathy," or, "Never bother your husband about his business, he has enough of that at his office. Make his home a place of rest."

What we ought to realize about marriage is, first of all, that, like every other human relationship, it is a problem that is never completely solved and settled, once and for all, until both parties are dead and buried. And secondly, that it is an intensely personal affair and that nobody on earth can know as much about it as the two people involved. Consequently, advice and pressure from the outside are always given on the basis of insufficient information, and have at least a fifty-fifty chance of being wrong.

If there is one single human relationship which more than any other cannot be run from the outside, it is the institution of marriage. There is no other which demands so inexorably from the people involved strength of character, intelligence and magnanimity, because, in the nature of things, the only strength of character, intelligence and magnanimity which can do married people any good is their own.

So that the best advice to give boys and girls about how to succeed in marriage is not to marry early or late, or to pick out blondes or brunettes, or to keep house or have a paid job; but to tell them from our hearts that the only thing that will help them to make a success of marriage is to grow up strong and wise and brave and gentle as possible, to use their own intelligence and to have the courage of their own convictions.

As a matter of fact, this won't do them any good, because, if they are wise enough to follow such advice, they will be wise enough not to need it. But we need not think, because there is no advice we can give them, that there is nothing we can do for them, once they are married. There is a priceless service we can, every one of us, render to married people, which, if conscientiously performed, would cure at least half the difficulties traditionally blamed on the institution of marriage.

What is this service? What could we do for them that would help them so greatly? We could let them alone; we could let them, without comment or blame, construct the sort of marriage which fits their particular case, rather than the sort which fits our ideas. We could leave them to struggle with a problem which, under the best circumstances, requires all their intelligence to solve, without crushing them under the weight of half-baked certainties and misquotations, such as: "No woman can be self-respecting if she is not a wage-earner." ... "A woman's place is the home, or there is no home." ... "No one can take the mother's place with children." ... "The care and education of children should be in the hands of experts, not of untrained girls who happen to be mothers."

Havelock Ellis says that married people should not live too much together; routine smothers love. Robert Herrick says that husband and wife should not be separated because people drift apart so easily.

We could allow, without adverse comment, a married woman to be a business woman, if that is the sort of person she is, and if she and her husband can bring their children up to be as happy and well-developed as the average of other children. (Bearing firmly in our minds that mothers in the home are by no means invariably and wholly successful in that job.) On the other hand, without sneering at her as an economic parasite, we could allow her to stay at home in what Zona Gale well calls the unpaid profession of housekeeping, if that is what she does best.

We could realize that every human being is different from every other, and hence each couple of human beings is different from every other couple: and, within the limits of possibility and decency we could leave people free to construct the sort of marriage that is best for their particular combination.

Don't we do this already? We do not. Not by a long shot. We have certain fixed convictions about which we are as intolerant as Spanish inquisitors. A part of us have the fixed conviction that the proper pattern for a marriage is a house in a suburb, with a lawn in front, a furnace in the cellar, doilies on the polished dining-room table, and some car better than a Ford in the garage. This collection of objects is to be kept in order by a woman with long hair who spends most of her days in the home, and paid for by a man with short hair who lives most of his time out of it.

According to what we may call Section One of humanity, this is a successful marriage, and Section One penalizes any departure from it by vigorious disapprobation, by social ostracism, by hurting the children's feelings, by any low-down means it can lay its hands to.

Section Two of humanity, observing the tyranny of Section One, disapproves, *not of the tyranny* (although it thinks it does) but of the particular mold which Section One is trying to force on marriage. Section Two, therefore, shouts out loudly (it is less numerous than Section One, but has much more capacity for making a noise) that the only self-respecting combination for two modern human beings is for both of them to be short-haired and latch-keyed, and for both of them to work outside the home, leaving the children to specially trained experts, to pay whom the short-haired parents work in offices like decent Twentieth Century folk.

Is Section Two satisfied to try to rescue from the clutches of Section One those couples who are unhappy in the suburban pattern? Not in the least. They are deeply annoyed because there are plenty of people who can construct happiness within that pattern, and they ardently desire to convince such people that there is something the matter with them or they couldn't be contented. They start with the excellent advice, "Don't believe implicitly what your mother-in-law's elderly preacher tells you from the pulpit about the right way to manage your marriage," but without a comma they continue at the top of their voices, "Believe implicitly what *we* tell you in our advanced books and magazines about how to manage your marriage."

vii

There is not, so far as my ear can detect, even one small still voice to be heard, saying, "Don't believe implicitly what anybody tells you about how to manage your marriage. Use your own sense to see what kind of woman you are, what kind of man you have married, what is the best possible relationship attainable between you, what is the best sort of life you can arrange together out of the materials handed down to you by your ancestors and laid before you by the Twentieth Century in which you live."

Anybody who knows anything knows how delicate and exacting a matter it is to try to tune in harmony two human beings, almost constitutionally out of tune even with themselves, full of strange complicated weaknesses and unexpected beauties and strength. Add to that the element of children, each of whom brings a full equipment of strange unexplored possiblities, and any fool can see that no outside complications are needed to make the problem a difficult one.

To try to unite, in one strong, healthful, happy, foward-sweeping current those diverse forces is enough of an undertaking for anybody. He ought not be required to spend part of his strength and time repelling people shouting in his ear, "No, no, that's not the way they'll do it a hundred years from now, so you're quite mistaken!" or "Our grandmothers didn't do it that way, so you must be wrong."

There is only one possible standard by which to judge any marriage. If a man and a woman manage to construct with their children a life-in-common which keeps them reasonably happy, healthy, good and strong, with a permanent affection for each other, they have made a successful marriage, no matter by which sort of pattern. And if they fail in this, their marriage has been more or less a failure.

—[Los Angeles *Examiner*, 1924]

THE HOME-MAKER

PART ONE

Chapter 1

I

SHE was scrubbing furiously at a line of grease spots which led from the stove towards the door to the dining-room. That was where Henry had held the platter tilted as he carried the steak in yesterday. And yet if she had warned him once about that, she had a thousand times! Warned him, and begged of him, and implored him to be careful. The children simply paid no attention to what she said. None. She might as well talk to the wind. *Hot* grease too! That soaked into the wood so. She would never get it clean.

She shook the surplus of water from her scrubbing-brush, sat back on her heels, sprinkled cleaning-powder on the bristles—the second can of cleaning-powder this month, and the price gone up so!—and setting her strong teeth hard, flew at the spots again, her whole body tense with determination.

A sober-faced little boy in clean gingham rompers,

with a dingy Teddy-bear in his arms, appeared at the door of the dining-room behind her, looked in cautiously, surveyed his mother's quivering, energetic back for an instant, and retreated silently without being seen.

She stopped, breathless, dipped her hand into the pail of hot soapy water, and brought out a hemmed, substantial floor-cloth, clean and whole.   When, with a quick twist, she had wrung this out, she wiped the suds from the floor and looked sharply at the place she had been scrubbing.

The grease spots still showed, implacably dark against the white wood about them.

Her face clouded, she gave a smothered exclamation and seized the scrubbing-brush again.

In the next room a bell tinkled.   The telephone! It always rang when it would bother her most.

She dropped her brush, stood up with one powerful thrust of her body, and went to wipe her hands on the roller-towel which hung, smooth and well-ironed, by the sink.

The bell rang again.   Exasperated by its unreasonableness, she darted across the dining-room and snatched the receiver from the hook.

"Yes, this is Mrs. Knapp."

. . . .

"Oh, it's you, Mattie."

. . . .

"Oh, all about as usual here, thank you. Helen has one of her awful colds, but not so I have to keep her at home. And Henry's upset again, that chronic trouble with his digestion. The doctor doesn't seem to do him any good."

. . . .

"No, my eczema is no worse. On my arm now."

. . . .

"How could I keep it perfectly quiet? I *have* to use it! You know I have everything to do. And anyhow I don't know that's it's any worse to use it. I keep it bandaged of course."

. . . .

"Oh, Stephen's well enough. He's never *sick,* you know. But into *every*thing! He drives me frantic when I'm flying around and trying to get the work done up; and I don't know what to do with him when he gets into those tantrums. It'll be an awful relief to me when he starts to school with the others. Perhaps the *teachers* can do something with him. I don't envy them."

. . . .

"Mercy, *no,* Mattie! How can you think of such a thing? I never can take the time for outings! I was right in the midst of scrubbing the kitchen floor when you rang up. I'm way behind in everything. I always am. There's not a room in the house that's fit to look at. And I've got to make some of those special health-flour biscuits for supper. The doctor said to keep trying them for Henry."

. . . .

"How can I go out more and rest more? You know what there is to do. *Somebody's* got to do it."

. . . .

"Yes, I know that's what the doctor keeps telling me. I'd just like to have him spend a day in my place and see how he thinks I could manage. Nobody understands! People talk as though I worked the way I do just to amuse myself. What *else* can I do? It's all got to be done, hasn't it?"

. . . .

"No, it's nice of you to suggest it, but I couldn't manage it. It would just waste your time to come round this way and stop. It's simply out of the question for me to think of going."

. . . .

"Well, thank you just the same. I appreciate your thinking of me. I'm sure I hope you have a lovely time."

An ominous silence in the house greeted her as she hung up the receiver and turned away. What could Stephen be up to, *now?* She had not heard a sound from him for some time. That was always alarming from Stephen.

"Stephen!" She called quickly and stood listening for an answer, her fine dark brows drawn together tensely.

The house waited emptily with her for the answer which did not come.

"Stephen!" she shouted, turning so that her voice would carry up the stairs.

"Tick-tick-tick-tick-tick-tick—" whispered the little mantelpiece clock hurriedly in the silence.

She was rarely quiet enough to hear that sound, but when it did come to her ears, it always said pressingly, "So much to do! So much to do! So much to do!"

She looked at it and frowned. Half-past two already! And that floor only half scrubbed. What possessed people to call you up on the telephone at all hours? Didn't anybody realize what she had to do!

"Stephen!" she called irritably, running upstairs. Was there anything more exasperating than to have a child not answer when you called? Helen and Henry had never *dreamed* of that when they had been his age. It was another one of his naughty tricks, a new one! He had a new one every day. And he always knew just when was the worst possible time to try one on. The water in her scrubbing pail was cooling off all the time and she had just filled up the reservoir of the kitchen stove with cold, so that she couldn't have another pailful of hot for an hour.

"Stephen!" The thought of the cooling water raised the heat of her resentment against the child.

She looked hastily into the spotless bathroom, the bedroom where Stephen's smooth white cot stood by his parents' bed, into Henry's little dormer-windowed cubby-hole—there! Henry had left his shoes in the middle of the floor again!—into Helen's room where a great bias fold in the badly made bed deepened the line between her eyes.

Still no Stephen. It was too much. With all she had to do, slaving day and night to keep the house nice for them all who never thought of appreciating it, never any rest or change, her hair getting thinner all the time, simply coming out by handfuls, and she had had such beautiful hair, so many things to do this afternoon while Mattie was out, enjoying herself, riding in a new car, and now everything stopped because of this naughty trick of Stephen's of not answering.

"Stephen!" she screamed, her face darkly flushed. "Tell me where you are this minute!"

In that tiny house he must be quite within earshot.

But the tiny house sent back not the faintest murmur of response. The echo of her screaming voice died away to a dead silence that closed in on her menacingly and laid on her feverish, angry heart the cold touch of terror.

Suppose that Stephen were not hiding from her! Suppose he had stepped out into the yard a moment and had been carried away. There had been those rough-looking men loitering in the streets yesterday —tramps from the railroad yards. . . . Oh, and the railroad yards so close! Mrs. Elmore's little Harry killed there by a freight-train. Or the river! Standing there in the dark upper hall, she saw Stephen's little hands clutching wildly at nothing and going down under that dreadful, cold, brown water. Stephen, her baby, her darling, the strongest and brightest of them all, her favorite. . . .

She flew down the stairs and out the front door into the icy February air, calling wildly: "Stephen! Stevie! Stevie, darling!"

But the dingy street was quite empty save for a grocer's wagon standing in front of one of the little clapboarded houses. She ran down to this and asked the boy driving it: "Have you seen Stephen since you turned into the street? You know, little Stephen Knapp?"

"No, I ain't seen him," said the boy, looking up and down the street with her.

A thin old woman came out on the front porch of the house next to the Knapp's.

"You haven't seen Stephen, have you, Mrs. Anderson?" called Stephen's mother.

"No, I haven't see him, Mrs. Knapp. I don't believe he'd go out this cold day. He's just hiding on you somewhere. Children will do that, if you let them. If he were *my* child, Mrs. Knapp, I'd cure him of that trick before he so much as started it— by the shingle method too! I never used to let *my* children get ahead of me. Once you let them get the start on you with some . . ."

Mrs. Knapp's anxious face reddened with resentment. She went back to her own house and shut the door behind her hard.

Inside she began a systematic search of every possible hiding place, racing from one to another, now hot with anger, now cold with fear, sick, sick with uncertainty. She did not call the child now. She hunted him out silently and swiftly.

But there was no Stephen in the house. He *must* have gone out! Even if he were safe, he would be chilled to the bone by this time! And suppose he were not safe! If only they didn't live in such an abominable part of the town, so near the railroad yards and the slums! Her anger dropped away. She forgot the barb planted in her vanity by old Mrs. Anderson. As she flung on her wraps, she was shivering from head to foot; she was nothing but loving, suffering, fearing motherhood. If she had seen her Stephen struggling in the arms of a dozen big hoodlums, she would have flown at them like a tigress, armed only with teeth and claws and her passionate heart.

Her hand on the doorknob, she thought of one last place she had not searched. The dark hole under the stairs. She turned to that and flung back the curtain.

Stephen was there, his Teddy-bear clutched in his arms, silent, his round face grim and hard, scowling defiantly at her.

II

When Mother was scrubbing a floor was always a good time for Stephen. She forgot all about you for a while. Oh, what a weight fell off from your shoulders when Mother forgot about you for a while! How perfectly lovely it was just to walk around in the bedroom and know she wouldn't come to the door any minute and look at you hard and say, "What are you doing, Stephen?" and add, "How *did* you get your rompers so dirty?"

Stephen stepped about and about in the room, silently, drawing long breaths. The bed, the floor, the bureau, everything looked different to you in the times when Mother forgot about you for a minute. It occurred to Stephen that maybe it was a rest to them, too, to have Mother forget about them and stop dusting and polishing and pushing them around. They *looked* sort of peaceful, the way he felt. He nodded his head to the bed and looked with sympathy at the bureau.

The lower drawer was a little open. There was something white showing. . . . Mother didn't allow you to open her bureau drawers, but that looked like . . . it *was!* He pulled the drawer open and snatched out his Teddy-bear . . . his dear, dear Teddy-bear. So *that* was where she had hidden it!

He sat down on the floor, holding the bear tightly in his arms, wave after wave of relief washing over him in a warm relaxing flood. All his life long, ever since he could remember, more than three years now, he had gone to sleep with his big Teddy in his arms. The sight of the faithful pointed face, like no other face, the friendly staring black eyes, the familiar feel of the dear, woolly body close to him—they were saturated with a thousand memories of peace, with a thousand associations of drowsy comfort and escape from trouble. Days when he had been punished and then shut, screaming furiously, into the bedroom to "cry it out," he had gone about blindly, feeling for Teddy through his tears, and, exhausted by his shrieking and kicking and anger, had often fallen asleep on the floor,

Teddy in his arms, exercising that mystic power of consolation. The groove in Stephen's brain was worn deep and true; Teddy meant quiet and rest and safety . . . and Stephen needed all he could get of those elements in his stormy little life, made up, so much of it, of fierce struggles against forces stronger than he.

The little boy sat on the floor of the quiet room, surrounded by the quiet furniture, resting itself visibly, and hugged his recovered treasure tightly to him, his round cheek pressed hard against the dingy white wool of the stuffed muzzle. He *loved* Teddy! He loved his Teddy! He was lost in unfathomable peace to have found him again. All the associations of tranquillity, the only tranquillity in Stephen's life, which had accumulated about Teddy, rose in impalpable clouds about the child. What the smell of incense and the murmur of prayers are to the believer, what the first whiffs of his pipe to the dog-tired woodsman, what a green-shaded lamp over a quiet study table to the scholar, all that and more was Teddy to Stephen. His energetic, pugnacious little face grew dreamy, his eyes wide and gentle. For a moment not only had Mother forgotten about him, but he had forgotten about Mother.

Was it only four days ago that this new bitter phase of Stephen's struggle for existence had come up? Mother had taken him to call on a lady. They

had walked and walked and walked, Stephen's short
legs twinkling fast beside Mother's long, strong
stride, his arm almost pulled out of the socket by
the firm grasp on his mittened hand by which she
drew him along at her pace. He had been breathless when they arrived, and filled with that ruffled,
irritable, nervous fatigue which walking with Mother
always gave him. Then, after long and intolerably
dull conversation, during which Stephen had been
obliged to "sit still and don't touch things," the
lady had showed them that hideous, pitiable, tragic
wreck, which she had said was a washed Teddy-
bear. "It suddenly occurred to me, Mrs. Knapp,
that the amount of dirt and microbes that creature
had been accumulating for two years must be beyond words. Molly drags it around on the floor,
as like as not. . . ."

"Yes, just like Stephen with his Teddy," Stephen's
mother said.

"And once I thought of it, it made me shudder.
So I just put it in the tub and washed it. You see
it came out all right."

She held up the dreadful remains, by one limp,
lumpy arm, and both the mothers looked at it with
interest and approval. Stephen's horror had been
unspeakable. If Mother did that to *his* Teddy . . .
his Teddy who was like a part of himself. . . . The
fierce fighting look had come into Stephen's eyes

and under the soft curves of rounded baby flesh he set his jaw.

But he had said nothing to Mother as they tore back across town, Mother in a hurry about getting her supper on time. Mother prided herself on never yet having set a meal on the table a single minute late. He said nothing, partly because he had no breath left over from his wild leaps from curb to paving and from paving to curb; and partly because he had not the slightest idea how to express the alarm, the bleeding grief, within him. Stephen's life so far had developed in him more capacity for screaming and kicking and biting than for analyzing and expressing his feelings in words.

That night Mother had taken Teddy away—treacherously, while Stephen was asleep. The next morning she announced that now she thought of the dirt and microbes on Teddy it made her shudder and as soon as she found time she would wash him and give him back to Stephen. Stephen had been filled with a silent frenzy every time he thought of it.

But now he had found Teddy, held him again in his arms that had ached for emptiness these three nights past. Stephen's hot little warrior's heart softened to love and quiet as he sat there; and presently there came to his calmer mind the plan to go to tell Mother about it. If he *told* her about it, maybe she wouldn't take Teddy away and spoil him.

He went downstairs to find Mother, his lower lip trembling a little with his hope and fear, as Mother had not seen it since Stephen was a little tiny baby. Nor did she see it this time.

He went to the kitchen door and looked in, and instantly knew through a thousand familiar channels that it would do no good to tell Mother, then—or ever. The kitchen was full, full to suffocation with waves of revolt, and exasperation, and haste, and furious determination, which clashed together in the air above that quivering, energetic figure kneeling on the floor. They beat savagely on the anxious face of the little boy. He recognized them from the many times he had felt them and drew back from them, an instant reflection of revolt and determination lurid on his own face. How could he have thought, even for a moment, of telling Mother!

He turned away clutching Teddy and looked about him wildly. All around him was the inexorable prison of his warm, clean, well-ordered home. No escape. No appeal. No way to protect what was dear to him! There fell upon him that most sickening and poisonous of human emotions, the sensation of utter helplessness before physical violence. Mother would take Teddy away and do whatever she pleased with him because she was stronger than Stephen. The brute forces of jungle life yelled loud in Stephen's ears and mocked at his helplessness.

But Stephen was no Henry or Helen to droop, to shrink and quail. He fled to his own refuge, the only one which left him a shred of human dignity: fierce, hopeless, endless resistance: the determination of every brave despairing heart confronted with hopeless odds, at least to sell his safety dear; to fight as long as his strength held out: never, never to surrender of his own accord. Over something priceless, over what made him Stephen, the little boy stood guard savagely with the only weapons he had.

First of all he would hide. He would hold Teddy in his arms as long as he could, and hide, and let Mother call to him all she wanted to, while he braced himself to endure with courage the tortures which would inevitably follow . . . the scolding which Mother called "talking to him," the beating invisible waves of fury flaming at him from all over Mother, which made Stephen suffer more than the physical blows which always ended things, for by the time they arrived he was usually so rigid with hysteria himself that he did not feel them much.

Under the stairs . . . she would not think of that for a long time. He crept in over the immaculately clean floor, drew the curtains back of him, and sat upright, cross-legged, holding Teddy to his breast with all his might, dry-eyed, scowling, a magnificent sulphurous conflagration of Promethean flames blazing in his little heart.

Chapter 2

WHEN Lester Knapp stepped dispiritedly out from Willing's Emporium, he felt, as he usually did, a thin little mittened hand slip into each of his.

"Hello, Father," said Helen.

"Hello, Father," said Henry.

"Hello, children," said Father, squeezing their hands up tightly and looking down into their upturned faces.

"How's tricks?" he asked, as they stepped off, his lagging step suddenly brisk. "What did the teacher say to that composition, Helen?"

"She said it was *fine!*" said the little girl eagerly. "She read it out to the class. She said maybe they'd get me to write the play for the entertainment our class is going to give, a history play, you know, something that would bring in Indians and the early settlers and the hiding regicides and what we've been studying. I wanted to ask you if you thought I could start it inside one of the houses, the night of an Indian attack, everybody loading muskets and barring the shutters and things, and the old hidden

23

regicide looking out through a crack to see where the Indians were."

"Oh, that would be *great!*" cried Henry admiringly, craning his neck around his father to listen. "What's a regicide?" Henry was three grades behind Helen in school and hadn't begun on history. His father and sister explained to him, both talking at once. And then they laughed to hear their words clashing together. They swung along rapidly, talking, laughing, interrupting each other, Henry constantly asking questions, the other two developing the imaginary scene, thrilling at the imaginary danger, loading imaginary muskets, their voices chiming out like bells in the cold evening air. Once in a while, Henry, who was small for his age, gave a little animated hop and skip to keep up with the others.

In front of the delicatessen-grocery store at the corner of their street, the father suddenly drew them to a halt. "What was it Mother asked me to bring home with me?" He spoke anxiously, and anxiously the children looked up at him. Suppose he should not be able to remember it!

But he did. It was a package of oatmeal and a yeast-cake. He dragged them triumphantly up from his memory.

They entered the shop and found Aunt Mattie Farham there, buying ginger cookies and potato salad and boiled ham. "My! I'm ashamed to have you Knapps catch me at this!" she protested with that Aunt Mattieish laugh of hers that meant that she wasn't really ashamed, or anything but cheerfully ready to make fun of herself. "It's not Evangeline Knapp who'd be buying delicatessen stuff for her family's supper at six o'clock at night! We went out in the new Buick this afternoon. . . . Oh, Lester, she's a dream, simply a *dream!* And we went further than we meant. You always do, you know. And of course, being me, there's not a thing in the house to eat. I put Frank and the children to setting the table while I tore over here. Don't you tell Evangeline on me, Lester. I tried to get her to go and take Stephen, but she wouldn't—had biscuits to make for supper and a floor to scrub or something. She *never* lets things go, as I do. She's a perfect wonder, Evangeline is, anyhow. An example to us all, I always tell 'em. After I've been in your house, I declare, I'm ashamed to set foot in my own!"

While the grocer wrapped up her purchases she stooped her fair smiling face towards Helen to say, "My gracious, honey, how swell we do look in our new coat! Where did Momma buy that for you?"

Helen looked down at it as if to see what coat it was, as if she had forgotten that she wore a coat. Then she said, "She made it, Mother made it, out of an old coat Gramma Houghton sent us. The collar and cuffs are off Cousin Celia's last-winter one."

Aunt Mattie was lost in admiration. She turned Helen around to get the effect of the back. "Well, your mother is the *wonder!*" she cried heartily, again. "I never saw anybody to beat her for style! Give Evangeline Knapp a gunny sack and a horse-blanket and she'll turn you out a fifty-dollar coat, I always tell 'em. Would anybody but her have dreamed of using that blue and light green together? It makes it look positively as if it came right from Fifth Avenue. I don't dare buy me a new hat or a suit unless Evangeline says it's all right. You can't fool her on style! What did *you* ever do, Lester Knapp, to deserve such a wife, I'd like to know."

She laughed again, as Aunt Mattie always did, just for the sake of laughing, gave Henry and Helen each a cookie out of her paper bag, and took up her boughten salad and boughten boiled ham and went off, repeating, "Now, folks, don't you go and give me away!"

The grocery store seemed very silent after she left. Mr. Knapp bought his yeast-cake and package of oatmeal and they went out without a word. They didn't feel like talking any more. The children were

eating fast on their cookies to finish them before
they reached home.

They turned up the walk to the house in silence,
stood for some time scraping the snow and mud off
their shoes on the wire mat at the foot of the steps
and went on their toes up to the cocoa-fiber mat in
front of the door.

When they finally opened the door and stepped
in, an appetizing odor of hot chocolate and something fresh out of the oven met them. Also the
sound of the clock striking half-past six. Good,
they were on time. It was very important to be
on time. Little Stephen sat on the bottom step of
the stairs, waiting for them, his face swollen and
mottled, his eyes very red, his mouth clamped shut
in a hard line.

"Oh, gee! I bet Stevie's been bad again!" murmured Henry pityingly. He went quickly to his
little brother and tried to toss him up. But the
heavy child was too much of a weight for his thin
arms. He only succeeded in giving him a great
hug. Helen did this too, and laid the fresh, outdoor coolness of her cheek against the little boy's
hot face, glazed by tears. They none of them made
a sound.

Lester Knapp stood silently looking at them.

Their mother came to the door, fresh in a well-
ironed, clean, gingham house-dress.

"Well, Evie dear, what's the news from home?" asked Lester, as the children separated and began quickly hanging up their wraps. Stephen slipped off back towards the kitchen.

"Oh, all right," she said in her clear, well-modulated voice, her eyes on Helen, to whom she now said quietly, with a crescendo effect of patient self-restraint, "Don't wriggle around on one foot that way to take off your rubbers. Sit down on a chair. No, not that one, it's too high. This one. Lay down your schoolbooks. You can't do anything with them under your arm. There are your mittens on the floor. Put them in your pocket and you'll know where to find them. Unless they're damp. Are they damp? If they are, take them into the kitchen and put them on the rack to dry." As the child turned away, she called after her, making her give a nervous jump, "Not too close to the stove, or they'll burn."

She turned to Henry now (Stephen had disappeared). He froze to immobility, looking at her out of timid shadowed eyes, as if like a squirrel, he hoped by standing very still to make himself small. . . .

Apparently Henry had taken off his coat and hat satisfactorily and had suitably disposed of his mittens, for, after passing her eyes over his small person in one sweep, she turned away, saying over her shoulder, "I'm just going to put supper on the table. You'll have time to wash your hands while I dish up the things."

Henry drew a long breath and started upstairs. His father stood looking after him till with a little start he came to himself and followed.

The supper-bell rang by the time their hands and faces were washed. Helen and Henry washed Stephen's. They did not talk. They kept their attention on what they were doing, rinsing out the wash-basin after they had finished, hanging the towels up smoothly and looking responsibly around them at the immaculate little room before they went downstairs.

The supper was exquisitely cooked, nourishing, light, daintily served. Scalloped potatoes, done to a turn; a broiled beefsteak with butter melting oozily on it; frothing, well-whipped chocolate; small golden biscuits made out of a health-flour.

The children tucked their clean napkins under their chins, spread them out carefully over their clean clothes and, all but Stephen, ate circumspectly.

"Nothing special happened to-day, then?" asked Mr. Knapp in a cheerful voice, looking over at the erect, well-coifed house-mother.

"Just the usual things," answered Mrs. Knapp, reaching out to push Henry's plate a little nearer to him. "I haven't been out anywhere, and nobody has been in. Stephen, don't eat so fast. Mattie telephoned. Their new car has come. Henry, do sit up straighter. You'll be positively hunchbacked if you keep stooping over so."

At the mention of Aunt Mattie and the new car, a self-conscious silence dropped over the older children and their father. They looked down at their plates.

"Helen, did you put salt on your potatoes?" asked her mother. "I don't put in as much as we like, because the doctor says Henry shouldn't eat things very salt."

"I put some on," said Helen.

"Enough?" asked her mother doubtfully. "You know it takes a lot for potatoes."

Helen tasted her potatoes, as though she had not till then thought about them. "Yes, there's enough," she said.

"Let me taste them," said her mother, holding out her hand for the plate. After she had tasted them she said, "Why, there's not nearly enough, they're perfectly flat. Here, give me that salt-cellar." She added the salt, tasted the potatoes again and pushed the plate back to Helen, who went on eating with small mouthfuls, chewing conscientiously.

There was another silence.

Mr. Knapp helped himself to another biscuit, and

said as he spread it with butter, "Aren't these biscuits simply great! You'd never know, by the taste,
they were good for you, would you?"

Helen looked up quickly with a silent, amused
smile. Her eyes met her father's with understanding mirth.

"Take smaller mouthfuls, Stephen," said Mrs.
Knapp.

Nobody said a word, made a comment, least of
all her husband, but she went on with some heat
as if in answer to an unspoken criticism. "I know
I keep at the children all the time! But how can
I help it? They've got to learn, haven't they? It
certainly is no *pleasure* to me to do it! *Some*body's
got to bring them up."

The others quailed in silent remorse before this
arraignment. Not so Stephen. He paid no attention
whatever to it. His mother often said bitterly that
he paid no attention to anything a grown-up said
unless you screamed at him and stamped your foot.

"Gimme some more meat," he said heartily,
pushing his plate towards his father.

"Say, 'Please, Father,' " commanded his mother.

He looked blackly at her, longingly at the steak,
decided that the occasion was not worth a battle and
said, "Please, father," in a tone which he contrived,
with no difficulty whatever, to make insulting.

His mother's worn, restrained face took on a

deeper shade of disheartenment, but she did not lift the cast-down glove, and the provocative accent of rebellion continued to echo in the room triumphant and unchecked. It did not seem to increase the appetite of the other children. They kept their eyes cast down and made themselves small in their chairs.

It had no effect on Stephen's enjoyment of his meal. He ate heartily, like a robust lumberman who has been battling with the elements all day and knows he must fortify himself for a continuation of the same struggle to-morrow. The mottled spots on his cheeks blended into his usual healthy red. He stopped eating for a moment to take a long and audible draught out of his mug.

"Don't make a noise when you drink your milk," said his mother.

The others ate lightly, sipping at their chocolate, taking tiny mouthfuls of the steak and potatoes.

"Helen's school composition had quite a success," said Helen's father. "They are going to have some dramatics at the school and . . ."

"What are dramatics?" asked Henry.

"Oh, that's the general name for plays, comedies, you know, and tragedies and . . ."

"What is a comedy?" asked Henry. "What is a tragedy?"

"Good Heavens, Henry," said his father, laughingly, "I never saw anybody in my life who could ask as many questions as you. You wear the life out of me!"

"He doesn't bother *me* with them," said his mother, her inflection presenting the statement as a proof of her superior merit.

Henry shrank a little smaller. His father hastened to explain what a tragedy was and what a comedy was. Another silence fell. Then, "Quite cold to-day," said Mr. Knapp. "The boys at the office said that the thermometer . . . " He had tried to stop himself the moment the word "office" was out of his mouth. But it was too late. He stuck fast at "thermometer," for an instant and then, hurriedly as if quite aware that no one cared how he finished the sentence, he added, "stood at only ten above this morning."

Mrs. Knapp had glanced up sharply at the word "office" and her eyes had darkened at the pause afterwards. She was looking hard at her husband now, as if his hesitation, as if his accent had told her something. "Young Mr. Willing didn't get back to-day, did he?" she asked gravely.

Mr. Knapp took a long drink of his hot chocolate. "Yes, he did," he said at last, setting down his cup and looking humbly at his wife.

"Did they announce the reorganization . . . the way he's going to . . . " asked Mrs. Knapp. As if she did not know the answer already!

They both already knew everything that was to be asked and answered, but there seemed no escape from going on.

"Yes, they did," said Mr. Knapp, trying to chew on a mouthful of steak.

"Who did they put in charge of your office?" asked Mrs. Knapp, adding in an aside, "Helen, don't hold your fork like that."

"Harvey Bronson," said Mr. Knapp, trying to make it sound like any other name.

"Oh," said Mrs. Knapp.

She made no comment on the news. She made it a point never to criticize their father before the children.

Helen's eyes went over timidly towards her father, sideways under lowered lids. She wished she dared give him a loving look of reassurance to show him how dearly she loved him and sympathized with him because he had not had the advancement they had all hoped for so long, because a younger man and one who was especially mean to Father had been put over his head. Her heart swelled and ached. She would get Father off in a corner after dinner and give him a big silent hug. He would understand.

But as it happened, she did not. Other things happened.

There was almost total silence during the rest of the meal. Mrs. Knapp did not eat another mouthful of food after her husband's news. The others made a pretense of cutting up food and swallowing it. Helen and Henry cleared off the table and brought in the dessert.

"Be careful about holding the meat-platter straight, Henry," cautioned his mother. "I scrubbed on those last grease spots till nearly five o'clock this afternoon. It makes it very hard for Mother when you and Helen are careless." Her voice was carefully restrained.

"How is your eczema, to-night, Eva?" asked her husband.

"Oh, about the same," she said. She served out the golden preserved peaches, passed the home-made cake, but took none herself. After sitting for a few moments, she pushed back her chair and said: "I don't care for any dessert to-night. I'll just go and start on the dishes. You can come out to help when you finish eating."

Her husband looked up at her, his face pale and shadowed. He tried to catch her eyes. But she averted them, and without a glance at him walked steadily out into the kitchen.

Her presence was still as heavy in the room as though she sat there, brooding over them. They conscientiously tried to eat. They did not look at each other.

They heard her begin to pile up the dishes at the sink, working rapidly as she always did. They heard her step swiftly back towards the kitchen table as though to pick up a dish there. They heard her stop short with appalling abruptness; and for a long moment a silence filled the little house, roaring loudly in their ears as they gazed at each other, across the table. What could have happened?

And then, with the effect of a clap of thunder shaking them to the bone, came a sudden rending outburst of sobs, strangled weeping, the terrifying sounds of an hysteric breakdown.

They rushed out into the kitchen. Mrs. Knapp stood in the middle of the kitchen floor, both hands pressed over her face, trying in vain to restrain the tears which rained down through her fingers, the sobs which convulsed her tall, strong body. From her feet to the dining-room door stretched a fresh line of grease-spots. Henry had once more tilted the meat-platter as he carried it.

She heard them come in; she gave a muffled inarticulate cry, half pronounced words they could not understand, and, rushing past them, still shaking with sobs, she ran upstairs to her room. They heard the door shut, the click of the latch loud and distinct in the silent house.

"I want another help of peaches," said Stephen greedily, taking instant advantage of his mother's absence. "I *like* peaches."

His father thought sometimes that Stephen was like the traditional changeling, hard, heartless, inhuman.

Henry's face had turned very white. He stood looking dully at his father and sister, his lips hanging half-open. He turned from white to a yellow-green, and a shudder shook him. He whispered hastily, thickly, unintelligibly (but they understood because they had seen those signs many times before), he murmured, his hand clapped over his mouth, his shoulders bowed, ". . . 'mfraid goin' be sick," and ran upstairs to the bathroom.

They followed and found him vomiting, leaning over the bowl, his legs bending and trembling under him. His father put one arm around the thin little body and held his head clumsily with the other hand. Helen stood by, helplessly sympathetic. Henry looked so *awfully* sick when he had those fits of nausea!

Henry vomited apologetically, as it were, trying feebly not to spatter any of the ill-smelling liquid on the bathroom wall or floor. In an instant's pause between spasms he rolled his eyes appealingly at Helen, who sprang to his side.

". . . 'mfraid got shome shstairs," he said thickly, the words cut short by another agonizing fit of retching.

Helen darted away. Her father called her back. "What is it? What did Henry say?" he asked anxiously. "I'll get him his medicine as soon as he is over this. I don't believe you can reach it. It's on that highest shelf." Helen stood up on tiptoe and whispered in her father's ear, "He said he was afraid he got some on the stairs, and I'm going to wipe it up."

Her father nodded his instant understanding. The little girl flew to the corner closet where the cleaning cloths were hung and disappeared down the stairs.

The door to the bedroom opened and Mrs. Knapp appeared. Her eyes were still red, and her face very pale; but her expression was of strong, kind solicitude. She came straight into the bathroom where Henry stood, half-fainting, wavering from side to side.

"Oh, poor Henry!" she said. "Here, I'll take care of him."

Mr. Knapp stepped back, self-effacingly, and with relief. She picked the child up bodily in her strong arms and carried him into the bedroom where she laid him on the bed. In an instant she had whisked out a basin which she held ready with one hand. "Bring me a wet washcloth, *cold*," she said to her husband, "and a glass of water." When it came she wiped Henry's lips clean, so that with a sigh of relief he closed his mouth; she held the glass to his lips, "Rinse out your mouth with this, dear. It'll make you feel better." When the next spasm came, she supported his forehead firmly, laying his head back on the pillow afterwards; and, sprinkling a little eau-de-cologne on a fresh handkerchief, she wiped the cold sweat from his face.

To lie down had relieved the strain on Henry. The eau-de-cologne had partly revived him. He began to look less ghastly; he began to feel less that this time he was really going to die. He drew strength consciously from his mother's calm self-possession. Nobody could take care of you like Mother when there was something the matter with you, he thought.

Mother now turned to inspect the contents of the basin. "What ever can have upset Henry *this* time? I planned that supper specially for him, just the things he usually digests all right."

A pause. Then, "What can those dark brown crumby lumps be?" she asked aloud. "We didn't have anything like that for supper."

Henry rolled his eyes at his father, and then closed them, weakly, helplessly.

His father said from the door, briefly, "We met Mattie when we were at Wertheimer's and she gave each of the children a cookie."

"*Store* cookies?" asked Henry's mother, more with an exclamation point than a question.

"The regular ginger cookie . . . a small one," said her husband.

"Oh," said Mrs. Knapp.

Behind Mr. Knapp in the obscurity of the hall, Helen slipped shadow-like, silently as a little mouse, back towards the closet where the cleaning cloths were kept. Her father hoped she had remembered to rinse the cloth well.

Mrs. Knapp sat down by Henry. She laid her hand on his forehead and said, "Mother doesn't *want* to be scolding you all the time, Henry, but you must try to remember not to eat things away from home. You know your digestion is very delicate and you know how Mother tries to have just the right things for you here. If I do that, give up everything I'd like to do to stay here and cook things for you, you ought to be able to remember, don't you think, not to eat other things?"

Her tone was reasonable. Her logic was unanswerable. Henry shrank to even smaller dimensions as he lay helpless on the bed.

She did not say a word to his father about having allowed Henry to eat the cookie. She never criticized their father before the children.

She got up now and put a light warm blanket over Henry. "Do you suppose you could get Stephen to bed, Lester?" she asked, over her shoulder. After he had gone, she sat holding Henry's cold little frog's paw in her warm hands till his circulation was normal and then helped him undress and get to bed.

When she went down to the kitchen she found that Helen and her father had tried to finish the evening work. The dishes were washed and put away. Helen was rinsing out the wiping-cloths, and Lester was sweeping. The clock showed a quarter of nine.

She looked sharply at what Helen was doing and plunged towards her with a gesture of impatience. "Mercy, Helen, don't be so back*handed!*" she cried, snatching a dripping cloth from the child's hands. "I've told you a thousand times you can't wring the water out of anything if you hold it like *that!*" She wrung the cloths one after another, her practised fingers flying like those of a prestidigitator. "Like *that!*" she said reprovingly to Helen, shaking them out and hanging them up to dry.

Seeing in Helen's face no sign of any increase of intelligence about wringing out dishcloths, but only her usual cowed fear of further criticism, she said in a tone of complete discouragement:

"Oh, well, never mind! You'd better get to bed now. I'll be up to rub the turpentine and lard on your chest by the time you're undressed." As the child trod softly out of the kitchen she threw after her like a hand-grenade, "Don't forget your teeth!"

To her husband she said, taking the broom out of his hand and looking critically back over the floor he had been sweeping, "Don't wait for me, Lester. I've got to change the dressings on my arm before I go to bed."

"Can't I help you with that, dear?" asked her husband.

"No, thank you," she said. "I can manage all right."

As he went out she was reflecting with a satisfaction that burned like fire that she was not as other women who "took it out" on their families when things went wrong. She never made scenes, not even when she was almost frenzied with irritation. She never lost her self-control—except of course once in a while with Stephen, and then never for more than an instant or two. Until the terrifying but really unavoidable breakdown of this evening, no one had ever seen her weep, heavy and poisonous as were the bitter tears she so frequently held back. She never forgot to say "thank you" and "please." Her heart swelled with an angry sense of how far beyond criticism she was. Come what might she would do her duty to the uttermost.

She went up to Helen's room, silently did the necessary things for her cold and kissed her goodnight, saying, *"Do* try to make your bed a little better, dear. There was a great fold across it today from one corner to the other."

Then she went downstairs and stepped about the house, picking up odd things and putting them in place: her usual evening occupation. As she hung up Henry's muffler which lay on the floor at the foot of the coat-rack in the hall, her eyes fell on Helen's coat. She looked at it with mingled pride and exasperation. There was not a woman of her acquaintance who could have taken those hopeless old materials and pieced and turned and fitted and made such a stylish little garment. She had always said to herself that no matter how poor they were, she would die before her little girl should feel humiliated for the lack of decent clothes. And yet . . . what a strange child Helen was! She had put on that coat as if it had been any coat, as if she didn't realize what a toilsome effort her mother had made to secure it. But children *didn't* realize the sacrifices you made for them.

She had a moment of complete relaxation and satisfaction as she dropped into a chair to feast her eyes on the sofa. What a success it was! Could anybody recognize it for the old wreck which had stood out in front of the junk-shop on River Street all winter! She had seen its lines through its ruin, had guessed at the fine wood under the many coats of dishonoring paint. Every inch of it had been re-created by her hand and brain and purpose.

How sweet of Mattie Farnham to give her that striped velours to cover it with. She never could have afforded anything so fine. What lovely, lovely stuff it was! How she loved beautiful fabrics. Her face softened to dreaminess as she passed her hand gently over the smoothly drawn material and thought with affection of the donor. What a good-hearted girl Mattie was.

Her children would not have recognized her face as she sat there loving the sofa and the rich fabric on it and thinking gratefully of her friend.

But how *funny* Mattie was about dressing her-self! Was there anybody who had less faculty for it? A flicker of amusement—the first she had felt all day—drew her lips into a good-natured smile at the recollection of that awful hat with the pink feather which Mattie had wanted to buy. What a figure of fun she had looked in it! And she knew it! And yet was hypnotized by the dowdy thing. All she had needed was the hint to take the small, dark-blue one that suited her perfectly. How queer she couldn't think of it herself.

She loved to go shopping with Mattie—with old Mrs. Anderson, with any of the ladies in the Guild who so often asked her advice. It was a real pleasure to help them select the right things. But—her softened face tightened and set—how horribly naughty Stephen was when you tried to take him into shops. Such disgraceful scenes as she had had with him when he got tired and impatient.

The clock behind her struck half-past nine, and she became aware of its ticking once more, its insistent whisper: *"So much to do! So much to do! So much to do!"*

She was very tired and found she had relaxed wearily into her chair. But she got up with a brisk energetic motion like a prize-fighter coming out of his corner. She detested people who moved languidly and dragged themselves around.

She went into the kitchen and put the oatmeal into the fireless cooker, and after this waited, polishing absent-mindedly the nickel towel-bar of the shining stove, till she heard Lester go out of the bathroom.

Then she went swiftly up the stairs, locked the bathroom door behind her, and began to unwind the bandages from around her upper arm. When it finally came off she inspected the raw patch on her arm. It was crusted over in places, with thick, yellowish-white pus oozing from the pustules. It was spreading. It was worse. It would never be any better. It was like everything else.

She spread a salve on it with practised fingers, wound a fresh bandage about her arm, fastened it firmly and then washed her hands over and over, scrubbing them mercilessly with a stiff brush till they were raw. She always felt unclean to her bones after she had seen one of those frequently recurring eczema eruptions on her skin. She never spoke of them unless some one asked her a question about her health. She felt disgraced by their loathsomeness, although no one but she and the doctor ever saw them. She often called it to herself, "the last straw."

Her nightgown hung on the bathroom door. They usually dressed and undressed here not to disturb Stephen who still slept in their bedroom, because there was no other corner in the little house for him. And now they would *never* be able to move to a larger house where they could live decently and have a room apiece, to a better part of town where the children would have decent playmates. *Never* anything but this . . .

She began to undress rapidly and to wash. As she combed her dark hair, she noticed again how rapidly it was falling. The comb was full of long hairs. She took them out and rolled them up into a coil. She supposed she ought to save her combings to make a switch against the inevitable time when her hair would be too thin to do up. And she had had such *beautiful* hair! It had been her one physical superiority, that and her "style." What good had they ever done her!

She began to think of the frightening moment in the kitchen that evening, when for an instant she had lost her bitterly fought-for self-control, when the taut cable of her will-power had snapped under the strain put upon it. For a wild instant she had been all one inner clamor to die, to die, to lay down the heavy, heavy burden, too great for her to bear. What was her life? A hateful round of housework, which, hurry as she might, was never done. How she *loathed* housework! The sight of a dishpan full of dishes made her feel like screaming out. And what else did she have? Loneliness; never-ending monotony; blank, gray days, one after another, full of drudgery. No rest from the constant friction over the children's carelessness and forgetfulness and childishness! How she hated childishness! And she must try to endure it patiently or at least with the appearance of patience. Sometimes, in black moments like this, it seemed to her that she had such *strange* children, not like other people's, easy to understand and manage, strong, normal children. Helen . . . there didn't seem to be anything *to* Helen! With the exasperation which passivity always aroused in her, Helen's mother thought of the dumb vacant look on Helen's face that evening when she had tried to show her how to perform a simple operation a little less clumsily. Sometimes it seemed as though Helen were not all *there!* And Henry with that nervous habit of questioning everything everybody said and the absent-mindedness which made him do such idiotic things. . . .

A profound depression came upon her. These were the moments in a mother's life about which nobody ever warned you, about which everybody kept a deceitful silence, the fine books and the speakers who had so much to say about the sacredness of maternity. They never told you that there were moments of arid clear sight when you saw helplessly that your children would never measure up to your standard, never would be really close to you, because they were not your kind of human beings, because they were not *your* children, but merely other human beings for whom you were responsible. How solitary it made you feel!

And Stephen. . . .

It frightened her to think of Stephen. What could you do for a child who *wanted* to be bad, and told you so in a loud scream? How could you manage a child whom no arguments touched, who went off like a dynamite bomb over everything and nothing; who was capable of doing as he did this afternoon, rushing right at his own mother in a passion, trying to bite and scratch and tear her flesh like a little wild beast?

And yet she had never spoiled Stephen because he was the baby of the family. She had always been firm with him just as she had with the others. Every one in her circle agreed that she had never spoiled him. What future could there be for Stephen? If he was like this at five, what would he be at fifteen, with all those slum boys at hand to play with? She couldn't *always* keep them away from him.

If they could only move to another part of town, the nice part, where the children would have nice playmates! But now she knew they never would. With this last complete failure of poor Lester's to make good, she touched bottom, knew hopelessness. There never would be anything else for her, never, never! How *could* Lester take things lying down as he did! When there were all those tragic reasons for his forging ahead? Why *didn't* he do as other men did, all other men who amounted to anything, even common laboring men—get on, succeed, provide for his family!

It was not lack of intelligence or education. He

had always been crazy about books and education. What good did Lester's intelligence and education do them? It was just that he didn't care enough about them to *try!*

Well, she would never complain. She despised wives who complained of their husbands. She had never said a word against Lester and she never would. Even to-night, at the table, struck down as she had been by that blow, that fatal blow, so casually, so indifferently announced, she had not breathed a word of blame. Not one!

But it was bitter! Bitter! She was fit for something better than scrubbing floors all her life. Her dark face in the mirror looked out at her, blazing. She looked as Stephen did when he was being whipped. She looked wicked. She felt wicked. But she did not want to be wicked. She wanted to be a good Christian woman. She wanted to do her duty. She began to pray, fervently, "O God, help me bear my burdens! God, make me strong to do my duty! God, take out the wild, sinful anger from my heart and give me patience to do what I must do! O God, help me to be a good mother!"

The right spring had been touched. Her children! She must live for her children. And she loved them, she did live for them! What were those little passing moments of exasperation! Nothing, compared to the passion for them which shook her like a great wind, whenever they were sick, whenever she felt how greatly they needed her. And how they did need her! Helen, with her delicate lungs, her impracticality, her helplessness—what could she do without her mother to take care of her? And Stephen—she shuddered to think of the rage into which some women would fly when Stephen was in one of his bad moods. Nobody but his own mother could be trusted to resist the white heat of anger which his furies aroused in the person trying to care for him. And Henry, poor little darling Henry! Who else would take the trouble, day by day, to provide just the right food for him? See what that one cookie had done to him this evening! Why, if Mattie Farnham had the care of that child, she and her delicatessen-store stuff . . .

Henry's mother swiftly braided up her thinning hair. Her face was calmer. She was planning what she would give him for lunch the next day.

Chapter 3

"**D**ON'T you want to sit by the window here, Mrs. Farnham?" suggested Mrs. Prouty, the rector's wife. "The light'll be better for your sewing. That dark material is hard on the eyes."

All the Ladies' Guild understood that Mrs. Farnham was being posted there to give the alarm when Mrs. Knapp turned into the walk leading to the Parish House, and they went on talking with an agreeable sense of security.

"It's pretty hard on those Willing's Emporium people, I say," Mrs. Prouty remarked, "after years of faithful service, to have everything turned topsy-turvy over their heads by a young whippersnapper. They say he's going to change the store all around too; put the Ladies' Cloak Department upstairs where the shoes always were; and he's taken that top floor that old Mr. Willing rented to the Knights of Pythias and is going to add some new departments. A body won't know where to find a thing! In my opinion he'll live to regret it."

They all reflected silently that if the young Mr. Willing had only been an Episcopalian like his defunct uncle, instead of a Presbyterian, Mrs. Prouty might not have taken the change of the Ladies' Cloak Department quite so hard.

"Poor Mrs. Knapp feels simply terrible about her husband's not being promoted," said Mrs. Merritt, the doctor's wife. "I saw her yesterday at Wertheimer's for an instant. Not that she said anything. She wouldn't, you know, not if she died for it. But you could feel it. All over her. And no wonder!"

"Poor thing!" (Mrs. Prouty had acquired the full, solicitous intonation of the parish visitor.) "She has many burdens to bear. Mr. Prouty often says that in these days it is wonderful to see a woman so devoted to her duty as a home-maker. She simply gives up her whole life to her family! Absolutely!"

"The children are such delicate little things, too, a constant care." Mrs. Merritt snatched the opportunity to display her inside information. "There's hardly a week that Doctor isn't called in there for one or another of them. He often tells me that *he* doesn't know what to do for them. They don't seem to have anything to do *with!* No digestions, no constitutions. Just like their father. All but little Stephen. He's *strong* enough!"

"He's a perfect imp of darkness!" cried old Mrs. Anderson, lifting her thin gray face from her sewing. "I've raised a lot of children in my day and seen a lot more, but I never saw such a naughty contrary child as he is in all my born days. Nor so hateful! He never does anything unless it's to plague somebody by it. The other day, in the last thaw it was, I'd just got my back porch mopped up after the grocer's boy—you know how he tracks mud in—and I heard somebody fussing around out there, and I opened the door quick, and there was Stephen Knapp lugging over a great pail of mud to dump it on my porch. He'd dumped one already and got it all spread out on the boards. I said, 'Why, Stephen Knapp, what makes you do such a bad thing?' I was really paralyzed to see him at it. 'What *makes* you be so bad, Stephen?' I said. And he said—he's got the hardest, coolest way of saying those wicked things—he said, as cool as you please, ' 'Tause I hate you, Mis' Anderson, 'tause I hate you.' And gave me that black look of his. . . . "

Through the tepid, stagnant air of the room flickered a sulphurous zig-zag of passion. The women shrank back from it, horrified and fascinated.

"Mr. Prouty says," quoted his wife, "that Stephen Knapp makes him think of the old Bible stories about people possessed of the devil. His mother is at her wit's end. Mr. Prouty says she has asked him to help her with prayer. And Stephen gets worse all the time. And yet she's always perfectly firm with him, never spoils him. And it's wonderful, her iron self-control when he is in one of his tempers. I never could keep *my* temper like that. It can't be due to anything about the way she manages him, for she never had a particle of trouble with the other two. Well, it'll be a great relief to her, as she often says, when he goes to school with the others."

Mrs. Merritt now said, lowering her voice, "You know she has a chronic skin trouble too that she never says anything about."

"Like St. Paul, Mr. Prouty says."

"Doctor has tried everything to cure it. Diet. Electricity. X-rays. All the salves in the drugstores. Oh, no," she explained hastily in answer to an unspoken thought somewhere in the room. "Oh, *no,* it's nothing *horrid!* Her husband is a *nice* enough man, as far as that goes. Doctor thinks it may be nervous, may be due to . . ."

"Nervous!" cried Mrs. Mattie Farnham. "Why, it's a real eruption, discharging pus and everything. I had to help her dress a place on her back once when Stephen was a tiny baby. Nervous!"

"Oh, Doctor doesn't mean it is anything she could help. He often says that just because you've called a thing nervous is no reason for thinking it's not serious. It's as real to *them,* he says, as a broken leg."

"Well, I'd have something worse than eczema if I had three delicate children to bring up and only that broken reed of a Lester Knapp to lean on," said Mrs. Prouty with energy. "They tell me that he all but lost his job in the shake-up at Willing's— let alone not getting advanced. Young Mrs. Willing told Mr. Prouty that her husband told her that he'd be blessed if he knew anything Lester Knapp *would* be good for—unless teaching poetry, maybe. Young Mrs. Willing is a Churchwoman, you know. It's only her husband who is a Presbyterian. That's how she happened to be talking to Mr. Prouty. She was telling him that if it depended on *her* which church . . . "

"He's a *nice* man, Lester Knapp is," broke in Mrs. Farnham stoutly. "You know we're sort of related. His sister married my husband's brother. The children call me Aunt. When you come to know Lester he's a real nice man. And he's a smart man too, in his way. When he was at the State University he was considered one of the best students there, I've always heard 'em say. If he hadn't married so young, he was lotting on being . . . " Her tone changed suddenly—"Oh, Mrs. Merritt, do you think I ought to hem this or face it?"

"It'd be pretty bungling to hem, wouldn't it?" Mrs. Merritt responded on the same note, "such heavy material—to turn *in* the hem, anyhow.

Maybe you could feather-stitch it down—oh, how do you *do*, Mrs. Knapp? So glad to see you out. But then you're one of the faithful ones, as Mr. Prouty always says."

They all looked up from their work, smiling earnestly at her, drawing their needles in and out rapidly, and Evangeline Knapp knew from the expression of their eyes that they had been talking of her, of Lester's failure to make good; that they had been pitying her from their superior position of women whose husbands were good providers.

She resented their pity—and yet it was a comfort to her. She loved coming to these weekly meetings of the Guild, the only outings of her life, and always went home refreshed and strengthened by her contact with people who looked at things as she did. She passed her life in solitary confinement, as home-makers always do, with a man who naturally looked at things from a man's standpoint (and in her case from a very queer standpoint of his own) and with children who could not in the nature of things share a single interest of hers; it was an inexpressible relief to her to have these weekly glimpses of human beings who talked of things she liked, who had her standards and desires.

She *liked* women, anyhow, and had the deepest sympathy for their struggle to arrange in a decent pattern the crude masculine and crude childish raw material of their home-lives. She liked too the respect of these women for her, the way they all asked her advice, and saved up perplexities for her to solve. To-day, for instance, she had scarcely taken out her thimble when Mrs. Prouty passed over a sample of blue material to ask whether it was really linen as claimed—when anybody with an eye in her head could see that it was not even a very good imitation. After that, Mrs. Merritt said she had noticed that Paisley effects were coming in. Would it be possible to drape one of those old shawls— she had a lovely one from her grandmother—to make a cloak—to simulate the wide-sleeved effect—without cutting it, you know—of course you wouldn't want to *cut* it!

Mrs. Knapp said she would think it over, and as she rapidly basted the collar on the child's dress she was making, she concentrated her inner vision on the problem. She saw it as though it were there —the great square of richly patterned fabric. She draped it in imagination this way and that. No, that would be too bungling at the neck—perhaps drawn up in the middle . . .

They felt her absorption and preserved a respectful silence, sewing and glancing up occasionally at her inward-looking face to see how she was progressing. Their own minds were quite relaxed and vacant. Mrs. Knapp had taken up the problem.

What need for any one else to think of it? They had such confidence in Mrs. Knapp.

Presently, "I believe you could do it this way, Mrs. Merritt," she said. "Mrs. Anderson, hand me that piece of sateen, will you, please. See, this is your shawl. You make a fold in the middle, so, halfway up—and catch it between with a . . ." They laid down their work to give their whole attention to her explanation, their eyes following her fingers, their minds accepting her conclusions without question.

She felt very happy, very warm, very kind. She loved being able to help Mrs. Merritt out this way. Dr. Merritt was such a splendid doctor and so good always to Henry and Helen. And she loved helping somebody to make use of something, to rescue something fine, as she had rescued the sofa. It would be a beautiful, beautiful cloak, especially with Mrs. Merritt's mink neckpiece made over into a collar, a detail that came into her mind like an inspiration as she talked.

Yes, she was very happy the afternoons when the Guild met.

Mr. Prouty usually brought his rosy-gilled face and round collar into the Guild Room before the group broke up and chatted with the ladies over the cup of tea which ended their meetings. He had something on his mind to-day—that was evident to every one of those married women the instant he stepped into the room. But he did not bring it out at once, making pleasant conversation with the pre-occupied dexterity of an elderly clergyman. As he talked, he looked often at Mrs. Knapp's dark intense face, bent over her work. She never stopped for tea. And when he said in his well-known, colloquial, facetious way, "Ladies, I've got a big job for you. Take a brace. I'm going to shoot!" it was towards Mrs. Knapp that he spoke.

He tried to address himself to them all equally as he made his appeal, but unconsciously he turned almost constantly to the keen attentive eyes which never left his for an instant as he talked. He spoke earnestly, partly because he feared lest the Presby-terians might steal a march on him, and partly be-cause of a very real sympathy with the wretched children whose needs he was describing. When he finished, they all waited for Mrs. Knapp to speak.

She said firmly, "There's just one thing to do. A good visiting nurse attached to our parish work is the only way we could get anywhere. Anything else —baskets of food, volunteer visiting—they never amount to a row of pins."

The feeble, amateur, fumbling plans which they were beginning to formulate fell to earth. But they were aghast at her.

"A *nurse!* How ever could we get the money to pay one?"

"Only big-city parishes can hope to. . . ."

"We could if we *tried!*" she said, quelling them by her accent. She looked around at them with burning eyes. She was like a falcon in a barnyard. "A visiting nurse would cost—let us say a thousand a year."

"Oh, more than that!" cried Mr. Prouty.

"Not if we supplied her with lodging and heat. Why couldn't we arrange the little storeroom at the head of the stairs here in the Parish House for a bedroom for her? We could . . ."

"How could you heat it? There's no radiator there."

"There's a steam-riser goes through that room. I noticed it when we were putting the folding chairs away last week. That would make it warm enough. We could furnish it by contributions, without its costing a cent in cash. Everybody has at least one piece of furniture she could spare from her house —in such a cause. About the pay, now. We have more than four hundred dollars in the Ladies' Guild Treasury, and next Christmas our Bazaar ought to bring in two hundred more; it always does. We could hire Hunt's Hall on Union Street for it, and have the bazaar bigger, and make more than two hundred easily. Then, there's Miss Jelliffe, the music supervisor in the public schools, you know. Now that she's joined St. Peter's, I'm very sure she would help us get up some concerts later on. We could give 'Songs of All Countries' in costume, with the children. When you have lots of children in a program, you can always sell tickets. Their folks want to see them. And we could get a certain amount from the poor families the nurse visits— perhaps enough to make up the rest of her salary. They'd appreciate the service more if they paid something for it. Folks do."

All this had poured from her effortlessly, as if she had been simply pointing out what lay there to see, not as though she were beating her brains to invent it.

They gaped at her breathlessly.

"I wish you would be chairman of the Committee," said Mr. Prouty deferentially, "and take charge of the campaign for funds."

Her face which had been for an instant clear and open, clouded and shut. "I'd *love* to!" she said passionately. "I see it all!" She began to roll her sewing together as though to give herself time to be able to speak more calmly. "But I mustn't think of it," she said at last. "I have too much to do at home. It's all I can manage to get to church and to Guild meeting once a week. I never leave the house for anything else except to go to market. I can take Stephen with me there. Of course, after he starts going to school . . ."

Yes, they all knew what a relief it was when the children started going to school, and you could keep the house in some kind of order, and have a little peace.

Their silent, sympathetic understanding brought out from her now something she had not meant to say, something which had been like a lump of lead on her heart, the dread that her only open door would soon close upon her. "Even for Guild-meetings," she said, speaking grimly to keep her lips from trembling, "I may have to give them up, too. Mr. Knapp has always been able to make an arrangement to get away from the store an hour and a half earlier on Thursdays to stay with Stephen and the other two after school. But I don't know whether he will be able to manage that now. Mr. Willing, I mean old Mr. Willing saw no objection. But now . . ."

Her voice was harsh and dry; but they all knew why. And she was quite aware of the silent glosses and commentaries she knew them to be supplying mentally. She pinned her roll of sewing together firmly. Nobody could put in a pin with her gesture of mastery. "My first duty is to my home and children," she said.

"Oh, yes, oh, yes, we all know that, of course."

Mr. Prouty gave to the aphorism a lip-service which scantily covered his bitter objection to it in this case.

"Our circumstances don't permit us to hire help," she added, making this resolutely a statement of fact and not a complaint. "I do the washings, you know."

"I know. Wonderful! Wonderful!" said Mr. Prouty irritably.

"She sets an example to us all, I always tell 'em," said Mrs. Farnham.

"Yes, indeed you *do*, Mrs. Knapp!" they all agreed fervently. Evangeline knew that this was their way of trying to make up to her for having a poor stick of a husband. She savored their compassion with a bitter-sweet mixture of humiliation over her need for it and of triumph that she had drawn this sympathy from them under the appearance of repelling it. "Nobody ever heard *me* complain!" she was saying to herself.

"Well, I'll do what I can," she said, standing up to go. "I'll think of things. I've just thought of another. If we can provide the nurse with dinner every day, that ought to cut down on cash expenses. There are twenty-four members of the Guild. That'd hardly mean more than one dinner a month for each of us. And it would cut off fifteen dollars a month from the money we'd have to provide. And in that way we could keep in closer touch with her.

Seeing her every day and hearing about her work, we'd be more apt to coöperate with her right along."

"Splendid! Simply splendid!" cried Mr. Prouty. "We will be the only parish of our size in the State to have a visiting nurse of our own." He saw himself at the next diocesan meeting the center of a group of envious clergymen, expounding to them the ingenious devices by which this remarkable result had been achieved. He had had a good deal of this sort of gratification since the Knapps had moved into his parish.

Chapter 4

"Who swoon in sleep and awake wearier."

As he woke up, Lester Knapp heard the words in the air as he so often heard poetry,

". . . and awake wearier!"

He was tired to the bone. He would have given anything in the world to turn over, bury his face in the pillow and swoon to sleep again.

And never wake up!

But the alarm-clock had rung, and Evangeline had risen instantly. He heard her splashing in the bathroom now.

With an effort as though he were struggling out of smothering black depths, he sat up and swung his feet over the edge of the bed. Gosh! How little good he seemed to get from his sleep. He was tireder when he woke up than when he went to bed.

On the cot opposite little Stephen lay sleeping as vigorously as he did everything, one tightly clenched small fist flung up on his pillow. What a strong, handsome kid he was. Whatever could be the matter with him to make him act so like the devil? Strange to see a *little* kid like that, so hateful, seem to take such a satisfaction in raising hell.

66

Well, there was the furnace fire to fix. He thrust his feet into slippers, put his dressing-gown over his pyjamas and shuffled downstairs, hearing behind him the firm, regular step of Evangeline as she went from the bathroom to the bedroom. On the way down he woke up enough to realize what made life look so specially intolerable that morning; the return of Jerome Willing and his own definite failure to make good in the new organization of the store. The significance of that and all that it foretold stood out more harshly than ever in the pale, dawn-gray of the cold empty kitchen. Oh, hell!

He flung open the cellar door and ran downstairs to run away from the thought. But it was waiting for him, blackly in the coal-bin, luridly in the fire-box.

"It looks just about like the jumping-off place for me," he thought, rattling the furnace-shaker gloomily; "only I can't jump. Where to?"

Well, anyhow, in the few minutes before breakfast, while his stomach was empty, he was free from that dull leaden mass of misery turning over and over inside him at intervals, which was the usual accompaniment of his every waking hour. That was *some*thing to be thankful for.

He strained his lean arms to throw the coal from his shovel well back into the firebox, and leveled it evenly with the long poker. Evangeline always found time to go down to see if he had done it right before he got away after breakfast.

Then he stood for a moment, struck as he often was, by the leaping many-tongued fury of the little pale-blue pointed flames. He looked at them, fascinated by the baleful lustfulness of their attack on the helpless lumps of coal thrown into their inferno.

> "The seat of desolation, void of light
>   Save what the glimmering of those livid flames
>   Casts, pale and dreadful. Yet from those flames
>   No light, but rather darkness visible,
>   Serves only to discover sights of woe."

He heard the words crackle in the flames. He said to himself gravely: "Sights of woe it surely is."

He heard Evangeline begin to rattle the shaker of the kitchen stove and started from his hypnotized stare at the flames. It was time for him to beat it back upstairs if he didn't want to be late. How he loathed his life-long slavery to the clock, that pervasive intimate negative opposed to every spontaneous impulse. "It's the clock that is the naysayer to life," he thought, as he climbed the cellar stairs. He hurried upstairs, dressed and began to shave.

In the midst of this last operation he heard lagging, soft little footsteps come into the bathroom behind him, and beyond his own lathered face in the glass he saw Stephen enter. Unconscious of observation, the little boy was gazing absently out of the window at the snow-covered branches of the maple tree. His father was so much surprised by the expression of that round baby face and so much interested in it that he stopped shaving, his razor in the air, peering at his little son through the glass darkly. Stephen was looking *wistful!* Yes, he was! Wistful and appealing! Wasn't his lower lip quivering a little as though . . .

Stephen caught his father's eye on him and started in surprise at being seen by somebody whose back was towards him.

"Hello there, Stevie," said his father in an inviting tone. "How's the old man to-day?"

Yes, Stephen's lower lip *was* quivering! He came closer now and stood looking up earnestly into the soapy face of his father. "Say, Father," he began, "you know my Teddy-bear—you *know* how . . ."

From below came a clear, restrained voice stating dispassionately, "Lester, you have only twelve minutes before it's time to leave the house." And then rebukingly, "Stephen, you *must*n't bother Father in the mornings when he has to hurry so. Either go back to bed this minute and keep warm or get dressed at once. You'll take cold standing around in your pyjamas."

The tone was reasonable. The logic unanswerable. But unlike Henry, Stephen did not shrink to smaller proportions under the reason and the logic. With the first sound of his mother's voice, his usual square-jawed, pugnacious little mask had dropped over his face. "I'll get dwessed when I get a-good-a-weady!" he announced loudly and belligerently, refreshed by his night's sleep and instantly ready to raise an issue and fight it out.

"*Stephen!*" came from below in awful tones. Stephen sauntered away back into the bedroom with ostentatious leisureliness, his face black and scowling. Mother had once more stolen Teddy away from him during the night.

Lester finished shaving in three or four swipes of his razor, put on his collar at top speed and tied his necktie as he ran downstairs, cursing the clock and all its works under his breath. Stephen had been on the point of *saying* something to him, something human, Stephen who never asked a question or made an advance towards any one, Stephen who lived in a state of moral siege, making sorties from his stronghold only to harry the enemy. And the accursed matter of punctuality had once more frozen out a human relationship. He never had *time* to know his children, to stalk and catch that exquisitely elusive bird-of-paradise, their confidence. Lester had long ago given up any hope of having time enough to do other things that seemed worth while, to read the books he liked, to meditate, to try to understand anything. But it did seem that in the matter of his own children . . .

"I didn't think you'd need your overshoes this morning, Lester. I didn't get them out. But if you think you would better . . . "

"Oh, no, no, dear, I won't. I hate them anyhow."

His breakfast, perfectly cooked and served, steamed on the white tablecloth. What a wonder of competence Eva was! Only it was a pity she let the children get on her nerves so. Lester never doubted that his wife loved her children with all the passion of her fiery heart, but there were times when it occurred to him that she did not like them very well—not for long at a time, anyhow. But, like everything else, that was probably his fault, because she had all the drudgery of the care of them, because she never had a rest from them, because he had not been able to make money enough. Everything came back to that.

He gulped down his hot, clear coffee and tore at his well-made toast, thinking that he was just about a dead loss anyway you looked at it. Not only had he no money to give his children, but no health either. That was another reason why Eva was so worn and took life so hard. He had given her sickly children—all but Stephen. And Stephen had other ways of wearing on his mother. Poor little Henry!

How sick he had been last night! It was damnable that the poor kid should have inherited from his good-for-nothing father the curse of a weak digestion, which made life not worth living—that and many other things.

He snatched his watch, relentless inquisitor, from the table beside his plate, thrust it into his pocket and jumped up to put on his overcoat and hat.

"Here are your gloves," said his wife, holding them out to him. "There was a hole in the finger. I've just mended it."

"Oh, that's awfully good of you, Evie," said Lester, kissing her cheek and feeling another ton of never-to-be-redeemed indebtedness flung on his shoulders. He felt them bend weakly under it like a candle in an over-heated room.

"Don't forget your soda-mints," said Evangeline.

Gee! it wasn't likely he would forget them, with that hideous demon of dull discomfort getting to work the instant he swallowed food.

Henry and Helen, half-dressed, came hurrying down the stairs to see him before he disappeared for the day. His heart yearned over them, their impressionable, delicate faces, their shadowed eyes, the shrinking carriage of their slim little bodies.

"Good-by, Father," they said, lifting their sweet children's lips to his. The poor kids! What business had he to pass on the curse of existence to other human beings, too sensitive and frail to find it anything but a doom. He tried to say, "Good-by there, young ones," as he kissed them, but the words could not pass the knot in his throat.

He saw Eva start up the stairs and, knowing that she was going to have it out with Stephen, crammed his hat on his head and ran. But not fast enough. As he fled down the porch steps he heard a combative angry roar. Helen and Henry would eat their breakfast to a cheerful tune! And then another scream, more furious, on a higher note. Hell and damnation! There must be something wrong with the way that kid was treated to make life one perpetual warfare. But his father was as helpless to intervene as if he were bound and gagged.

Well, he *was* bound and gagged to complete helplessness about everything in his life and his children's lives, bound and gagged by his inability to make money. Only men who made money had any right to say how things should go in their homes. A man who couldn't make money had no rights of any kind which a white man was bound to respect —nor a white woman either. Especially a white woman. The opinion of a man who couldn't make money was of no value, on any subject, in anybody's eyes. The dignity of a man who could not make money—but why talk about non-existent abstractions? He had about as much dignity left him as a zero with the rim off.

His after-breakfast dyspepsia began to roll crushingly over his personality as it always did for a couple of hours after each meal. His vitality began to ebb. He felt the familiar, terrible draining out of his will-to-live. At the thought of enduring this demoralizing torment that morning, and that afternoon, and the day after that and the day after that, he felt like flinging himself on the ground rolling and shrieking. Instead he pulled out his watch with the employee's nervous gesture and quickened his pace. He was just then passing Dr. Merritt's office. If only there was something the doctor could do to help him. But he'd tried everything. And anyhow, he understood perfectly that a man who doesn't make money has no right to complain of dyspepsia—of anything. Illness only adds to his guilt.

He put a soda-mint in his mouth, turned a corner and saw, down the street, the four-story brick front of Willing's Emporium. Was it possible that a human being could hate anything as he hated that sight and not drop dead of it? Before this new phase it had been bad enough, all those years when it had been a stagnant pool of sour, slow intrigue and backbiting, carried on by sour, slow, small-minded people, all playing in their different ways on the small-minded, sick old man at the head of it. Lester had always felt that he would rather die than either join in those intrigues or combat them. This aloofness, added to his real incapacity for business, had left him still nailed to the same high stool in the same office which had received him the day he had first gone in. That first day when, vibrant with the excitement of his engagement to that flame-like girl, he had left his University classes and all his plans for the future and rushed out to find work, any work that would enable him to marry! Well, he had married. That had been only thirteen years ago! The time before it seemed to Lester as remote as the age of Rameses.

He had hated the slow régime of the sick, small-minded old man, but he hated still more this new régime which was anything but slow. He detested the very energy and forcefulness with which Jerome Willing was realizing his ideals, because he detested those ideals. Lester felt that he knew what those ideals were, what lay behind those "pep" talks to the employees. Jerome Willing's notion of being a good business-man was to stalk the women of his region, as a hunter stalks unsuspecting game, to learn how to catch them unawares, and how to play for his own purposes on a weakness of theirs only too tragically exaggerated already, their love for

buying things. Jerome Willing's business ideal, as
Lester saw it, was to seize on one of the lower human
instincts, the desire for material possessions, to feed
it, to inflame it, to stimulate it till it should take on
the monstrous proportions of a universal mono-
mania. A city full of women whose daily occupation would be buying things, and things, and more
things yet (the things Jerome Willing had to sell,
be it understood): that was Jerome Willing's vision
of good business. And to realize this vision he joyfully and zestfully bent all the very considerable
powers of his well-developed personality. Lester
Knapp, the barely tolerated clerk, hurrying humbly
down the street to take up his small drudging task,
gazed at that life-purpose as he had gazed at the
lurid baleful energy of the coal-flames half an hour
before.

Lester did not so much mind the way this subtly
injected poison ate into the fibers of childless women.
They might, for all he cared, let their insane hanker-
ing for a cloak with the "new sleeves" force them
to put blood-money into buying it, and allow their
drugged desire for such imbecile things to wall them
in from the bright world of impersonal lasting satis-
factions. They hurt nobody but themselves. If
the Jerome Willings of the world were smart enough
to make fools of them, so much the worse for them.
Although the spectacle was hardly an enlivening one

for a dyspeptic man forced to pass his life in contact with it.

But what sickened Lester was the unscrupulous exploitation of the home-making necessity, the adroit perversion of the home-making instinct. Jerome Willing wanted to make it appear, hammering in the idea with all the ingenious variations of his advertising copy, that home-making had its beginning and end in good furniture, fine table-linen, expensive rugs. . . . God! how about keeping alive some intellectual or spiritual passion in the home? How about the children? Did anybody suggest to women that they give to understanding their children a tenth part of the time and real intelligence and real purposefulness they put into getting the right clothes for them? A tenth? A hundredth! The living, miraculous, infinitely fragile fabric of the little human souls they lived with—did they treat that with the care and deft-handed patience they gave to their filet-ornamented table linen? No, they wrung it out hard and hung it up to dry as they did their dishcloths.

And of course what Jerome Willing wanted of every employee was to join with all his heart in this conspiracy to force women still more helplessly into this slavery to possessions. Any one who could trick a hapless woman into buying one more thing she had not dreamed of taking, he was the hero of

the new régime! That was what Jerome Willing
meant when he talked about "making good." Making good what? Not good human beings! That
was the last thing anybody was to think of. And
as to trying to draw out from children any greatness
of soul that might lie hidden under their immatu-
rity . . .

"You're late again, Mr. Knapp," said Harvey
Bronson's voice, rejoicing in the accusation.

Lester Knapp acknowledged his three-minute
crime by a nervous start of astonishment and then
by a fatigued nod of his head. All the swelling
fabric of his thoughts fell in a sodden heap, amount-
ing to nothing at all, as usual. He hung up his
coat and hat and sat down on the same old stool.
He was no good; that was the matter with him
—the whole matter. He was just no good at all—
for anything. What right had he to criticize anybody at all, when anybody at all amounted to more
than he! He was a man who couldn't get on in
business, who couldn't even get to his work on time.
He must have been standing on the sidewalk outside, not knowing where he was, lost in that hot
sympathy with childhood. But nine o'clock is not
the time to feel sympathy with anything. Nine
o'clock is sacred to the manipulation of a card cata-
logue of customers' bills.

The spiked ball within him gave another lurch

and tore at his vitals. Lord, how sick of life that dyspepsia made you! It took the very heart out of you so that, like a man on the rack, you were willing to admit anything your accusers asserted. He admitted thus what everybody tacitly asserted, that the trouble was all with him, with his weakness, with his feeble vitality, with his futile disgusts at the organization of the world he lived in, with his unmanly failure to seize other men by the throat and force out of them the things his family needed.

Sympathy for childhood nothing! If he felt any real sympathy for his own children, he'd somehow get more money to give them. What were fathers for, if not for that? If he were a "man among men," he would do as other manly men did: use his wits to force the mothers of other children to spend more money than they ought on material possessions and thus have that money to spend in giving more material possessions to his own.

And even the bitter way he phrased his surrender —yes, he knew that everybody would say that it was a weak man's sour-grapes denunciation of what he was not strong enough to get. And they would be right. It was.

He bent his long, lean, sallow face over the desk, looking disdainful and bad-tempered as he always did when he was especially wretched and unhappy.

Harvey Bronson glanced at him and thought,

"What a lemon to have around! He'd sour the milk by looking at it!"

Presently, as often happened to Lester, a lovely thing bloomed there, silent, unseen. Through the crazy, rhythmless chatter of the typewriters in the office, through the endless items on the endless bills, he heard it coming, as from a great distance, on radiant feet. It was only rhythm at first, divine, ordered rhythm, putting to flight the senseless confusion of what lay about him.

And then there glowed before him the glory of the words, the breath-taking upward lift of the first one, the sonorous cadences of the lines that followed, the majestic march of the end.

"Soaring through wider zones that pricked his scars
    With memory of the old revolt from awe,
    He reached a middle height, and at the stars
    Which are the brain of heaven, he looked, and sank.
    Around the ancient track marched, rank on rank
    The army of unalterable law."

Lester Knapp's heart swelled, shone bright, escaped out of its misery, felt itself one with the greatness of the whole.

The words kept singing themselves in his ear . . . " . . . he looked, and sank." " . . . marched, rank on rank." "The army of unalterable law."

The weighty, iron clang of the one-syllabled word

at the end gave him a sensation of an ultimate strength somewhere. He leaned on that strength and drew a long free breath.

His lean sallow face was lighted from within, and shone. He leaned far over his desk to hide this. He tried to think of something else, to put away from him this unmerited beauty and greatness. A man who is a failure in a business-office ought not for an instant to forget his failure. The least he can do is to be conscious of his humiliation at all times.

But in spite of himself, his lips were curved in a sweet, happy smile.

Harvey Bronson glanced at him and felt irritated and aggrieved by his expression. "What call has a dead loss like Lester Knapp got to be looking so dog-gone satisfied with himself!" he thought.

Chapter 5

THAT afternoon when at half-past four he stepped out on the street again, his long lean face was quite without expression. But it was not sallow. It was very white.

He walked straight before him for a step or two, stopped short and stared fixedly into the nearest show-window, one of Jim McCarthy's achievements.

Mrs. Prouty happened to stand there too. She was looking at a two-hundred-dollar fur coat as tragically as though it were the Pearly Gates and she sinking to Gehenna. She dreamed at night about that fur coat. She wanted it so that she could think of little else. Unlike Mrs. Merritt, she had no resources of fine old Paisley shawls to fall back on.

She looked up now, saw who had come to a stop beside her, and said, with the professional cordiality of a rector's wife, "Oh, how do you *do*, Mr. Knapp," and was not at all surprised when he did not answer or notice that she was there. Lester Knapp was notoriously absent-minded. It was one of his queer trying ways. He had so many. Poor Mrs. Knapp! But how brave she was about it. It was splendid to see a woman so loyal to a husband

82

who deserved it so little. She looked sideways at him, forgetting for an instant her heartache over the coat. Mercy! What a sickly-looking man! Bent shoulders, hollow chest, ashy-gray skin . . . no physique at all. And the father of a family! Such men ought not to be allowed to have children.

The coat caught her eye again, with its basilisk fascination. She sighed and stepped into the store to ask to see it again, although she knew it was as far out of her reach as a diamond tiara. To handle its soft richness made her sick with desire, but she couldn't keep away from it when she was downtown.

Her moving away startled Lester from his horrified gaze on nothingness, and he moved on with a jerky, galvanized gait like a man walking for the first time after a sickness.

He had lost his job. He had been fired. At the end of the month there would be no money at all to keep things going, not even the little they had always had.

Was it the earth he was treading, solid earth? It seemed to sway up and down under him till he was giddy. He *was* giddy. He was going to faint away. Oh, that would be the last disgrace. To faint away on the street because he had lost his job. The world began to whirl around before his eyes, to turn black. He caught at a tree.

For an instant his eyes were blurred, his ears

rang loudly; and then with racking pains, consciousness began to come back to him. He still stood
there, his arm still flung around the tree. He had
not fainted.

In the pause while he fought inwardly for strength
to go on, when every step seemed to plunge him
more deeply into the black pit of despair, he was
conscious of a steady voice, saying something in his
ear—or was it inside his head? The street was
quite empty. It must be in his head. How plainly
he heard it—another one of those tags of poetry
which haunted him. . . .

> "But make no sojourn in thy outgoing,
>   For haply it may be
>   That when thy feet return at evening
>   Death shall come in with thee."

At once it was as though strong wine had been
held to his lips, as though he had drunk a great
draught of vigor. His eye cleared, his heart leaped
up, he started forward with a quick firm step.

> "When thy feet return at evening
>   Death shall come in with thee."

There was no need to despair. He was not helplessly trapped. There was a way out. A glorious
way! The best way all around. The rightness of
it blazed on him from every point as he hurried

up the street. It meant for the children that at last
he would be able to give them money, real money,
just like any father. There would be not only the
ten thousand dollars from his insurance policy but
five thousand at least for the house and lot. He had
been offered that the other day. Actual cash. And
not only actual cash, but emancipation from the
blighting influence of a futile and despised father.

The children didn't despise him yet, but they
would soon, of course. Everybody did. And Eva
never lost a chance to bring home to them with
silent bitterness the fact of their father's utter worth-
lessness. Not that he blamed her, poor ambitious
Eva, caught so young by the senses, and rewarded by
such a blank as he!

And what a glorious thing for Eva—freedom
from the dead weight of an unsuccessful husband
whom she had to pretend to put up with. An easier
life for Eva all around. She would sell the house—
Eva would probably get more than five thousand
dollars for it!—and with that and the insurance
money would move back to her parents' big empty
village home in Brandville as the lonely old people
had so many times begged her to do. People lived
for next to nothing in those country towns; and as
a widow she could accept the proffered help from
her prosperous store-keeping father which her pride
had always made her refuse as a wife.

That's what it would be for his family; and for himself— Good God! an escape out of hell. Not only had he long ago given up any hope of getting out of life what he wanted for himself,—an opportunity for growth of the only sort he felt himself meant for, but he had long ago seen that he was incapable of giving to Eva and the children anything that anybody in the world would consider worth having. The only thing he was supposed to give them was money, and he couldn't make that.

The words sang themselves in his head to a loud triumphant chant:

> "For haply it may be
> That when thy feet return . . ."

He was brought up short by a sudden practical obstacle, looming black and foreboding before his impracticality, as life had always loomed before him. How could he manage it? His insurance policy was void in case of suicide, wasn't it? He would have to contrive somehow to make it look like an accident. He was seared to the bone by the possibility that he might not be able to accomplish even that much against the shrewd business sense of the world which had always defeated him in everything else.

At the idea he burst into strange, loud laughter, the mad sound of which so startled even his own ears that he stopped short, stricken silent, looking apprehensively about him.

But there was nobody in sight, except far at the end of the street, three small figures which seemed to be running towards him and waving their arms. He looked at them stupidly for a moment before he recognized them. His own children! Oh, yes, of course, this was Thursday afternoon, Ladies' Guild day, one of those precious Thursday hours that were different from all the others in the week. The children often got Stephen's wraps on and brought him out to meet their father, to "start visiting" that much sooner.

They were nearer now, running, Stephen bouncing between them, holding tightly to their hands. They were all smiling at him with shining welcoming eyes. He heard the sweet shrillness of their twittering voices as they called to him.

The tears rushed to his eyes. They loved him. By God, they loved him, his children did! Yes, perhaps even Stephen a little. And he loved them! He had for them a treasure-store of love beyond imagination's utmost reach! It was *hard* to leave them.

But so the world willed it. A father who had only love and no money—the sooner he was out of the way the better. He had had that unquestioned axiom ground into every bleeding fiber of his heart.

"Oh, Father, Stevie got on his own coat and buttoned every . . ."

"*Yubbers* mineself too," bragged Stephen breathlessly.

"Teacher says the first half of my play . . ."

They had come up to him now, clambering up and down him, clawing lovingly at him, all talking at once. What good times they had together Thursday afternoons!

"Father, how does the 'Walrus and the Carpenter' go after 'It seems a shame, the Walrus said'? Henry and I told Stevie that far, but we can't remember any . . ."

Lester Knapp swung Stephen up to his shoulder and took Henry and Helen by the hand.

"It seems a shame, the Walrus said," he began in the deep, mock-heroic voice they all adored,

> "To play them such a trick
> After we've brought them out so far
> And made them trot so quick."

"Oh, yes," cried the older children. "Now we know!" And as they swung along together, they all intoned delightedly,

> "The Carpenter said nothing *but*
> 'The butter's spread too thick!'"

Chapter 6

MRS. ANDERSON never forgot a detail of what happened that afternoon, and she soon became letter-perfect in her often-repeated statement of the essential facts. She told and retold her story word for word like a recitation learned by heart, without alteration; except as she allowed herself from time to time to stress a little more heavily her own importance as the only witness who had seen everything, to insist yet more vehemently on her absolute freedom from responsibility for the catastrophe.

"It was icy that afternoon, you know how it had thawed in the morning and then turned cold, and I was real nervous about slipping. I'm not so steady on my feet as I was fifty years ago and when I saw Mrs. Knapp putting on her things to leave the Guild meeting I said to her, 'Mrs. Knapp,' I said, 'won't you let me go along with you and take your arm over the icy places? I'm real nervous about slipping,' I said. And she said, 'Yes, of course,' and we started out and I felt so relieved to have her to hold to. She's the kind you couldn't imagine slipping, you know, the kind you'd *want* to take her arm over hard places. She's a wonderful woman, Mrs. Knapp is. I always said so even before all this happened. There's nothing she can't do. You ought to see the parlor furniture she recovered with her own hands, as good as any upholsterer you ever saw. And then didn't her Henry pester her to let him have a dog, and a *white* dog at that! Of course she didn't let him—you know how a white dog's hairs will show. When I was a girl I remember my Aunt Esther had a white dog —but I was telling you about how we first saw the fire. We had just turned the corner by Wertheimer's and I was looking down to pick my way, and Mrs. Knapp said, 'Good gracious, Mrs. Anderson, what's that on your roof?' I looked quick but I couldn't see anything, and she said, 'It looks like a—oh, yes, I see, a flame right by your chimney.'

"And then I knew it must be so, for that end chimney of mine had had a crack in it for ever so long, and I'd tried and *tried* to get a mason to come, but you know how they hate a little tinkering repair job, and anyhow for a *woman!* Well, Mrs. Knapp she started on a run for her house to telephone the fire department and I scuffled along as fast as I could for fear of slipping. I wasn't anywhere near my front walk yet when Mr. Knapp came running out from their house, bareheaded in all that cold with a pail in each hand. He could see me coming along slow and he hollered to me, 'Where's your long ladder, Mrs. Anderson?' And I hollered back, 'It's hung up under the eaves of the barn, but don't you go trying to climb up that steep icy roof, Mr. Knapp! You'll break your neck if you do!' I said to him just as I'm saying to you. I did my *best* to keep him from it! I feel bad enough without that. And I give you my word I hollered to him just as I told you, 'Don't you go trying to climb up that steep icy roof, Mr. Knapp. You'll break your neck if you do!' I said.

"He didn't say anything back so I don't know whether he heard me or not, though I hollered at the top of my voice, I promise you. He ran around through my back yard and I after him, only I had to go slow on account of the ice, and before I turned the corner of the house, I heard somebody yelling my name back of me, 'Mrs. Anderson! Come and let us in quick! Your house is on fire!' It was Mr. Emmet and his two boys from across the street. They had axes and they wanted me to let them in and up attic because they thought they could get at it from the inside. It seems they had a fire once in their chimney that they—well, while I was trying to get my latch-key in the keyhole— you can just better believe that by that time I was so mixed up I didn't know which end my head was on, and Mr. Emmet had to take the key away and open the door himself—that was after the fire-engine drove up and you know what a terrible clatter they always make, and I was wild about their getting out their big hose because my sitting room ceiling had just been replastered and I was afraid the water would run down and spoil it, and by that time any-how I had something else to worry about, for all creation was there, the way they do, you know, run wherever the fire engine goes, more men and boys than you ever *saw!* Awful tough-looking too, lots of them, from those low-down tenement houses near the tracks. . . . My, wasn't I glad to see Mrs. Knapp coming back! She's a master hand for man-aging things. She shooed all those hoodlums out double-quick. They were crowding right in after Mr. Emmet, bold as brass. I tell you there don't anybody stay long when *she* tells 'em to go. And then she headed off the firemen from turning on their hose till some of them had gone up attic to see how the Emmets were getting along, and some others had gone around back to see what Mr. Knapp was up to. She ran upstairs with them to the attic, and I went out on the porch and leaned around to see if I could make out what they were doing back of the house—and then—oh, then—I'll never forget it to my dying day! I saw a couple of firemen come around from the back of the house carrying some-thing. I couldn't see what it was, it was so dark, but the way they carried it, the way they stepped—when you're as old as I am, and have seen as many dead people . . . you *know!*

"I screamed out at them, 'Oh, oh, oh, what is it? What has happened?' But I knew before they said a word. One of them said, 'It's Mr. Knapp. Don't let Mrs. Knapp know till we can get the body over to the house!' And the other one said, 'He must have fallen off the roof and broken his back.' "

PART TWO

Chapter 7

IT was after an almost continuous thirty-six-hour session of work that Jerome Willing finally stepped out of his office, walked down the dark aisles between brown-linen-covered counters, nodded to the night-watchman, and shut the front door behind him. He crossed the street and turned to take a last affectionate survey of the building which sheltered his future. He was very tired, but as he looked at it he smiled to himself, a candid young smile of pride and satisfaction. It did not look to him like a four-storied brick front, but like a great door opened to the opportunity he had always longed for.

He stood gazing at it till a passer-by jostled him in the dusk. "Well, well . . ." he shook his head with a long, satisfied sigh, "mustn't stand mooning here; must get home to Nell and the little girls."

As he walked up the pleasant street, between the double rows of well-kept front yards and comfortable homes, he was thinking for the thousandth time how lucky he was, lucky every way you looked at it. For one thing lucky just this minute in having an ex-business-woman for a wife. Nell would understand his falling head over ears into work that first day and a half of his return after an absence. She never pulled any of that injured-wife stuff, no matter how deep in business he got. Fact was, she was as deep as he, and liked to see him get his teeth into it. She surely was the real thing as a wife.

When he let himself into the front door of the big old house, he heard the kids racketing around upstairs cheerfully, with their dog, and was grateful, as he and Nell so often were, for the ease and freedom and wide margin of small-town life. It wasn't in a New York flat that the children could raise merry hell like that, with nobody to object.

Through the open door he saw his wife's straight, slim, erect back. She was in the room they had set apart for her "office," and she was correcting a galley of proof, the ads. for to-morrow's papers.

"Hello there, Nell," he cried cheerfully. "Got my head above water at last. I'm home for a real visit to-night."

His wife laid down her fountain pen, turned around in her chair and smiled at him.

"That's good," she said. "What's the news?" Although she saw that he looked haggard with fatigue, she made no comment on it.

"The news is, Mrs. Willing," he said, bending over her for a kiss, "that I've got it just about all worked out."

*"Every*thing?" she said skeptically. "Even the bonus for the—"

"Pretty much! The store is surely tuning up! Give her a month to work the bearings in, and then watch our dust!"

They looked at each other happily, as he sat down in an armchair and leaned back with a long breath almost of exhaustion.

"Just like a dream, isn't it, all of it?" said Nell.

"You've said it! When I remember how I used to hope that perhaps if we scrimped and saved we might be able to buy a part interest somewhere, after I'd put in the best years of my life working for other men! Doesn't it make you afraid the alarm clock will ring and wake you up any minute?"

"But did you really settle the bonus question for the non-selling force?" asked Mrs. Willing, returning relentlessly to the most difficult point.

"I worked it out by giving it up for the present," he answered promptly.

She laughed. "Well, that's *one* way."

"I tell you, I've given up trying to make it all fit together like clockwork. Jobs in a store aren't alike. Salespersons are one thing, and you can find out exactly what they're worth in dollars and cents and pay them what they *earn*. But when they don't sell, it's different. What I'm going to do is to decide on basic wages for all the employees who don't sell—

just about enough to get along on. And then pull the really good work out of them with a bonus— I'll call it a bonus. It's really a sort of disguised fine for poor work. . . ."

"I wish you'd start at the beginning and get somewhere," said his wife rigorously. "If I put woolly statements like that into my advertising copy . . ."

"Well, here's the idea. Take the delivery crews for example.—There's only one of them now, of course, but there are going to be more soon. I offer them—oh, anything you like, twelve or fifteen dollars a week. That much they're sure of until they're fired, no matter how they do their work! 'But if you do your work perfectly,' I tell 'em, 'there's ten dollars a week more,' or something like that—I haven't made up my mind about the details. . . . 'There's ten dollars apiece for each of you if you get through the week with a perfect record.'—No, that doesn't put emphasis enough on team spirit; I'll make it ten or fifteen for the crew to divide— that'll give them an incentive for jacking each other up. We put the money in dimes and quarters in a box with a glass cover where they can look at it. Then every time they run without oil, or with a dirty car, or lose a package, or let a friend ride with them, out comes a dollar or a quarter or fifty cents, depending on how serious the case may be. Don't you just bet when they see their bonus shrinking before their eyes they'll buck up and *try?* Of course I couldn't use such a raw line with the better class— the accounting department, for instance, but something with the same idea.—By the way, that reminds me. I had to let Lester Knapp go—remember him? That dyspeptic gloom, second desk on the left as you go in."

Mrs. Willing nodded. "I don't know that I ever noticed him, but I've heard about him through the St. Peter's women. I thought you said you could manage."

"I never really thought that. I knew I couldn't right along. But I tell you, Nell, the truth is I'm soft when it comes to telling folks they can go. I hate to do it! I kidded myself into thinking Knapp might buck up. But it wouldn't do. For one thing Bronson can't stand him and I've got to back up my heads of departments. They've got to like their help or they can't get any work out of them." He sat forward in his chair and began playing with his watch chain.

"How did Mr. Knapp take it?"

"Oh, very decently—too decently! It made it all the harder. He admitted, when I asked him, that his work didn't interest him—that he hated it. When I half-way offered to give him a try at the selling end, he said he was sure he wouldn't like it any better,—was sure he wouldn't do even so well there. He said he knew he'd hate selling. Then when I put it up to him whether he thought a man can ever do good work if he doesn't like his job, he didn't say a thing, just kept getting whiter and whiter, and listened and listened. I did my best to let him down easy. Thanks of the firm for long and faithful service, take plenty of time to look for something else, no hurry. But it was no go. He's got plenty of brains of a queer sort, enough to see through that sort of talk. It was damned unpleasant. He has a very uncomfortable personality anyhow. Something about him that rubs you the wrong way." His voice was sharp with personal discomfort. He looked exasperated and aggrieved.

Out of her experience of his world and her knowledge of him, his wife's sympathy was instant. "It *is* hard on *you* having all those uncomfortable personal relations!" she said. "It always seems unfair that I can stay here at home with the children and draw a salary for writing advertisements that I love to do without sharing any of the dirty work."

"It's no joke," he agreed rather somberly. He looked at his watch. "Will I have time for a cigar before dinner?" he asked.

"Just about. I didn't know when you might be in, so the children and I have had ours. I told Kate to start broiling the steak when she heard you come in, but she's always slow."

He clipped and lighted his cigar with an air of immense comfort. Wasn't it something *like* to come back to such a home after working your head off, and find everything so easy and smooth!

"I've often thought," said his wife, "that letting people go would be the hardest part of administrative work for me."

He drew his first puff from his cigar and relaxed in his chair again. "Did I ever happen to tell you about the first time I had to fire any one?" He had told her several times but she gave no intimation of this, listening with a bright eager attention as he went on. "Way back when I'd only just pulled up to being head of the hosiery department at Burnham Brothers. She was a weak-kneed, incompetent, complaining old maid who was giving the whole department a black eye with the customers—ought to have been cleared out long before. Well, at last I got my nerve up to telling her to go, and she took it hard— made a scene, cried, threatened to kill herself, said her sick sister would starve. She was ninety per cent hysteric when she finally flung out of my office; and I was all in. So I beat it right up to the chief's office and sobbed out the whole talk on old J. P. Burnham's bosom."

Nell smiled reminiscently. "Yes, how we all used to lean on old J. P. when things went wrong. He always made me think of a dog-tired old Atlas, holding everything up on those stooped old shoulders of his. What did he say?"

"Oh, he didn't look surprised. I suppose I wasn't the first youngster to lose my nerve that way. He limped over and shut the door as if he was going to give me a long talk, but after all he didn't say much. Just a few pieces of advice with long pauses to let them sink in. But I've never forgotten them."

"No, you never did forget what he said," agreed Nell. She was very anxious to get on to another matter of importance but she saw by her husband's manner that he was talking himself out of his discomfort, so she gave him another chance to go on, by remarking, "But I don't see what *any*body can say about dismissing employees that would help a bit. It's just horrid and that's all there is to it."

"Well, he sort of stiffened me up, anyhow. Reminded me that running a store isn't philanthropy, that everybody from the boss down is there not to make a living for himself but to get goods sold. Made me see that for a department manager to keep an incompetent salesperson is just as dishonest as if he'd put his hand in the cash register. Worse, because the firm can stand losing a little cash enough sight better than having its customers snapped at and slighted. But what made the biggest impression on me was when he made me think of the other girls in the department who *did* do

their work, how unfair it was to them to keep a
lame duck that shoos everybody away from the department so they can't make any sales. They don't
come into the office and throw a fit, but they don't
get a fair deal just the same. Besides incompetence
is as catching as measles."

"That's so." Nell saw the point, thoughtfully.
"But it doesn't make it any pleasanter when the one
you're dismissing *is* throwing the fit."

"You bet your life it does not," agreed her husband, drawing with satisfaction on his excellent
cigar, "and old J. P. didn't put up any bluff about
it. He never said he enjoyed it. He said it was
just a part of the job, and you've got to stand up
to it if you're going to grow up to carry a man's
load. You're there to do your best for the business. He got another point over to me, a good
one—even for the lame ducks, it's kinder to
throw 'em right out as soon as you're sure they can't
make good. Don't let 'em stay on and gather mold
till they can't make a good try at anything else.
That's what made it so hard to tell Knapp he was
through. Uncle Charley ought to have told him
that, after he'd been a month in the store, twelve
years ago. It's a crime to let a man stay on and
vegetate and get mildewed like that. It must have
been clear for anybody but a blind man to see,
after he'd been a month at his desk, that he'd never

be anything but a dead loss in the business-world,
what with his ill health, and his wool-gathering, and
his tags of poetry! Uncle Charley ought to have
pushed him off to be a dish-washer, or a college professor, or one of those jobs that a man without any
jump in him can hold. It's just a sample of the way
poor Uncle Charley let the business run downhill
ever since he knew he had that cancer. You can't
blame him, in a manner of speaking. But the fact
is that the whole works from the stock-room to the
heating plant was just eaten up with dry rot."

"I'm sorry about that Mr. Knapp though, personally," said his wife. "He has a wife and three
young children, you know."

"The devil he has!" said Jerome annoyed. "Isn't
that just like him? Well, I'll try to look him up
to-morrow and see if I can't suggest *some*thing else.
Or give him a check with the thanks of the firm.
That'd be the cheapest way out. I know right now
there's no getting any decent work out of him.
Wherever I put him, he'd be like a bit of cotton
waste clogging up an oil-pipe."

"How about the accounting department, anyhow?" asked Nell. "Have you got it straightened
out?"

"Yes, now that Knapp has gone I guess it will
run all right. Thank heavens, there's one department in the department-store business that's pretty

well standardized.   That young expert accountant McKenzie and Blair sent on has straightened out the awful mess it was in.   You can tell where you stand now without closing down and taking a month's work to unravel the snarls.   And I guess Bronson is young enough to keep it running.   I'll give him the chance anyway; he's the livest wire on that side of the business if he is an awful roughneck! If he'll come through, it'll save time having to break somebody else in."

"I rather think Mr. McCarthy may be good enough, too," said Mrs. Willing.   "Since you spoke about him, I've been watching his window displays. Of course they're crude and he's a bit old.   But he has temperament and if you took him with you a time or two on buying trips to New York to let him look at the real thing and bought him a good modern manual on window-dressing—poor thing! I don't suppose he dreams there are books on his subject. . . ."

Her husband grunted.   "Yes, there's stuff in him. He's pretty red-headed and touchy, but there never was a good window-dresser yet that wasn't as prickly and unreasonable as a teething baby.   We'd have to put up with that from any one who had the temperament to do the work the way it ought to be done.   But that's about *all* the temperament I can stand.   Thank the Lord, I won't have to put up with a professional buyer. The more I think of it the more I'm sure I want to keep the buying in my own hands, every bit of it—unless *you* want to come along sometimes, of course. But no highly paid expert buyers in mine! You know them as well as I do. Did you ever see one that wasn't domineering and stuck on himself and dead sure he never made a mistake in his life?"

"Never!" Nell burned with a resentment of as long a date and as hot as her husband's. *"Never!* What always made me the tiredest about them was the way they blamed everything on the selling force or the advertising office. If the goods didn't move, was it ever *their* fault? Not once in a million times. It was because the salespeople couldn't sell or the ad.-writers couldn't write."

"And yet look at the times they get suckered into buying a carload of what everybody knew was lemons, only we mustn't let on, for fear of hurting their sacred temperamental feelings! No, by George, none of that in mine! I feel like sending up a Hallelujah when I think I'll never have to baby one of them again and smooth him down and calm his nerves. I've had the experience and training to handle that whole thing for myself. And I'm going to do it!"

A gong boomed pleasantly behind him. "Dinner," said Nell, getting up from her desk.

He threw away what was left of his cigar and went into the comfortable dining-room, his appetite whetted by the odor of steak, onions and fried potatoes.

"I bought a case of that near-beer Wertheimer's has," said his wife, uncorking and pouring out a foaming brown glassful. "I can't see that it's not just as good as it ever was."

"Yes, tastes pretty good to me to-night, that's sure," said Jerome, taking a long drink and smiling as he cut into the thick steak. His wife let him alone while he took the sharpest edge off his appetite. She herself had often come in after working overtime in an office! But as he started in on a second round of everything, she said, "It'll be a surprise for the old store, won't it, to have somebody really *buying* for it after the junk that's been loaded onto its shelves?"

"Uncle Charley," pronounced Jerome, "never got beyond the A. T. Stewart 1872 notion of stocking up four times a year with 'standard goods.' " They both laughed at the old phrase.

"Standard goods!" said Nell. "How funny it sounds! When you can't sell a button the year after it's made nowadays!"

"I just *hope*," said Jerome, "I just hope to the Lord that some of that gang of crooks who used to sell Uncle Charley try to work the same game on

me just once! Where in the world did they *get* the
out-of-the-ark junk they used to work off on him?
Must have had it stored in a barn somewhere!"

His wife thought silently that now, after he had
eaten and was beginning on his pie, with a second
cigar in prospect, perhaps she might get to the question she had really wanted to ask all along. "Did
you see that young Crawford at Jordan Marsh's?"
she asked.

"Yes," said Jerome.

And Nell knew that for some reason it was all off.
"Won't he do?" she said in disappointment. "You
do need a store superintendent so awfully if you're
going to be away on buying trips."

"Well, it's better to wait and get the right person
than rush in and take somebody who'd gum the
whole works. Oh, nothing wrong with Crawford.
He's a comer. But the more I talked with him the
surer I was that he wouldn't fit. Nobody like him
would fit into the organization the way we want it.
That corking slogan of yours says it all—"The
Homelike Store." Well, no smooth, big-city proposition like Crawford could be homelike, not in a
thousand years. He wouldn't want to be. He
wouldn't see the point. He'd be too smart for the
town. He wouldn't go to church. He'd play golf
on Sundays. He wouldn't belong to any of the
societies or clubs. He'd drive a snappy runabout

and beat it off to the city. The long and the short of it is that he'd be bored by the town and show it."

Nell saw all that. She nodded her head. She tried to imagine him at a church supper in the basement of the First Congo Church—and gave it up.

"Worse than that, it came to me," said Jerome, "that any man with pep enough for the job would have too much pep. He'd want to look forward to being taken into the business. And I don't want any partner but you. This is *our* store! But leave that alone. He wouldn't know how to handle the girls. He'd be used to flip, knowing, East-side tenement-house kids. How would he get along with our small-town American high-school graduates who're as good as anybody and know it? He might try to get gay with them—you haven't forgotten Ritchie at Burnham's? None of that for *our* store. We've got little girls of our own—and besides in a little place like this scandal gets round so quick and people take it so personally."

"But you've got to have somebody. There are some pretty keen business women," suggested his wife. "Why not try one of them—they give more value for the same salary. They stick to their work and don't make trouble. Mostly they have tact enough not to antagonize the customers. Don't you think the business could afford one of the really good ones?"

"It can afford pretty much any salary for the right party. Nothing's too good for our store, Nell! Yes, I'd rather have a woman any day. I've thought about one or two of the best I know. They're good, good as the best—wear the right sort of quiet clothes, don't make a noise, always on the job, and they'd never make a row about not being taken into the firm. Yes, I like the idea of a woman for store manager—but—well—none of the ones I can think of are exactly right. They don't quite stand for the idea I've got for the business, don't make the personal friendly appeal. You know how they are—quiet enough and efficient enough, but they've got the big-town label plastered all over them, with their smart clothes and their permanent waves and their voices going up and down the scale. Half our customers would be afraid of them. And you hate people you are afraid of. I suppose a woman like that would *do,* but I'd rather wait a while to see if better material doesn't come along. I want somebody the customers would think of as one of *themselves.*"

"Yes, of course that would be better," acquiesced Nell. "But you have to take what you can get. Are you sure there's nobody in the store?"

"I've been over the selling force with a fine-toothed comb. There's nobody there who can go higher than floor manager. Miss Flynn, the head of the Cloak-and-Suits, is the nearest. She's a wise old bird, with lots of experience. But she plays favorites with her girls, picks on certain ones for no special reason and protects others, no matter what they do. That's the Irish of it. More temperament!"

"I suppose, anyhow, it's always better policy to get an outsider. It means less friction. But it does seem as though we ought to be able to find some one in this town, some one who's respected and liked by the people here."

"If we could, she'd draw all the women into the store after her, as though they were her sisters and her cousins, especially if it was somebody known as a good buyer already. There are always some such in any community. We'd want a woman old enough to take care of herself but young enough to have all her physical stamina left, a nice woman, a first-rater, who could learn and grow into the job. Isn't it exasperating how, when you have a grand opening like that for just the right person, you can't lay your hand on her!"

"I could do it myself," said Nell, "even although all my training has been in the ad. department. I know I could."

"You could walk away with it, Nell. But we need you for the advertising, and besides that job would take you away from home all the time. And of course somebody has to be here for the children."

"No, I'd never consent to leave the children," said Nell. "I didn't really mean it. I was just thinking what fun it would be if there were two of me."

"I wish there were!" said her husband, fervently.

"On second thought, I'm not at all sure *I* do!" she said, laughing.

They went back now into the living-room and sank down in armchairs, Nell with a cigarette. She had looked first to be sure that the curtains were down so that she was not visible from the street. "No," said Jerome, "we'd better not consider either of us taking it. It would be a waste not to stick to the lines we've been trained for. I suppose it's just a pipe-dream to think I can find exactly the right person. But you can bet your last cent I won't tie up for any long contract to anybody who isn't exactly the right person. I've got a hunch that some day the right one will walk into the store and let me lasso her. And I've faith enough in my hunch to believe I'll know her when I see her, and . . ."

"Isn't that the 'phone?" asked his wife, suspending her cigarette in mid-air.

"Oh, Lord! I hope not, just when we're settled for the evening!" cried her husband.

"I'll answer it," she said, going out into the hall.

When she came back she looked grave. "Oh, Jerome, what do you think? That Mr. Knapp has just had a terrible accident, they say. Fell off a roof and killed himself."

Jerome's impulse was to cry out blamingly, "Isn't that just like him! Why couldn't he choose some other time!" But he repressed this decently. "Well, what do you think we ought to do?" he asked Nell.

He was frightfully tired. The idea of stirring out of his chair appalled him. But he wanted to establish a tradition in the town that the store looked after its employees like a father.

She hesitated. "Let me run upstairs and start the children to bed. I believe we'd better go around to their house and offer to do anything we can to help out."

Chapter 8

A^S they stepped quickly along in the dark, they tried to piece together the chronology of the late afternoon for Knapp and decided that this tragic ending to his feeble life must have come even before he could have seen his wife to tell her of his dismissal from the store. "I'm so glad of *that!*" said Nell Willing, softly. "Now she need never know."

Her husband gave a hearty inward assent. It was the devil anyhow to be so intimately concerned in other people's lives as an employer was.

They found the little house alight from top to bottom, and full of people, whispering, moving about restlessly and foolishly, starting and turning their heads at any noise from upstairs. An old woman, who said she was the Knapps' next-door neighbor and most intimate friend, stopped crying long enough to tell them in a loud whisper that the doctor said Mr. Knapp was still alive, but unconscious, and dying from an injury to the spine. The children, she said, had been taken away by a sort of relative, Mrs. Mattie Farnham, who would keep them till the funeral. Asked about Mrs. Knapp, she replied that Mrs. Knapp was with the doctor and her dying husband and was, as always, a marvel of self-possession and calm. "As long as there's anything to do, Mrs. Knapp will be right there to do it," she said. "She's a wonderful woman, Mrs. Knapp is."

The Willings sat for a time, awkwardly waiting, with the other people awkwardly waiting, and then went away, leaving behind them a card on which Jerome had penciled the request to be allowed to be useful in any way possible "to the family of a highly respected member of the Emporium staff."

As they walked home through the darkness, they exchanged impressions. "That old neighbor's head is just like a snake's, didn't you think?" said Jerome.

"She seemed very sympathetic, I thought," said Nell extenuatingly.

"She did seem to think a lot of Mrs. Knapp," admitted Jerome.

"All the women in St. Peter's do," said Nell. "Mrs. Prouty says she doesn't know what they would do in parish work if it weren't for Mrs. Knapp. She's one of the *workers*, you know. And a good headpiece too."

"I imagine she's had to develop those qualities or starve to death," conjectured Jerome, forgetting for an instant that the man he was criticizing lay at the point of death.

The memory of this kept them silent for a moment and then Nell asked, "Did you notice that living-room?"

"You bet your life I did," said her husband with a lively professional interest. "The only living-room I've seen in this town that had any style to it. Did you see that sofa? And those curtains?"

"They say she's a wonderful housekeeper. The kind who stays right at home and sticks to her job. You never see her out except at church."

"No, I don't believe I've ever laid eyes on her," said Jerome.

"And people are always talking about how beautifully her children are brought up. With real manners, you know. And such perfect ways at table. How *do* you suppose she does it?"

"What *did* she ever see in Knapp?" Jerome cast out the age-old question with the invariable, ever-fresh accent of amazement which belongs with it.

"Oh, they married very young," said thirty-year-old Mrs. Willing wisely. "I believe he hadn't finished his course at the State University. He was specializing in English literature."

"He *would!*" ejaculated Jerome, pregnantly.

His wife laughed. And then they both remembered again that the man was dying.

When they heard through Dr. Merritt that poor Lester Knapp would not die but would be a bed-ridden invalid, a dead-weight on his wife, the Willings along with everybody else in town were aghast at the fatal way in which bad luck seems to heap up on certain unfortunate beings.

"That poor wife of his! What has she ever done to deserve such a tragic life!" cried young Mrs. Willing pityingly.

"For the Lord's sake, what's going to keep them from being dependent on public charity?" thought Jerome, apprehensively.

He sent up to the house with a tactfully worded letter a check for a hundred dollars, saying he thought the store was under a real obligation to its faithful employee of long standing. "But," he thought, "you can't keep that sort of help up forever."

"I needn't have worried!" he told himself the next morning, when he found his check returned with a short, well-written expression of thanks, but of unwillingness to accept help which could only be temporary. "We shall have to manage, somehow, sooner or later," the letter ran. It was signed Evangeline Knapp. "What a fool name, Evangeline!" thought the young merchant, somewhat nettled by the episode.

After this he was away on a buying expedition

that lasted longer than he intended, and when he came home they had a set-to with leaking steam-pipes in the store. He thought nothing more of the Knapps till, meeting Dr. Merritt on the street, he remembered to ask for news. Knapp was better now, he heard, suffering less atrociously, with periods of several hours of relative quiet. There had been no actual fracture of the spinal bones, but the spinal cord seemed affected, probably serious effusion of blood within the spinal canal, with terrible nervous shock.

How doctors do run on about their cases if you get them started! Mr. Willing cut short any more of this sort of medical lingo by asking to be told in plain terms if the man would ever walk again.

"Probably not," said Dr. Merritt, "though he will reach the wheel-chair stage and perhaps even crutches. Still, you never can be sure. . . . But he is not a robust man, you know. I told you about his obstinate dyspepsia. I never saw a worse case."

Mr. Willing's healthy satisfied face expressed the silent disgust of a strong, successful man for a weak and unsuccessful one. "What in hell are they go-ing to *do?*" he inquired. He added, blamingly, "Three children! Lord!"

Dr. Merritt found nothing to answer and went on, looking grave. He had helped all three children into the world, had worn himself out over the two older ones in their constantly recurring maladies, and felt for them the tenderness and affection we have for those who have given us much anxiety.

Jerome Willing was sitting at his office-desk, but he was not working. He was dreaming. Into the quiet of his office filtered a hum of activity exquisite to his ears, the clicking of billing-machines, the whirr of parcel-carriers, the sound of customers' voices, buying merchandise. Out there the store was smoothly functioning, supplying modern civilization to ten thousand men and women. And it was *his* store! Not only did he reap the profit—that was a small part of his pleasure. It was his personality which gave all those people the opportunity to satisfy their needs, that was educating them to desire better things. He called that a pretty fine way of doing your share in raising the American standard of living. It was a whale of a job to get it into shape, too. What a mess the business had got into during the stagnant passivity of the last ten years of poor Uncle Charley's life. It was a wonder that so much as four walls and a roof were left.

Well, that just showed what an unheard-of favorable position it had, the old store. It hung on and kept alive like a rugged old lilac bush that you'd tried to cut down. What wouldn't it do, now that it had somebody to water it and enrich it—somebody who cared more about it than about anything else in the world? And somebody who had the right training, the right experience and information to do the job. That was what had struck him most forcibly during the last six months, when he had been walking round and round his new work, getting ready to take hold of it. He saw that there was wonderful opportunity not only for him, but just as wonderful for the store. And to take advantage of it every scrap of his knowledge of business would come in, all that he had picked up at trade conventions, what he'd learned out of books on administration, above all, every hour of experience. Yes, every one, from his first bewildered week as a salesman to the later years of the intoxicating battle of personalities in the Market, when on his weekly buying trips to New York, he had gone the round of the wholesalers, comparing values, noting styles, making shrewdly hidden calculations, keeping an inscrutable face before exquisite things that made him cry out inwardly with admiration, misleading buyers from other stores, keeping his own counsel, feeling his wits moving swiftly about inside his skull with the smooth, powerful purr of a high-class motor. If he could do all that just to be in the game, just to measure up to other buyers, what couldn't he do now!

What a half-year he had had! What a wonderful

time he and Nell had put in together in this period
of waiting and preparation. No matter how fine
the realization might be, he was old enough to know
that nothing could ever be for them like this period
of creative planning when, moving around his problem, he had studied it, concentrated on it and felt
that he had the solution in his own brain and personality. It fitted him! It was his work! It was
like something in a book, like a missionary going out
into the field, like a prophet looking beyond the veil
of the present. Yes, that was what it was—he
looked through to the future, right past what was
there, the little halting one-horse affair, with its
meager force of employees, so many of them super-
annuated, others of good stuff, but in the wrong
places, all of them untrained and uninformed, dull,
listless, bored, without a notion of what a fascinating job they had. He had looked through them and
had seen the store he meant to have by the time he
was forty-five; for he knew enough to look far
ahead, to take his time, to build slowly and surely.
There it stood, almost as plain to his eye as the poor
thing that now took its place. He saw a big, shining-
windowed building, the best in all that part of the
state, with eighty or a hundred employees, trained,
alert, on their toes, sure of their jobs, earning big
money, developing themselves, full of personality
and zip, as people can be only when they are in

work they're meant for and have been trained for.

It would never be what a man from the city would call a *big* business. He never wanted it so big that he couldn't keep his hand on it all. It would be *his* business, rather than a big one. But at that, he saw now, especially with Nell getting a salary for doing the advertising, it would bring them in more income than anybody else in town dreamed of having. They could live as they pleased as far as spending went. Not that that was the important part,—but still a very agreeable one.

He was sure of all this, sure! By God, he couldn't fail! The cards were stacked for him. A prosperous town, just the right size; good-will and a monopoly of trade that ran back for forty years; no big city within fifty miles—why, even the trains providentially ran at hours that were inconvenient for people who wished to go to the city to shop. And no rivals worth mentioning; nobody he couldn't put out of business inside ten years. He thought again, as he had so many times, how miraculous it was that in the ten years since Uncle Charley had lost his grip, no Jew merchant had cut in to snatch the rich heart out of the situation. Nobody could do that now. He had the jump on the world.

With half-shut eyes he let himself bask for a few minutes in this glorious vision; then, picking up his hat and overcoat he left the office and, alert to every impression behind his pleasant mask of affability, moved down between household linens and silk goods to the front door and stepped out into the street. He had seen out of the tail of his eye how that Boardman girl was making a mess of showing lining silks to a customer, and made a mental note to call in Miss Atkinson, the floor superintendent, and tell her to give the girl a lesson or two on draping silks as you showed them and making sure that the price-tag was where the customer could get the price without having to ask for it.

He was really on his way to the bank, but as he stood in the front door, he saw that McCarthy was dressing a window for the sporting-goods department and decided to go across the street to look at it. Jerome was convinced that window-dressers never back far enough off from their work, never get the total effect. Like everybody else they lose themselves in details. He stepped across to the opposite side of the street and stood there, mingling with the other passers-by.

As he looked back towards the store, he noticed a tall woman coming rapidly down the street. His eye was taken at once by the quality of her gait. He sometimes thought that he judged people more by the way they walked than by any other standard. He always managed to get a would-be employee to walk across the room before taking her on. This tall, dark-haired woman in the well-made dark coat had just the sort of step he liked to see, vigorous and swift, and yet unhurried. He wondered who she was.

He saw her slow her pace as she approached the store and stand for a moment looking in at McCarthy fussing with his baseball bats and bicycle-lamps. She really looked at him, too, as few people ever look at anything, as if she were thinking about what she was looking at, and not about something in her own head. He had a good view of her face now, a big-featured, plain face that looked as though she might be bad-tempered but had plenty of motive-power. She was perhaps forty years old. He wondered what she was thinking about McCarthy.

She turned into the store now. Oh, she was a customer. Well, she was one they wanted to give satisfaction to. He stepped back across the street and into the store to make sure that the salesperson to whom she addressed herself was attentive. But she was nowhere to be seen. Perhaps she had gone directly upstairs.

He went along the aisle, casting as he went that instinctively attentive look of his on the notions and ribbons, and up the stairs to the mezzanine floor where his office was. He meant to leave his hat and coat there and go on in search of the new cus-

tomer. He heard a woman's voice inside the accounting-room saying, "Will you tell me, please,
where Mr. Willing's office is."

He knew in a moment, without seeing her, that the
voice belonged to the woman he had seen. That
was the kind of voice she *would* have.

"This is Mr. Willing," he said, coming into the
accounting-room behind her. "Won't you come with
me?"

Arrived in his office, she took the chair to which
he motioned her and said at once, in a voice which
he divined to be more tense than usual, "This is
Mrs. Lester Knapp, Mr. Willing. You said, you
remember . . . You wrote on a card that you would
do something to help us. I thought perhaps you
could let me try to fill my husband's place. We
need the money very much. I would do my best
to learn."

Mr. Willing had the sure prescience of a man
whose antennæ are always sensitive to what concerns his own affairs. He had an intuition that something important was happening and drew himself
hastily together to get the best out of it for the
business. First of all, to make talk and have a
chance to observe her, he expressed his generous
sympathy and asked in detail about poor Knapp.
He assured her that he was more than willing to
help her in any way to reconstruct their home-life

and said he was in no doubt whatever that they could find a place for her in the business, though not in Mr. Knapp's old place. "That office is entirely reorganized and there are no vacancies. But in the sales department, Mrs. Knapp. There are always opportunities there. And for any one with a knack for the work, much better pay. Of course, like all beginners, you would have to begin at the bottom and learn the business."

She answered in a trembling voice, with an eagerness he found pitiful, that she was quite willing to start anyhow, do anything, for a chance to earn.

He guessed that she had been horribly afraid of him, had heard perhaps from her husband that he was hard and cold, had dreaded the interview, and was now shaken by the extremity of her relief. He liked the gallant way she had swung straight into what she had feared.

To give her time to recover her self-control, he turned away from her and fumbled for a moment in his drawer to get out an employment blank, and then, as he held it in his hand and looked at its complicated questions, he realized that it was another of the big-city devices that did not hit his present situation. It would be foolish to give it to this woman, with its big-city rigmarole of inquiry, —"Give the last three places you worked; the address in full of last three employers; what was your position; reason for leaving," etc., etc. He put it back in the drawer and instead asked the question to which he already knew the answer, "You have, I suppose, had no experience at all in business?"

But after all, he did not know the answer, it seemed, for she said, "Oh, yes, before I was married. My father keeps the biggest store in Brandville, up in the northern part of the state. It's only a general store of course. Brandville is a small place. But I used to help him always. I liked it. And Father always made a good thing out of the business."

Jerome was delighted, "Why, that's the best sort of training," he told her. "I always maintain that country-store methods are the ideal: where you know every customer personally, and all about their tastes and needs and pocketbooks. Did you really work there? Sell goods?"

"Yes, indeed. From the time I was a little girl— after school in the afternoons and in vacation time. Father had a special little step-ladder made for me so that I could carry it around and climb up to the shelves. I am the only child, you know. Father was proud that I liked to work with him."

The vivid expression of her face as she told him of this childhood memory made Jerome Willing wonder that he could have thought she looked bad tempered. She looked like a live wire, that was all.

And they never, in the nature of things, looked like feather beds.

"Well . . ." he said, to give himself time to think. "Well . . ." He pulled an official-looking loose-leafed book over to him and began looking through it as though its contents had some connection with placing the applicant before him. But as a matter of fact the book contained nothing but some of his old reports from the Burnham days. He was turning over in his mind the best way to handle the situation. Should he put her in a slow-moving department like furniture or jewelry till she got used to things? That was the safe, conservative way. But he didn't believe in the safe and conservative if a chance to move faster looked good. And at that it wouldn't be much of a chance. If she didn't pan out, he could move her back into the table-linen, and no harm done.

He looked at her keenly to see the effect of his announcement. "I believe the thing for you," he said, "is the Ladies' Cloak-and-Suit department. I can put you right in as stock-girl till you get the hang of things. I always think stock-girl work is the finest sort of training for salesmanship."

He saw by her expression that she did not know what a stock-girl was, that she did not realize what a privilege it was to be put at once in the coveted Cloak-and-Suits. But she rose at once. He liked

the way she stood up, with one thrust of her powerful body. That was the way he liked to have salespeople get up, alertly, when a customer came in. It
expressed willingness to serve and strength to give
good service. The sale was half made, right there,
he told his salespeople.

"I could go to work to-day," she said. "I didn't
know . . . I hoped . . . perhaps. I put on a black
dress to be ready in case you might have . . ."

By George! She was ready to step right into it
this minute. She slipped off her well-cut cloak
and showed a severe black serge dress.

"Why, yes, if you like," he said negligently. She
took off her hat showing magnificent dark hair,
streaked with gray.

He said casually, as if making talk, "I happened
to see you watching our window-dresser at work as
you came in. What was your impression of what
he was doing?"

She said seriously, reflectively, "Well, Mr. Mc-
Carthy always seems to me to put too many things
in his windows. I've thought a good many times
that if he chose his things with more care and had
fewer it might catch the eye better."

"Well, Great Scott!" said Mr. Willing to himself
in extreme surprise. Aloud he said impassively, "We
haven't talked wages yet. Stock-girls only get ten
dollars a week to begin with, you know."

"That is a great deal better than nothing," she said firmly. "We have a few savings that will keep us going till I can get a start. And perhaps I may learn the business fairly quickly."

"You bet your life you will," said the proprietor of the store inaudibly. Aloud he said, "The cloakroom for salespeople is at the other end of the second floor. If you'll put your things there and come back here, I'll take you to your department and introduce you to Miss Flynn."

When Jerome Willing came back to his office he stood for a while motionless, frowning down at his desk. "Yes, of course it was preposterous," he told himself. He'd known her less than half an hour—all the same he'd backed those crazy hunches of his before—it had paid him to play his hunches! And if something like that *did* pan out . . . he fell once more into a reverie. She was just the kind of woman he was looking for, mature, with a local following, somebody the women of the town trusted. He could hear their voices plain, "Ask Mrs. Knapp to step here a minute, won't you please? She has such good taste, I'd trust her judgment. . . . " And she'd be tied up so tight with a sick husband and family of children there'd be no chance of some one snatching her away and marrying her just after he'd taught her the job.

It would be *fun* to teach somebody who wanted to learn. Creative work—it always came back to that if you were going to do anything first-rate. You took raw material and shaped it with your own intelligence. If only she might be the raw material! If she turned out to have only a little capacity to study and get information out of books as well as the character and personality he was pretty sure she had. Wilder dreams had come true. His thoughts ran on again to the future of the store . . . with a competent manager keeping the wheels and cogs running smoothly . . . with him to do the buying . . . small lots at a time . . . every fortnight . . . quick sales . . . rapid turnovers that made low profits possible. With Nell handling the advertising campaign as only an intelligent college woman could, with just the right adaptation of those smart modern methods of hers to this particular small town they were serving. She was a first-rater, Nell was! It always had been fun to work with her even before they were married! And what a lark to work with her now! Good thing for Nell too! It had been asking a great deal of a real, sure-enough business-woman like Nell to give it all up for *Kinder, Küche,* and *Kirche.* Nell had been willing, had been happy, had loved having the babies, had made them all happy. But now the children were both going to school it stood to reason she'd find time hang heavy on her hands, whip-stitch that she was! And life in a small town was Hades if you didn't have lots of work to do in spite of the big lawns and comfortable roomy homes. As far as that went, life anywhere was Hades if you didn't have a job your size. You could see Nell had thought of all that (though she had been too good a sport to speak of it) by the way she had grabbed at this chance to get back into the old work, the work she'd loved so, and done so well at Burnham's. Now if this Mrs. Knapp would only come through!

He brought himself up short again. . . . What a kid he was to let his imagination reel it off like this —but a minute later he was thinking how he and Nell would enjoy giving an apt pupil steers, show-ing her how to use a microscope in fabric tests, how to know the right points of a well-made garment, how to handle her girls as she got along to execu-tive work. . . . Oh, well, probably it was only a pipe dream—and he knew enough to keep it to him-self.

The clock in the National Bank opposite began striking. Jerome glanced at it and saw with aston-ishment that the hands pointed to twelve o'clock. Time to go home to lunch. As he got his hat and coat, he was wondering whether he had wasted a forenoon or whether perhaps on the contrary . . .

Chapter 9

MRS. WILLING was as much interested as her husband in the arrival of Mrs. Knapp in the store. When he had finished telling her about the interview and they had laughed and wondered over the acuteness of the novice's criticism of McCarthy's window-dressing, Nell said reflectively: "Do you know, from all I've heard about her from the St. Peter's women—I wouldn't be a bit surprised . . . "

Jerome recognized the idea to which his wife's imagination, like his own, had leaped, but he did not think it at all necessary to let Nell know that the same possibility had occurred to him.

He shook his head disapprovingly. "No, nothing doing," he said. "Anybody that's got so much pep to begin with, they're always hard to handle. Want to boss everything."

He was pleased to have his wife point out what had already occurred to him, the strangle-hold which their relative economic situations gave them over Mrs. Knapp. "I don't believe she'd ever be hard to handle or want more than you wanted to give her—with all those reasons at home for holding onto a job," said Nell. She had as good a business head as Jerome, however, felt as well as he how visionary it was to build even the slightest hopes on so slight a foundation, and now contributed her own share of cold water to the prudent lowering of their expectations. "But a woman with no experience of business! Women who have spent fifteen or twenty years housekeeping are no good for anything else."

"I forgot to tell you," said Jerome, "that she had worked some before she was married. Her father keeps the stcre in Brandville. I looked him up. Very good rating. She may get some of her ability from him. Those country-store men sometimes acquire a real business hunch. But see here, how can her family manage if she's away all day? I didn't feel like asking her. But I wondered if she could be depended on. There's nothing more of a bother in a store than somebody who is always having to miss a day."

"Mrs. Prouty was telling me how she's got everything organized there. They are all saying it's just like her. Mr. Knapp is fairly comfortable now and can read, and sit up in bed, and doesn't need constant care. There's nothing anybody can *do* for him, now, poor thing! The two older children are big enough to take care of themselves and dress their little brother and help around the house. It seems that several of the people at the store are being very helpful—not salespeople or anybody in Mr. Knapp's office but a couple of the delivery boys and one of the cleaning women. The cleaning woman, old Mrs. Hennessy, works at the store you see, before and after hours, so she can go to the Knapp house in the daytime an hour or so to do up the work. And the delivery boys take turns dropping in nights and mornings to look out for the furnace and empty ashes and do the heavy things. They stop in daytimes too as they go by to see if he wants anything. Oh, they manage, somehow."

"How good poor people are to anybody in trouble," remarked Jerome comfortably, pulling on his pipe and wondering for the first time if perhaps there really might be some truth in that threadbare remark which he had heard and repeated so many times and never believed a word of.

"They say Mr. Knapp was always very kind to them at the store," said his wife, "the work people, I mean—was lovely to old Mrs. Hennessy when her grandson had to be sent to the sanatorium. And he helped one of the delivery boys out of a scrape."

The proprietor of the store frowned and took his pipe hastily out of his mouth. "He *did!* Which boy I wonder? What do you suppose he'd been doing? I'd like to know more about that!" He was very much vexed at the idea that something about which he had no information had been happening at the store. It was just like that impractical, weak-kneed Knapp to shield an erring employee and interfere with discipline! He felt again a wave of the inexplicable annoyance which every contact with Knapp had caused him from the first time he ever laid eyes on the man. Helping the delivery boys to cover up their tracks, was he? Lord! what a dead loss that man was every way you looked at him. He didn't blame Harvey Bronson for being rubbed the wrong way by him and snapping his head off. Who wouldn't?

He remembered suddenly that the man was now a bed-ridden cripple, cooled down, put his pipe back in his mouth and said aloud: "Well, I wish you'd drop in to the Cloak-and-Suits after a week or so and just get an impression of her yourself."

Miss Flynn, the veteran head saleswoman in the Cloak-and-Suits told Mrs. Willing that the new employee was a wonder, and that the way she had taken hold made them all sit up. "She's just eating it up, Mrs. Willing, just eating it up. She's learned her stock quicker than anybody you ever saw, as if she loved it. Now I never expect a stock-girl to know where things are inside the first week; they do *well* if they do. But Mrs. Knapp—every minute there wasn't a customer on hand, would she fluff up her hair and get out her vanity box or put her head together with the other girls, turning their backs on the stairs—not much! Mr. Willing had told her the way he's told every stock-girl we've tried, that the first thing to do was to learn her stock and she went to it as if 'twas to a wedding! With never a word from me, she just tore off into the stock-cabinet every chance she got. First off, she made a list of the things, the way they hung and then as she worked I could see her look at her piece of paper, her lips moving, just like a kid learning a spelling lesson. And yet for all she was so deep in that, she'd keep her eye out for customers—yes, she did! You wouldn't believe a *stock-girl* would feel responsible about customers, would you, Mrs. Willing, when there's nothing in it for her? But for a fact she'd keep poking her head out of the stock-cabinet to make sure nobody had come in; and once I saw her, when she didn't know I was looking, spot a customer coming up the stairs, and go to stir up that lazy Margaret Donahue to get busy, and she reading a novel under the counter the sly way she does behind my back!" Miss Flynn perceived that she had wandered from the sequence of her narrative and added now, "Well, by studying her work like that, it wasn't three days—really, I mean it, Mrs. Willing, not *three days* before she knew where every cloak and suit in this entire department was hung, or if it had been sold. I heard Ellen O'Hern that can't remember a *thing* ask her to bring out that blue knit cape with the astrachan collar, and Mrs. Knapp say to her, in a nice quiet tone, so the customer couldn't hear, "That was sold day before yesterday, don't you remember, to Mrs. Emery," and go and get a blue broadcloth cape with a white wool collar that was the closest thing to the other cape. And Ellen O'Hern made the sale too. It was a good choice. I asked Mrs. Knapp how she ever happened to think of picking out just that and she said the customer just looked to her as though that blue broadcloth would be her style. I believe she slept nights on that list of stock she made and said it over as she did her hair in the morning. Lovely hair she's got, hasn't she, if she *is* so very plain in the face. And yet look at the style of her! Sometimes I think that the plain ones have more style than the pretty ones, always."

Before she had finished this aphorism, her Celtic wit perceived that her Celtic fluency had led her into what was rather a difficult position when she considered that she was talking with that important personage, the young and very pretty wife of the proprietor; and her Celtic tongue added smoothly, without so much as a comma, "though of course there *are* certain lucky people that have all of everything." She smiled meaningly as she spoke,

and told herself with an inward grin that she had
got out of that pretty well, if she did say so . . .

"Selling goods does polish people up to be the
smooth article," thought the wife of the proprietor,
"but Miss Flynn thinks she's just a little too smart.
Flattery that's too open is not the *best* salesmanship.
It wears thin if you use it too often. I wouldn't be
surprised if Miss Flynn had lost more sales than
she thinks with that oily manner. It's more than
probable that some of the silent country women who
come in here go away without buying because they
think that Miss Flynn is trying to make fools of
them. No, she's not really Grade A. But she's so
old she'll have to get out before so very long anyhow."

After this silent, inward colloquy, the voices of the
two women became audible once more.

"Don't you believe, Miss Flynn, that Mrs. Knapp
could be tried out in saleswork soon?"

"I'd try her to-morrow if it was me," said Miss
Flynn promptly. "I bet a nickel she could knock
the spots off that Margaret Donahue this minute."

"Oh, yes," Mrs. Willing remembered, "Jerome
had told her that Miss Flynn had that objectionable
habit of 'playing favorites' among her girls—the
Irish were so *personal* anyhow! No abstract ideas
of efficiency and justice."

Aloud she said, "I'm going to suggest to Mr. Will-

ing that you let her have a try at noon hours, for the
next week, when some of the girls are out to lunch."
She added tactfully to avoid seeming to commit the
unpardonable offense of coming in from another department to dictate to a head salesperson about her
girls, "We're both of us so sorry for Mrs. Knapp
in her great trouble we would like to help her
along."

"Yes, indeed, poor thing! Poor thing!" said Miss
Flynn at once, in a sympathetic tone. But all the
same, something of the substance of the younger
woman's silent observation had reached her dimly.
What was Mrs. Willing up to? She didn't like
people nosing around her department that hadn't any
business there. What was Mrs. Willing, anyhow,
when you got right down to it? Just the advertising
woman, wasn't she? And what was all this interest
in Mrs. Knapp about? Were they thinking perhaps
of getting rid of another faithful gray-haired employee, as they had already in other departments.
Her Irish blood warmed. There'd be something said
before . . .

A few days later, "We were mistaken about that
Mrs. Knapp, Mr. Willing," said Miss Flynn somewhat belligerently. "Mrs. Willing said you wanted
to have me try her out in saleswork, so I gave
her a salesbook yesterday, and explained how to

record sales and all, and turned her loose at the noon hour. But she hasn't got the stuff in her. I'm sure of it."

"What makes you think so, Miss Flynn?" asked the proprietor of the store mildly. As always when it was a question of the welfare of the store, he called in peremptorily every one of his five senses and all his attention, experience and acumen. On the aspect, attitude, voice and intonation of Miss Flynn he focused all of those trained faculties in a burning beam of which she was happily unaware. What she saw was his negligent attitude as he tipped back in his swivel chair, sometimes looking up at her, sometimes down at the blotting paper on his desk, on which he drew, as if absent-mindedly, an intricate network of lines, like a problem in geometry. She thought that perhaps after all the Willings were not so dangerously interested in Mrs. Knapp's advancement as she had feared, and she relaxed a little from what had been her intention on entering the room. It certainly was a fact that Mrs. Knapp did need a job something terrible, with those three children and a bed-ridden husband and all. "Well, I don't mean that she's not all right, well enough, and a good worker and all, but no salesgirl. Why, let me tell you how she let a customer get away to-day. *Let* her get away! Pushed her right out of the store, I might say; wouldn't let her buy what she wanted. I was watching from across the aisle, without letting on, to see how she'd do. She was helping out in sweaters because they were short of help this noon. I saw her showing the goods to a customer. I heard the customer say, 'My, isn't that lovely!' and I heard Mrs. Knapp say,—you'd hardly believe it, I heard her say just as bossy, 'No, I don't believe that is really what you want, Mrs. Something-or-other, it wouldn't be suitable for the purpose you . . . ' And the customer looking at the goods as though she wanted to eat it . . . it was a dandy sports sweater too, one of the chickest we have. Somebody called me off just then, and I didn't see what happened afterwards, but after Mrs. Knapp had gone back to the stock-closet at two, I went to look and the sweater was still there, *and no sale of a sweater on Mrs. Knapp's salesbook either!*"

Her horror at such an utter absence of any natural feeling for the standards of her profession was sincere and deep. She felt that the recital of the bare fact needed no embellishment to make its significance apparent to any man in retail selling.

As she expected, Mr. Willing lowered the corners of his mouth and raised his eyebrows high as he listened. He looked down at the geometrical design he was drawing on the blotting paper. He thought silently for a moment, gnawing meditatively on one corner of his lower lip. Then, "I believe I'd better have a talk with Mrs. Knapp myself," he said weightily; "send her in at closing time, won't you?"

Miss Flynn went off, walking softly, and well satisfied.

He had made a point of not speaking to Mrs. Knapp except for a casual salutation since he had taken her up to the Cloak-and-Suits three weeks before, and now as she came into the office he looked at her hard to see what the experience had done for her, and make out if he could gather from her aspect, attitude, voice and intonation anything like the rich illustrative commentary which Miss Flynn had involuntarily given him.

"How do you like the work, Mrs. Knapp," he asked her, in a dry, business-like way, "now that you have had a little experience of it?"

He was touched, he was actually moved by the flush of feeling which came into her dark, ardent face as she answered, "Oh, Mr. Willing, I *love* it! I do hope I'll give satisfaction, for I love every bit of it."

Jerome Willing loved it so himself that he felt warm towards the kindred spirit. "I'm glad of that," he said heartily, swept away for an instant from his usual prudent reserve, "and I think there's no doubt whatever that you'll give satisfaction."

He added with an instant return to his dry manner, "I mean, of course, when you've learned the work. There is a great deal to learn."

"Yes, I know," she said humbly. "I feel how ignorant I am. But I try to pick up whatever I can. I've been watching with all my might how the salespeople work. The job of stock-girl gives you such a splendid chance to watch customers and salespeople. And yesterday Miss Flynn gave me a salesbook and let me come out on the floor at noon. It is very exciting to me," she said, smiling a little, deprecating her inexperience and ignorance.

"How did you get along?" asked Jerome, with an increase of the nonchalant in his tone.

"I was so interested I could hardly breathe," she told him. "You're so used to it all, Mr. Willing, you can't think how fascinating it is to me. I've always loved shopping, anyhow, though I've had very little chance to do much. And I've thought about it a great deal, of course, from the customer's point of view. Now to be on the other side and to be able to try to do what I've always thought salespeople ought to do . . . it's wonderful! Of course, nothing very extraordinary. Just what any experienced salesperson knows, without thinking about it, I suppose."

"Yes, I dare say. What kind of thing?" asked the proprietor of the store, finding it hard to keep up his decent appearance of indifference when he really felt like a hound who, after weary beating about the bush, strikes a trail as fresh as paint and longs to give tongue to his joy in a full-throated bay.

"Oh, all kinds of things, too little to mention. Just what I've noticed in all the years I've shopped . . . why, here's one. The way a salesperson gets up and comes toward you when you come in. I've always loved to have a girl get up quickly, as if she were glad to see me, and come towards me, looking right at me with a pleasant welcoming look. It's always made me feel cross when they drag themselves up and come sagging over to me, looking down at their blouse-fronts or over my head . . . or especially at their finger-nails. Isn't it queer how it rubs you the wrong way to have a salesperson look at her finger-nails?"

"Yes, that's a good point," said Mr. Willing guardedly, baying inwardly for joy.

"And then another thing I just love to be able to do is to know just where to lay my hand on anything. I'm afraid I'm very quick-tempered and irritable by nature, and I know I've started up and gone right out of a store, many's the time, because the girl who was waiting on me would look and look for something I wanted, fumbling around absent-mindedly as if she weren't really thinking about it, and then call across to another girl, 'Say, Jen, where'd you put that inch-and-a-half binding?' "

The proprietor of the store repressed with difficulty a whoop of delight over the exactitude of this snapshot. He looked down neutrally at his desk.

The new saleswoman went on, "I'd always supposed that it must be ever so hard to know where things are back of a counter from the way the girls often act about it. But it's not! Not for me anyhow! No harder than knowing where your baking-powder and salt stand on the kitchen shelf!"

"Oh, no, it's not hard at all for any salesperson who puts her mind on it." Mr. Willing tossed this off airily and negligently. So successful was his manner that his employee thought she was being indiscreet and had forgotten to keep her place. "I'm taking too much of your time," she said apologetically, turning to go.

He kept her with an indulgent gesture, "Oh, no, you'll find I'm always interested in anything that concerns the Store," he said grandly. "And you haven't told me yet about the sales you made in your first try."

She looked at him earnestly now and spoke seriously, "Mr. Willing, there is something that troubled me, and I'd like to tell you about it. I'd made two or three sales all right, and then a customer,

Mrs. Warner it was, perhaps you know her, came in to look at sweaters. We're just out of the plain, one-color, conservative kind, though Miss Flynn said you had some ordered and they'd be here any day. That was the kind Mrs. Warner asked for. But she saw another one in the show-case, a bright emerald-green one with pearl-gray stripes, the conspicuous kind that young girls wear with pleated gray crepe-de-chine skirts and pearl-gray stockings and sandals, and it sort of took her eye. I knew it would look simply terrible on her —she's between forty and fifty and quite stout— the kind who always runs her shoes over. And I persuaded her to wait till the plain ones came in. I thought she'd be better satisfied in the end and feel more like coming back to the store. But Miss Flynn thought it was very wrong in me to have let her get away without making a sale."

"Why didn't you try to sell her both sweaters?" asked the merchant testily.

"Oh, her husband is only a clerk in Camp's Drug Store! They haven't much money. She'd never have felt she could afford two. If she'd taken the bright sporty one she'd have had to wear it for a year. And I know her husband and children wouldn't have liked it."

"Oh, you know her personally?" asked Jerome.

"No, not what you'd call personally—just from

what I've seen of her here in the store. She's quite a person to come around 'just looking,' you know. I guess she loves to look at pretty things as much as I do. And several times when I hadn't any customer on hand, I've had a little talk with her to make friends, and I showed her some of our nicest things, letting her see that I knew they were nothing she wanted to buy. I *love* to show off some of the pretty young things to women like that, who have to work hard at home. It's as good as going to a party for them. And it gives them the habit of coming to the store too when they *do* want something. Then she happened to mention her name. I put it down on my list to memorize. I remember how I always used to like it when a salesgirl remembered my name."

"Well, for God's *sake!*" ejaculated the young merchant inaudibly, moved to an almost solemn thankfulness. Aloud he said, clearing his throat and playing with a paper-cutter, "Don't you find it hard to remember the names of the customers?"

"No," she said. "I've got a good memory for names naturally. And it interests me. I try to find out something about the customer, too, to put together with the name. It seems to keep me from getting them mixed. This Mrs. Warner, for instance, I looked up her address in the 'phone book and found out that she lives near one of my friends in St. Peter's parish, and I asked my friend about her and she told me that Mr. Warner works for Camp's. It helps to know something personal, I think. In odd moments, when I'm walking down to the store in the morning, for instance, I have my list in my hand, and try to hitch the people to the names,—this way—'J. P. Warner, drug-store husband, about fifteen hundred a year. Laura J. Pelman, teacher in Washington Street School, about twelve hundred. Mother lives with her.' Inexperienced in selling as I am, I feel as though I could tell so much more what people want in merchandise if I know a little about them."

"Yes, that's so," he admitted this point without comment.

He could hardly wait to get home and report this talk to Nell. She wouldn't believe it, that was all. Well, he wouldn't have believed it either if he hadn't heard it with his own ears. And such perfect unconsciousness on the woman's part! Apparently she thought that this was the way that *all* salespeople took hold of their work—save the mark!

"That'll do for to-day, Mrs. Knapp," he said with dignity. "I'm glad to hear you like the work. You seem to be giving very good satisfaction. We . . . we . . . " he hesitated, wondering just how to phrase it. "We have been meaning to add one more salesperson to the Cloak-and-Suits, to see if the department would carry one more. If you like, we will try you out there, beginning with next week. The pay is no higher. But of course you get a bonus on all sales after your weekly quota is reached."

"Thank you very much, Mr. Willing," she said, with some dignity of her own, the dignity of a mature woman who knows that she is useful.

He liked her for her reserve. She turned away.

He called after her, as though it were a casual notion, just come into his head, "Are you anything of a reader? Would you be interested in looking at a manual on retail selling? I have a pretty good one here that gives most of the general principles. Though of course nothing takes the place of experience."

Her reserve vanished in a flash. Her strongly marked, mature face glowed like a girl's. She came swiftly back towards him, her hand outstretched, "Oh, are there *books* written about the business?" she cried eagerly. "Things you can study and learn?"

Chapter 10

EVANGELINE KNAPP was eating her breakfast with a good appetite, the morning paper propped up in front of her, so that she could study attentively Mrs. Willing's clever advertising for the day. She admired Mrs. Willing's talent so much! That was something *she* could never do, not if her life depended on it! She had always hated writing, even letters. Everything in her froze stiff when she took up a pen. But she knew enough to appreciate somebody who could write. And Mrs. Willing could. Her daily advertisements were positively as good as a story—better than most stories because there was no foolishness about them. This morning, for instance, as Evangeline sipped her coffee, she enjoyed to the last word the account of the new kitchen-cabinets at the Emporium, and Mrs. Willing's little story about the wonderful way in which American ingenuity had developed kitchen conveniences! Good patriotism, that was, too. She knew that all over town women were enjoying it with their breakfast and would look around their own kitchens to see how they could be improved. The kitchen-ware department would have a good day, she thought unenviously, her pride in the store embracing all its departments.

She moved to the cashier's desk to pay for her breakfast, for she took her breakfast downtown, as the easiest way to manage things at home in the morning. The children didn't need to be off to school until an hour after she left the house, and this plan left them more time to get their breakfast without hurrying. The cashier gave her a pleasant good morning as he handed over the change, and asked how all the family were that morning. Everybody in town knew what troubles Mrs. Knapp had, and how brave she was about them. As he asked the question he was thinking to himself, "Nobody ever heard her complain or look depressed— and yet how forlorn for a home-body such as she had always been to get her breakfast in a cafeteria like a traveling-man!"

"Mr. Knapp is really pretty well," she answered cheerfully; "he gets about in his wheel chair wonderfully well, considering. Takes care of himself entirely now, even dressing and undressing. And the children are splendid. So helpful and brave."

"Your children *would* be!" said the cashier, who was a distant relative of Miss Flynn's. But he really did admire Mrs. Knapp very much. Evangeline smiled to acknowledge the compliment, which she took very much as a matter of course. That was the kind of thing every one always said to her. She corrected the smile with a sigh and said earnestly, "Of course it is dreadfully hard for a mother to be separated from her children; but we all have to do the best we can."

"Oh, yes, dreadfully," agreed the cashier sympathetically. Mrs. Knapp had made the same remark to him several times before, but he was used to that. Customers always repeated themselves. It was part of the business not to notice it. She went on now, repeating herself again, and he listened with his usual patience. "The *hard*est part for me was to make up my mind to let things go at the house. If I do say it, I'd always done my duty by my housekeeping."

The cashier murmured his usual ejaculation of assent.

"Dr. Merritt had just put his foot *down* that I was not to do one thing at the house after I got home from the store. But you know how it is, you can't help yourself when you see all there is to be done. I used to turn right in those first weeks and clean house every Sunday from morning till night. But I had to give it up. I found I was no good at the store on Mondays, unless I got my rest. And of course, *that* . . . "

"Yes, of course *that!*" acquiesced the cashier.

"So now I just look the other way and think about

something else," she said bravely, bestowing the change in her purse.

The cashier nodded as she turned away, noticing that she folded her morning paper and put it under her arm with the exact gesture of any other business-man.

He had sent her away, as he had intended, well-satisfied with life, and as she walked along to her work, she was turning over in her mind some of the reasons for her satisfaction. The children were coming along splendidly, she thought, remembering lovingly how sweet they had looked this morning as she kissed them good-by; Helen still in her petticoat, combing her hair, turning a freshly washed, rosy face up towards her tall mother; Henry pulling on his little trousers and reading out of that absurd conundrum book Lester had borrowed of Mattie for him; Stephen poking his head out from under Lester's bedclothes like a chicken sticking its downy crest through the old hen's wings! Stephen slept downstairs, beside his father's bed, in a little cot that slipped under Lester's bed in the daytime. He was always scrambling into bed with Lester in the morning. As she dressed upstairs, she often heard their voices, talking and laughing together. Lester had of course plenty of time for that sort of thing, since he did not have to hurry about getting an early breakfast for any one. And Stephen seemed to have passed a sort of turning-point in his life and was much less troublesome than he had been. Mattie Farnham had always said that perhaps Stephen would just outgrow those naughty spells! She said children often did between five and six.

As always she was the first of the selling force in at the doors of the Emporium and the first in her department. She loved this tranquil taking possession of the day's work. It was one of the reasons why she breakfasted at the cafeteria. She liked to check up on all the necessary, before-opening-time activities, and be sure they were all finished in good shape by the time the first customer came in. This was not really her business of course, but as she always willingly lent a hand, the stock-girls and cleaning-women did not object. This morning she found that the stock-girls had not finished taking off the covers, and at once began to help, reminding the stock-boy over her shoulder about the thorough morning airing which Mr. Willing thought so important.

What a wonderful man he was! It was an education to work for him. He never forgot a detail. "If the air in the store is close and low in oxygen, the whole selling pace is slower," he had told her; "customers are dopy and salespersons can't stay right up on their toes as they ought." How true that was! And how wise! She had had no idea there was so much *to* retail selling.

As her long, quick fingers folded the great covers, she was thinking of those fascinating books Mr. Willing had loaned her, books she had devoured as a child devours fairy-tales, which she was now re-reading slowly and making her own. The chapter on textiles, how to distinguish linen from cotton and all that—how absorbingly interesting that had been! She had sat up till midnight to finish it. She had never dreamed that anything in a book could hold her attention so. How like amateur guess-work it made all her earlier information seem. And then to have Mrs. Willing loan her that microscope, "to keep as long as you need," to study and analyze fabrics. How good the Willings were to her! Such kind young people as well as such awfully clever and educated ones.

Together with the stock-girl she began running through her stock to make sure everything was right before the real business of selling began. She had timed herself and found that it took her just forty seconds per suit or cloak to make sure that hooks and eyes were firmly on, buttons all right, belts properly tacked in place, and the price-ticket on. There was therefore no reason why she shouldn't go through all the stock for which she was responsible every morning and lay to one side any garment that needed attention. Afterwards, rapidly as she sewed, a quarter of an hour of work with needle and thread, and there she was, ready for the day, her mind at peace about her merchandise. If there was anything she detested it was to see a garment offered to a customer with a hook hanging loose, or a button dangling, or to see a saleswoman paw it all over without finding any price-ticket. It gave her a warm feeling of comfort to be quite sure that this could not happen with any of the garments in her department. Also she enjoyed, sensuously enjoyed, handling those beautiful, well-made garments, with their exquisitely tailored details which she who had struggled so long with the construction of garments could so professionally appreciate.

And the new merchandise, as it was brought in from the receiving-room! What a joyful excitement to welcome the newcomers, with their amusing and ingenious little novelties of finish and style and cut! What a wonderful buyer Mr. Willing was! Nobody had ever seen such garments in town before, so simple, so artistic, so perfect! They filled one's cup to overflowing with speechless satisfaction, they were so exactly *right!* Here was that new homespun suit, just in yesterday, in that lovely new shade of mauve. Whoever in *that* town had heard of a mauve tailor-made suit? And yet how lovely it was, and how suitable, even for a middle-aged woman. Why, yes, especially for a middle-aged woman! It would be a real comfort to a woman who had just begun to feel sad over losing her youth. Every time she put the suit on it would be a kind, strong reassurance that although youth was going, comeliness and a quieter beauty were still within reach.

Evangeline held the suit up, looking at it and thinking gratefully how it would help some woman through a difficult year in her life. She remembered suddenly the Mrs. Warner who had so pathetically longed for that bright green sports sweater. This would satisfy her wistful, natural longing for pretty things and yet be quite suitable for her age. Evangeline had so much sympathy for women struggling with the problem of dressing themselves properly at difficult ages! Of course this suit was much, much more expensive than anything Mrs. Warner had ever worn. But, thought Evangeline earnestly, wasn't it always the truest wisdom to make any sacrifice for the sake of getting the *real thing?*

She slipped it back on the hanger and turned to that black velours-de-laine fur-trimmed cloak that had been so slow to sell. What ever was the matter with it? Why couldn't they get rid of it! Marked down as it was by this time, it was a wonderful bargain! How queer it was about some things, how

—quite mysteriously—they simply did not take. That black cloak was known all over the floor, and when a saleswoman got it out to show a customer, all the other salespersons turned their heads to watch if this time it wouldn't go. But it never had.

She looked at it hard, boring her mind into the problem as deep as she could drive it. But no inspiration came. The garment went back on the hanger after an inspection of its fastenings. Ah, here was the first customer! She turned to greet her warmly, with the exhilarated dash of a swimmer running out along the spring-board for the first dive of the day. "Good morning, Mrs. Peterson," she said, smiling her welcome. "Come to see that sports suit for your daughter again? I'm so thankful I can tell you that it is still here. It was almost sold yesterday. Mrs. Hemingway was considering it. But it is really much more suitable for your Evelyn, with that glorious coloring of hers."

She had plunged off the spring-board with her athletic certainty of movement. And now she was in her real element, glowing and tingling, every nerve-center tuned up to the most heartily sincere interest in what Mrs. Peterson's daughter would wear that spring. Evelyn Peterson would look simply stunning in that sports suit, with those rose-pink cheeks and her glistening blonde hair! Evangeline gloried in the brilliant good looks of girls! There was a period between eighteen and twenty-three when it was as good as a feast to dress one.

Mrs. Peterson was drawn along after her enthusiasm as a piece of paper is drawn fluttering after an express train. She said, "Well, I *had* come to say that Mr. Peterson and I have about decided that it was too expensive a suit for Evelyn, but now I'm here, I guess I'll look at it again."

Mrs. Knapp's day had begun.

That evening after supper they had the comfortable game of whist which had come to be one of the family institutions of late. Lester had taught Helen and Henry how to play and after Stephen was in bed in his little cot, sociably close to them, they usually moved into the next room for a rubber. Evangeline thought that she thought it rather a foolish waste of time; but she did not demur, because she did not like to refuse poor Lester anything that would lighten his dreary life. She had liked to play cards in her youth and found that she had still quite a taste for the game. She played well, too, and usually held good hands. Henry had, it now appeared, inherited from her considerable "card sense" and with her as a partner, they more then held their end up. Lester and Helen, notoriously absent-minded, often made fearful mistakes, which set them all into gales of laughter and ad-

vanced the cause of their opponents notably. One
of the family jokes was the time when Lester, holding only one trump, had triumphantly led it out as
a sneak lead!

"If it amuses Lester and the children . . ."
thought Evangeline, dealing the cards swiftly and
deftly, and enjoying herself very much, she and
Henry just now having won their third game in succession.

She did not know that they were all frightfully
uneasy that evening. Stephen had been coming in
and out of the house all day, and just the instant
before Mother was expected, they discovered that
on one occasion he must have climbed up on the
sofa with his muddy rubbers! There were lumps
of crumbling, drying mud all up and down it.
They were wildly brushing it off when they heard
Mother's quick strong step on the porch and had
scurried to cover. There were lots of lumps left
yet. Suppose Mother should see them.

It was all right so long as they were playing whist.
They had put Mother's chair with its back to the
sofa. But afterwards, when she and Father settled
down to their evening of reading and studying, what
would happen?

When nine o'clock struck, Helen and Henry stood
up to start to bed. And Mother . . . oh! . . .

after strolling about absently a moment she went
and sat down on the sofa!

And never said a word. Never noticed a thing!
Just sat there for a moment, thinking, and then
jumped up to make a note in her store-book where
she methodically put down her every idea! How
was that for luck, their shining eyes said to each
other silently, as the children kissed their father
and mother good night, and went off upstairs.

It had come to her, right out of nowhere, as one's
best thoughts always come, that the thing to do with
that black, fur-trimmed velours-de-laine cloak was
to sell it to Mrs. Prouty in place of the fur coat
which she coveted so and couldn't possibly afford.
It would actually, honestly, look better on Mrs.
Prouty's too-rounded dumpy figure than the fur
coat. Her conviction was instantly warm! The
earnest words came rushing to her lips. She heard
herself saying fervently, "You see, Mrs. Prouty, a
fur coat has no *line*. The only people who look
well in one are the flat, long, bean-pole variety. But
a well-cut, well-tailored coat like this . . . just see
how that flat, strap trimming carries the eye up
and down and doesn't add to the bulk. And those
great fur cuffs and collar give all the *richness* of
the fur coat without the . . . " Oh, she knew she

could do it! She could just see Mrs. Prouty's wistful eyes brightening, her anxious face softening into satisfaction and content.

And what a feather in her cap if she could be the one to work off that unsalable cloak!

PART THREE

Chapter 11

IN the hurly-burly of the rearrangement of life, nobody had been able to pay much attention to Stephen, and he had reveled in this freedom from supervision. He had always steered his small, hard life on a line of his own, a line he strove to make parallel to the course of the rest of the family, and never intersecting. Contact with others always meant trouble in Stephen's experience—except with Henry and Helen. Now that the grown-ups had almost forgotten his existence, he was enjoying life as never before, under his dirty, crumpled rompers, stiff with spilled egg-yolk and cold bacon grease.

His father's accident had made no impression on his emotions. Events that did not touch Stephen personally never made any impression on his emotions. The only element in the new situation which interested him was that Mother seemed to have forgotten all about Teddy. This was important. It made Stephen very glad that Father had fallen off the roof and broken his legs all up, or whatever it was. As long as Father stayed in bed, he couldn't bother anybody, even when he and Stephen were left alone.

For, after a time, they were left alone. When the sick man began to improve so that he was conscious, and later, occasionally out of pain, there were hours when the round of volunteer neighbors and helpers thinned out, when he was left in his bed in the dining-room, a glass of water, a book, something to eat and the desk-telephone on a table by his side, with instructions to telephone if he needed anything.

"Don't you hesitate a minute now, Mr. Knapp," said old Mrs. Hennessy heartily; "if it's no more than to put a shovelful of coal on the kitchen fire, you call fourteen ring thirty-two and I'll be right over."

"And when Stephen gets to acting up, just shake the window-curtain real hard and I'll drop everything to come over and settle him," said Mrs. Anderson zestfully.

So far Stephen had not "acted up." Probably, so Mrs. Anderson told Mrs. Knapp, "because as things are now he's let to do just what he pleases and goodness knows what *that* is!" Stephen had even been a stimulating element in his father's days when they first began to emerge from the endless nightmare of pain and to become, once more, successive stages in a human life.

Lester never spoke to any one about those first weeks after his fall and thought of them himself as little as possible. The mere casual mention of them afterwards brought the cold sweat out on him. No circle in any hell would have contained more concentrated suffering than was crowded into his every conscious moment—horrible, brute, physical suffering, tearing at every nerve, suffering that degraded him, that left him no humanity. When this was deadened for an instant by opiates or exhaustion, there were terrible hallucinations—he was again on the steep, icy roof, turning, death in his heart, to throw himself down into cold nothingness —he was falling, falling, endlessly falling . . . and now he knew what intolerable anguish awaited him at the end of his fall. He screamed out dreadfully at such times and tore at the bedclothes as if to save himself. These moments of frenzy always ended by his coming to himself with a great start and finding himself burning and raging once more in unendurable physical pain.

Later, once in a while, there were fleeting instants almost of lucidity during which, as he was flung through space by the whirlwind of that inhuman, impersonal agony, he yet caught glimpses as it were of his own personality lying there prone, waiting for him to come back to enter it. This half-consciousness always brought the same thought to him.

. . . "Poor weak wretch! He had not even force enough to kill himself!" He thought it as of some one else, half-pityingly, half-contemptuously.

Then came periods of freedom from pain, incredulous, breathless bliss, poisoned by his horrified apprehension of being touched; for the slightest touch, even of the bed, plunged him again into the abyss.

During one of those respites when he lay, scarcely daring to breathe, there came to him the first personal sensation since his fall. He chanced to lie with his head turned towards the room, and for a moment he saw it, as it was, a part of human life, and not merely the background for this endless dying of his! On the floor sat Stephen, very dirty and uncared for, playing with his Teddy-bear! The expression on his face reminded Lester of something . . . something, it seemed, which had begun, something with which he had wanted to go on. But just then Eva had brushed his pillow, and this glimpse back into the human life out of which he had hurled himself vanished in the molten lava of his physical pain.

Little by little, some unsuspected and implacable vitality hidden in his body slowly pushed him, groaning and unwilling, out of the living death which he still so passionately desired to make dead death. The weeks passed, he suffered less. He lay passive and empty, staring up at the ceiling, counting and cataloguing all the small blemishes and stains in the plaster. A little strength seeped slowly back into his body. One day he found that he could read for a few moments at a time. He became aware of the life that went on about him. Chiefly it was Stephen's life, because Stephen was generally in the foreground of the room.

Lester began to look down at the child as he played about the floor, watched languidly the expression on his round, pugnacious face, almost always dirty now, but, so it seemed to his father, not always so darkly grim as he remembered it. But then, he thought again (one of the slow thoughts which occasionally pushed their way up to his attention), he had never seen Stephen except in active conflict with authority.

"I never saw one of my children just living before," he meditated. As he lay in bed, a book was usually open before him, but he looked over it at the far more interesting spectacle of his undiscovered little boy.

His first voluntary move back towards life was on the day when he had his talk with Stephen about his Teddy.

It began by his remembering suddenly what it had been which had begun, and with which he had

wanted to go on. The little memory, presenting itself so abruptly out of his subconsciousness, startled
him into saying impulsively, "Oh, Stephen, come
here a minute. What was it you started to tell me
that day—up in the bathroom, when I was shaving—about your Teddy?"

The moment he had spoken he realized how foolish the question was. The day seemed like yesterday to him because there had been only blackness for
him ever since. But it was two months ago; and
two months for a little boy—how could he have
thought that Stephen would remember?

But, as a matter of fact, Stephen looked as though
he remembered very well indeed. He had started at
the word "Teddy," had turned instantly suspicious
eyes on his father and had made a clutch at the
stuffed bear over whose head he now stared at the
man in bed, silently, his mouth a hard line, with
the dogged expression of resistance which was so
familiar.

Lester's enforced observation of Stephen made
this pantomime intelligible to him, in part. Stephen
was afraid something would happen to Teddy. Why
in the world should he be afraid?

On this question he put his attention, watching
Stephen closely as he said laughingly, "What's the
matter with you, old man? Do you think I want to
take Teddy away to play with him myself?"

Stephen's face relaxed a very little at this. His eyes searched his father's, deeply and gravely, with an intense wary seriousness, as a white traveler, lost in a jungle amongst savages, might search the eyes of one of the tribe who offered a friendly aspect. Could he be trusted? Or was this just another of their cannibalistic wiles?

"I like your Teddy fine," continued Lester, conversationally. "I always liked the way he snuggles up to you in your bed. I used to wake up and look over at him sometimes. But I'm afraid I'm too old to play with him, myself."

At the mention of Teddy's sleeping beside him, Stephen looked away and down into the bright, opaque eyes of his fetish, and as he did this, his father felt an acute shock of surprise. The child's face was passionately tender and loving. He looked as his own mother had looked when she held her first baby in her arms. Lester was so astonished that he was obliged to wait a moment before he could command his voice to casual negligence.

"So you don't remember what it was you were going to ask me about Teddy?" he said, presently. "Well, it *was* quite a while ago."

So far he had not induced Stephen to say a single word. That was always Stephen's way of resisting talk, and persuasion, and attempts to reach him.

Lester held his book up again and waited.

He waited a long time.

But waiting was one thing which circumstances made easy for him. There was little else a paralyzed man could do. Stephen sat motionless, his face a blank, staring into space. His father felt the uncertainty and questioning going on under that self-protective front of stolidity. Presently, a long time afterwards, the little boy got up and came slowly towards his father's bed. "Yes, I 'member what it was," he said in a low tone, keeping his eyes fixed intently on the expression of his father's face. "I wanted to ask you . . . to ask you not to let Mother . . ." his voice dropped to a solemn, quavering whisper, " . . . not to let Mother *wash* Teddy."

Lester survived the entire and grotesque unexpectedness of this with no more sign of his amazement than a flicker of his eyelids. He considered a dozen different ways of advancing into the undiscovered country and rejected them all in favor of the neutral question, "Was Mother going to wash Teddy?"

At this it all came out in a storm, the visit to the lady, the horrible, misshapen, shrunken Teddy there, Mother's stealing Teddy away at night, the devouring dread in Stephen's mind, a dread so great that it now overcame even his fierce pride and his anger, as he sobbed out at the last, "Don't let him be washed, Father! *Don't* let him!" He raised his streaming eyes agonizingly towards his father, his whole face quivering.

Lester was so horrified that for a moment he could not speak. He was horrified to see Stephen reduced so low. He was more horrified at the position in which he found himself, absolute arbiter over another human being, a being who had no recourse, no appeal from his decisions. It was indecent, he thought; it sinned against human dignity, both his and the child's. . . . "As I would not be a slave, so I would not be a master!" he cried to himself, shamed to the core by Stephen's helpless dependence on his whim, a dependence of which Stephen was so tragically aware, all his stern bulwarks of anger and resistance broken down by the extremity of his fear—fear for what he loved! Fear for himself would never so have transfigured Stephen, never!

Lester understood this. More, he felt it himself, felt himself ready to fight for Stephen as Stephen had been ready to fight for Teddy; he, Lester, who had never felt that he had the right to fight for anything of his own.

His gaze on the child had passion in it as he said firmly, weightily, "I'll never have anything done to your Teddy that you don't want, Stephen. He's yours. You've got the right to have the say-so about him."

Stephen looked at his father blindly, as if he did not understand these strange words. But though they were unfamiliar, though he could not understand them, they gave him hope. "You won't have him washed?" he asked, clinging to the one point he understood.

"Not washed or anything else if you don't want it," said his father, reiterating his own point. It seemed to him he could not live another day if he did not succeed in making Stephen understand that.

To his astonishment, again to his shame, Stephen burst out with a phrase which had never before passed his lips except under protest, "Oh, thank you, Father! Oh, *thank* you!" he cried loudly, his lips trembling.

Lester found the child's relief shocking. It made him sick to think what a dread must have preceded it, what a fathomless blackness of uncertainty in Stephen's life it must represent. He spoke roughly, almost as he would to another man, "You don't have to thank me, Stevie," he said. "Great Scott, old boy, it's none of *my* business, what you do with your own Teddy, is it?"

Even as he spoke—like a lurid side-glimpse—was it possible that there were people who would *enjoy* thanks extorted on those infamous terms? Were they ever set over children?

His insistence seemed to have penetrated a little

way through Stephen's life-long experience of the nature of things. The little boy stood looking at him, his face serious and receptive, as if a new idea were dawning on him. It was so new that he did not seem to know what to do with it, and in a moment turned away and sat down on the floor again. He reached for his Teddy and sat clasping him in his lap.

The two were silent, father and son.

Lester said to himself, shivering, "What a ghastly thing to have sensitive, helpless human beings absolutely in the power of other human beings! Absolute, unquestioned power! Nobody can stand that. It's cold poison. How many wardens of prisons are driven sadistically mad with it!"

He recoiled from it with terror. "You have to be a superman to be equal to it."

In the silent room he heard it echoing solemnly, "That's what it is to be a parent."

He had been a parent for thirteen years before he thought of it. He looked over the edge of his bed at Stephen and abased himself silently.

The child sat motionless, clasping Teddy, his face bent and turned away so that Lester could not see its expression. His attitude was that of some one thinking deeply.

Well, reflected Lester, there was certainly good reason for the taking of thought by everybody concerned! He let his head fall back on the pillow and, staring up, began for the first time since his fall to think connectedly about something other than his own wretchedness. For the first time the ugly blemishes on the ceiling were not like blotches in his own brain. Presently he forgot them altogether.

That sudden contact with Stephen's utterly unsuspected suffering had been like dropping his fingers unawares upon red-hot iron. His reaction had been the mere reflex of the intolerable pain it gave him. Now, in the long quiet of his sick-room, he set himself to try to understand what it meant.

So that had been at the bottom of Stephen's fierceness and badness in those last days of the old life. So it had been black despair which had filled the child's heart and not merely an inexplicable desire to make trouble for his mother. For Heaven's sakes, how far off the track they had been! But however could they have guessed at the real cause of the trouble? What possessed the child to keep such a perverse silence? Why hadn't he told somebody? How could they know if he never said a word.

He thought again of the scene in the bathroom that last morning and saw again Stephen's wistful face looking up into his. Stephen had *tried* to tell him. And those sacred itemized accounts of Willing's Emporium had stopped his mouth.

But Evangeline was always on hand. Why hadn't Stephen . . .

Without a word, with a complete perception that filled all his consciousness, Lester knew why Stephen had never tried to tell his mother.

And yet—his sense of fairness made him take up the cudgels for Eva—it hadn't been such an unreasonable idea of hers. Teddy was certainly as dirty as it was possible for anything to be. You have to keep children clean whether they like it or not. Suppose Teddy had been played with by a child who had scarlet fever? They'd have to have him cleaned, wouldn't they? He'd gone too far, yielded to a melodramatic impulse when he'd promised Stephen so solemnly they'd never have anything done to Teddy that he didn't like.

But as a matter of fact Teddy never had been near scarlet fever or anything else contagious. And even if he had, weren't there ways of dry-cleaning and disinfecting that would leave the personality of the toy intact? You didn't have to soak it in a tub of soapy water. What was the matter with wrapping it in an old cloth and baking it in the oven, as you do with bandages you want to sterilize. If anybody had had the slightest idea that Stephen felt as he did. . . . *But nobody had!* And that was the point.

He saw it now. Nothing turned on the question

of whether Teddy should or should not be cleaned. That purely material matter could have been arranged by a little practical ingenuity if it had occurred to anybody that there was anything to arrange. The question really was why had it not occurred to anybody?

What was terrifying to Lester was the thought that the conception of trying to understand Stephen's point of view had been as remote from their minds as the existence of the fourth dimension.

And even now that the violent shock of this little scene with Stephen had put the conception into his brain, how under the sun could you ever find out what was felt by a child who shut himself up so blackly in his stronghold of repellent silence.

Why *had* Stephen so shut himself up?

The question was as new to Lester as a question of the cause of the law of gravity. It had never occurred to him that perhaps Stephen had not been born that way.

But even a sullen stronghold of badness was better than that dreadful breakdown of human dignity. Lester felt he could never endure it again to have Stephen look into his face with that slavish, helpless searching of his eyes. No self-respecting human being could bear that look from another.

Could there be human beings—women—mothers —who fattened on it, fought to keep that slave's look in the eyes of children? He turned from this thought with a start.

Well, what good did all this thinking do him? Or Stephen? What could he do now, at once, to escape out of this prison and take Stephen with him?

With a heat of anger, he told himself that at least he could start in to make Stephen feel, hour by hour, in every contact with him, that he, even a little boy, had some standing in the world, inviolable by grown-ups, yes, *sacred even to parents*.

He breathed hard and flung out his arm.

For the first time he desired to get well, to live again.

Chapter 12

H ELEN and Henry Knapp were skipping home from school, hand in hand, to the tune of

"Skippety hop to the barber-shop
To buy a stick of candy.
One for you and one for me
And one for . . ."

They were interrupted by their Aunt Mattie Farnham, who ran out of the house and pounced on them. "For goodness' sakes, Helen 'n' Henry, tell me about your folks! I've been worried to death about you all."

She stopped, looked down at the new black dress she wore and said, with a decent sigh, "Poor Aunt Emma passed away a week ago, you know. The funeral was day before yesterday. I just got home this morning."

The children tried, not very successfully, to put on a decent soberness to match her sigh, and were silent, not knowing what comment to make. They had, as a matter of fact, heard (although they had long since forgotten it) that Aunt Mattie had been called away clear up to Maine by a telegram announcing the sickness of her husband's old aunt. Usually they missed Aunt Mattie fearfully when she was away from town. But this time the two months of her absence had been filled far too full with other events.

Due respect to the abstract idea of death having been paid, after their fashion, by each of the three, they reëntered ordinary life with the exclamation from Aunt Mattie, "Now do tell me how ever in the living world you've managed! How do you get along? I haven't heard a thing, not really to say heard. Mr. Farnham means to do all right, but he's no hand to write letters. I'd write and write and ask him about a million questions about you all, and all he'd write back would be some little smitch of news and a lot about the weather! He did tell me that your Momma has got a job down at Willing's and is doing fine. She would! She's a wonderful woman, your Momma is. Everybody knows that. But however do you *manage* with your poor Momma away all day and your Poppa the way he is. How *is* he? Awful bad?" Her kind fair face bent anxiously towards them.

It was again as if the children tried, not very successfully, to put on a decent soberness to match her expression. They hesitated as if they did not know exactly what was decorous to say. Then Helen murmured, "Father was awfully bad at first, they

said.   Mother sent us children off to Brandville
to stay with Gramma and Grampa Houghton so we
didn't know anything about that first part.   But
Gramma got sick, and we had to come home.   And
Father was lots better by that time."

"But how do you manage?" queried Aunt Mattie
again.   "How can you, with your poor Momma
away?   I never thought that house could run a
minute without her.   She did *e*verything!"

"Oh, we manage all right," said Helen.   "Father
and us children keep the house."

"Your father!   I thought he was in bed!"

"No, he's able to be up in a wheel chair now.
The janitor of the store's old father had a wheel
chair and they didn't sell it after he died and it
was up attic and he brought it to Father.   He said
Father had helped him out at the store when his
little boy was sick.   Oh, lots of the folks from the
store have come to help out.   The delivery driver,
he said he couldn't ever forget what Father did for
him one time.   He won't tell what it was because
he's ashamed.   Only he wanted to help out, too, and
as long as we had to have a furnace fire he came
in every morning and night to look out for the furnace.   And he steps in daytimes now, when he's
going by, to see if everything is all right.   And old
Mrs. Hennessy, she's the cleaning woman, she kept

coming all the time to help and bring in things to eat, pies, you know! She came in nights and mornings when Father was so bad to do up the work and wouldn't take any pay for it. She doesn't have to now, do the work, I mean. But she still does the washings. Only we pay her, of course."

Aunt Mattie's look of bewilderment sharpened to distraction. "You have only got me more mixed up than ever!" she cried vacantly. "Mercy me! the furnace, the washings . . . Yes, I see about those. But all the rest! The meals! The housework! *Stephen!* When I think of how your poor mother slaved to . . . " She looked at them almost sternly as if suspecting them of levity.

Henry said, "Father and all of us get along. You see Father's all right now, only his legs. He can do anything except walk. And Helen and I do the walking for him."

Mrs. Farnham made an exasperated gesture at their refusal to take in her meaning. *"Who does the cooking?"* she shouted desperately, getting down to bed-rock.

"Father does. We all do," said Helen. "Father's a lovely cook. He's learning out of the cook-book. And so am I—learning, I mean. We're learning together."

Aunt Mattie's face instantly smoothed into com-

prehension of everything. She had wondered how
they managed without a woman to keep house for
them. Now she knew. They didn't manage.

"*Oh* . . ." she said, and, "Well . . ."

She looked at them compassionately. "I'll have to
get over to your house as fast as ever I can," she
said as if to herself.

As her eyes dwelt half-absently on the children,
she observed aloud, "Seems to me Henry's looking
better. Not so peaked. Did that pepsin treatment
of Dr. Merritt's really do him some good? I never
thought much of pepsin, myself."

The children looked at each other as if surprised
by something they had not noticed before.

"Why, Henry, that's so. You haven't had one
of your sick spells for ever so long, have you?" said
Helen. To her Aunt Mattie she explained, "We've
had so much else to think about we haven't noticed."

Mrs. Farnham rejected pepsin for another diag-
nosis. "*I* know what 'tis. The visit to your
Gramma and Grampa Houghton! I always told
your Momma that what Henry needed was country air. There's nothing like a change of air,
nothing!"

Helen said now, "We've got to run along, Aunt
Mattie. We help about lunch. Father gets it ready,
but we clear off and take Stephen out to play a
while."

"Oh, that reminds me. How about Stephen? What does . . . Is he . . . How does your . . ."

Her ingenuity was not enough to contrive a presentable form for her inquiry, but the child came to her rescue understandingly, "Why, Stephen seems to be growing out of those naughty streaks," said Helen. "He's lots better, somehow. He still has a tantrum once in a while, but not nearly so often, nor so bad. You see, he *likes* Father's being sick!" She knew how shocking this was on Stephen's part, and added apologetically, "He's so little, you know. He doesn't understand how terrible it is for poor Father. And Father tells him stories. All the time, almost. Stephen loves them. Mother was always too busy to tell stories, you know."

"Well, I should say so indeed!" cried Aunt Mattie, outraged at the picture, even hypothetical, of poor Evangeline's attempting to tell stories on top of everything else she had to do.

"Step along with you, children," she said now. "I hadn't ought to have kept you so long, as 'tis. But I've been worrying my head off about you all. Tell your Poppa that I'm coming right over there this afternoon to see him just as soon as I get my trunk unpacked and things straightened around a little."

Chapter 13

"He that is down need fear no fall,
He that is low, no pride,"

said Lester Knapp aloud to himself. It was a great pleasure to him to be able to say the strong short Saxon words aloud. For years he had been shutting into the cage of silence all the winged beautiful words which came flying into his mind! And beautiful words which you do not pronounce aloud are like children always forced to "be quiet" and "sit still." They droop and languish.

But before this it would have been too foolish to repeat the lovely lines that came into his mind. What would Harvey Bronson have thought to hear "the army of unalterable law" pronounced in the office of Willing's Emporium? Lester Knapp smiled to himself at the idea! And if it hadn't been Harvey Bronson at hand it would have been some one else just as scandalized.

But now there was no one to hear, no one but little Stephen playing with his toy train on the newspapers spread out over the floor. A blessed healing solitude lay about Lester as he sat in his wheel chair in the sunny kitchen peeling a panful of potatoes. It had been when he looked down at the gingham apron spread over his paralyzed knees that the song of the little shepherd had come to his mind. A gingham apron on a man! And peeling potatoes!

He supposed that Harvey Bronson would die of shame if anybody put a gingham apron on him and expected him to peel potatoes. And yet there was nobody who talked louder than he about the sacred dignity of the home which ennobled all the work done for its sake—that was for *Mrs*. Harvey Bronson of course!

Lester Knapp smiled again, his slow, whimsical smile which Harvey Bronson especially detested and feared. Then he stopped thinking about his old associate at the office. The lines which had come into his mind brought with them all the world to which they belonged, the strong-hearted, simple, passionate world of the old cobbler-pilgrim. Where were those lines? Towards the end of the book, wasn't it, just below that quaint marginal note of *Men thrive in the Valley of Humiliation.* It was where the pilgrims were going—yes, now he remembered the very words with that exactitude of memory which had been such a golden thing in his life, "They were going along talking and espied a boy feeding his father's sheep. The boy was in very mean clothes, but of a fresh, well-favored countenance; and as he sat by himself he sang. 'Hark!'

said Mr. Greatheart, 'to what the shepherd's boy saith.' So they harkened."

Lester Knapp, peeling his potatoes, harkened with them as he said aloud again,

> "He that is down need fear no fall,
> He that is low no pride.
> He that is humble ever shall
> Have God to be his guide.
> I am content with what I have
> Little be it or much. . . ."

He perceived that Stephen had stopped playing and was looking at him steadily as he said the words aloud. With a flourish of his paring knife he went on, smiling at the little boy, "Then said the guide, 'Do you hear him? I will dare to say that this boy lives a merrier life and wears more of that herb called heart's ease in his bosom than he that is clad in silk and velvet!'

"Silk and velvet!" he said with a humorous scorn, lifting a fold of his gingham apron.

"Is it a 'tory?" asked Stephen, coming up beside his father's chair.

"You bet your life it is a story, a crackajack of a story."

"Tell it to me," said Stephen. He leaned both elbows on the arm of the chair, put his round chin in his hands, tipped his head to one side and turned his shining dark eyes up towards his father's face.

A phrase came to Lester's mind, the description
of the day when Bunyan had first seen the great
invisible world henceforth to be his heart's home,
and how it had begun by his seeing in one of the
streets of Bedford, "three or four poor people sitting at a door in the sun talking of the things of
God." He and Stephen were poor people too, sitting in the sun—such golden sunshine as came
through the window into the quiet room and fell
on the head of his little boy.

"Well, Stephen, once upon a time there was a
man," he began, deciding that the rolling off of the
burden and the fight with Apollyon were most in
Stephen's line. He wondered if he could find in the
old story stuff to interest a modern little boy, and in
a moment was carried away by it. What a tale it
was! How full of pith and meat and savor!

The potatoes were all peeled before he finished
the story of the fight, so that he laid down his paring knife and turned entirely to Stephen as they
came to the climax. They had adventured down the
terrible Valley of Death and were now in the hand-
to-hand combat, cut! slash! forward! back! "Then
Apollyon began to gather up close to Christian and
wrestling with him, gave him a dreadful fall; and
with that, Christian's sword flew out of his hand!"

He paused dramatically. Stephen's wide eyes
grew wider! His lips were parted. He did not

seem to breathe, all his being suspended on his father's words. It was plain he had forgotten where he was, or who. "Then said Apollyon, '*I am sure of thee now!*'" said Lester, and Stephen shivered.

"But Christian reached out quick, quick and snatched up his sword and ran it deep into that horrible old Apollyon and made him stagger back to get his breath! And then Christian scrambled up on his feet and ran at the dragon, shouting! And with that Apollyon spread out his dragon wings and sped him away and Christian saw him no more."

Stephen drew a long breath. "Golly!" he said fervently.

"Yes, I should say as much," agreed his father, pushing his chair over to the stove and dropping the potatoes into the boiling water. How exciting it was, he thought, how absorbing, to see those first impressions of power and courage touch a new human soul. And when it was your own little boy . . . To share with him one of the immortal fine things created by the human spirit!

He sat still for a moment, remembering the book, soaking himself in its flavor and color, tasting some of the quaint, posy-like phrases,

> "Some things are of that nature as to make
> One's fancy chuckle while his heart doth ache!"

Harvey Bronson for instance.

And, "Some people are never for religion until it walks with silver slippers in the sunshine." Was that Mr. Prouty?

Still musing, he wheeled himself into the dining-room and began to set the table for lunch. Through the clicking of the silver, Stephen could hear him say, "His daughter went through the Dark River, singing, but none could understand what she said . . . none could understand what she said."

It sounded like a song to Stephen, although Father was only talking to himself.

When he came out again into the kitchen and began to slice the bacon, he was saying in a loud, strong voice, "So he passed over, and all the trumpets sounded for him on the other side! All the trumpets sounded . . ."

The words rang in Stephen's ears. He said them over to himself in a murmur as he handled his top absently. "All the twumpets sounded. All the twumpets sounded on the other side."

After a time he asked, "Father, what's a twumpet?"

A question from Stephen!

His father turned his head from the frying-pan from which the bacon sent up its thin blue wreaths of smoke. "What's a trumpet? It's a great, gleaming brass horn which always, always has been blown where there has been a victory—like this!" He flung up his arm, holding an imaginary trumpet to his lips, "Taran*ta!* Taran*ta!*" He sounded it out ringingly! "That's the way they sounded when Mr. Valiant crossed the Dark River."

"Taran*ta!*" murmured Stephen to himself. "And all the twumpets sounded."

He sat in the sun on the kitchen floor, looking up at his crippled father frying bacon. For both of them the kitchen was ringing with the bright brazen shout of victory.

Men thrive in the Valley of Humiliation.

Chapter 14

LESTER was glad to see Mattie Farnham come bustling in the very afternoon of the day she returned from Maine. He liked Mattie—indeed he almost loved her—in spite of the fact that so far as he had been able to ascertain she had never yet understood anything he ever said to her. They did not use at all the same vocabulary, but they held friendly communication by means of sign-language, like a dog and cat who have grown up in the same house and have an old affection for each other.

"Hello there, Mattie," he welcomed her, as she entered. "How are the potatoes in Maine? Ours have spots in them."

It amused him with Mattie to disconcert her decent sense of what was the suitable attitude to strike. He knew that both she and her husband were relieved to have their ninety-year-old, bed-ridden aunt safely and painlessly in the next world. Blessed if he'd go through the motions of condoling with her.

But he saw at once that he had shocked not her sense of the proper attitude about Aunt Emma but about himself. She had come over prepared to "sympathize" with him. Mattie always had to go through the proper motions.

"How are you getting *on*, Lester?" she asked earnestly, with her best Ladies'-Guild flatness of intonation. "You can't imagine how I have worried about you and poor Eva and the dear children. I've been sick to think I wasn't here to help out in this sad time. Now I'm back you must let me do everything I can."

"You might come and call on Stephen and me once in a while and bring us some of your famous home-cooking," he suggested mischievously. She laughed, in spite of herself, at his jibe over her weakness for delicatessen potato-salad. "You miserable *sinner!*" she cried, in her own voice, dropping for an instant into their old joking relationship. She sobered at once, however, into what Lester called to himself the "mourners-waiting-for-the-benediction manner" and said, "I was planning as I walked over how I could arrange my own work to have two hours free every afternoon and come here to do for you."

"You'll find it all done," he told her genially. "You can't beat me to it. Come along all the same, and we'll play cribbage." She was perplexed as well as shocked by his levity and at last simply threw herself on his mercy, "Lester, do tell me all about things," she said in an honest, human tone of affection and concern which brought from him an answer in kind.

·"Well, Mattie, I will. It was hell at first . . . all the kinds of hell there are. But you know how folks are, how you get used to everything. And I got better, got so it didn't make me faint away with pain to have somebody touch the bed. And then little by little I settled down to where I am now. Both legs incurably paralyzed, I'm told, but the rest of me all right. In the meantime, Eva—you know how Eva never lies down and gives up—as soon as I could be left, hustled right out and got a job. She's in the Cloak-and-Suits at Willing's now, and making good money. What with her commissions on extra sales, she's making just about what I did. With the promise of a good raise soon. The Willings have treated her very white, I must say. And I imagine she is the wonder of the world as a saleswoman."

"She would be, at anything!" breathed Mattie devoutly.

"She surely would," agreed her husband heartily. "Well, here at the house we've shuffled things around into a new pattern, and we're getting on. I can do anything that needs to be done on this floor with Henry and Helen's help, and the doctor says I'll soon be on crutches and able to get up stairs once a day. It seemed queer to be doing housework, but there isn't another mortal thing I can do but to keep things running. So I do."

"Poor Lester!" said Mattie, just as he knew she would.

"Not on your life!" he told her. "I don't mind the work a bit, now I've got used to the idea. I can't say it is exactly enlivening to be tied up to half your body that's dead but not buried, but I haven't got anything else to complain of. As to the housework, I haven't had such a good time in years. You know what an absent-minded scut I am, with my head always full of odds and ends of book-junk I like to mull over. Well, housework doesn't interfere with thinking as account-keeping does, believe me! I can start my hands and arms to washing dishes or peeling potatoes or setting the table, and then leave them to do the job while I roam from China to Peru. Every time I tried that at the office—the bottom dropped out. Here I've more time for thinking and for reading too in the evenings! The children bring the books to me from the Library."

"Well, it's very *brave* of you to take it that way, I'm sure," said Mattie with a decent sigh of sympathy.

He thought to himself with exasperation that Mattie's mental indolence was invincible. She never made the slightest effort of her own accord to escape from the rubber-stamp formula in which she had been brought up. By lively joshing you could occasionally jolt her into a spontaneous perception of her own, but the minute you stopped, back she sank and pulled the cover of the Ladies' Guild mummy-case over her. And she was so human under it,—one of the most human people he had ever met. As he was thinking all this, by no means for the first time in his life, she caught out of the corner of her eye a glimpse of something in the kitchen over which she now exclaimed in amazement. "What in the name of *time* is all that litter of papers on the kitchen floor?"

"All that litter?" he protested. "That's not litter, that is an original exercise of the human intelligence in contact with real life. You encounter so few of those you don't recognize one when you meet it. That is one of the patented inventions of the Knapp Family, Incorporated."

She looked at him dumbly with the patient expression of bewilderment which always brought him to time. He began to explain, literally and explicitly, "We have executive sessions, the children and I, to figure out ways and means to cope with life and not get beaten by small details. We all got together on this floor proposition. We put it to ourselves this way: the kitchen floor has to be scrubbed to keep it clean. None of us are smart enough to scrub it. What's the answer? Of course

Eva must simply do nothing whatever about the house. The doctor issued an ultimatum about *that*. She has all she can do at the store. Well, you wouldn't believe it, but Stephen got the answer. He said, 'When I paint with my water-colors, Mother always 'preads papers down on the floor.'

"Done! The attic was piled to the eaves with old newspapers. Every day Helen or Henry brings down a fresh supply. We spread them around two or three thick, drop our grease on them with all the peace of mind in the world, whisk them up at night before Eva comes in, and have a spotless floor to show her. What's the matter with that?"

"Why, I never heard of such a thing in my life!" cried Mattie.

"People seemed to think," reflected Lester, "that they make an all-sufficient comment when they say that."

She got up now and walked to the kitchen door to gaze down on the paper.

"That's a sample of the way *we* do business," said Lester to her back. He wheeled himself over to the table and took out of a work-basket a pair of Stephen's little stockings which he prepared to darn.

Mattie turned, saw what he was doing and pounced on him with shocked, peremptory benevolence. "Oh, *Lester*, let me do that! The idea of *your* darning stockings! It's dreadful enough your having to do the housework!"

"Eva darned them a good many years," he said, with some warmth, "and did the housework. Why shouldn't I?" He looked at her hard and went on, "Do you know what you are saying to me, Mattie Farnham? You are telling me that you really think that home-making is a poor, mean, cheap job beneath the dignity of anybody who can do anything else."

Mattie Farnham was for a moment helpless with shock over his attack. When she slowly rose to a comprehension of what he had said she shouted indignantly, "Lester Knapp, how dare you say such a thing! I never *dreamed* of having such an awful idea." She brought out a formula again, but this time with heartfelt personal conviction, "Home-making is the noblest work anybody can do!"

"Why pity me then?" asked Lester with a grin, drawing his needle in and out of the little stocking.

"Well, but . . ." she said breathlessly, and was silent.

There was a pause. Then she asked meekly, climbing down with relief from the abstruse and unfamiliar abstract to the friendly concrete, "However in the world did you *learn* to darn, Lester?"

"Out of a book," he told her tranquilly. "While I

was still in bed I sent to the Library for any books they had on housekeeping. They sent me some corking ones—as good reading as ever I saw."

"Why, I didn't know they had books about house-keeping at the Library!" said Mattie, who was a great reader of novels.

"I bet I know more about cooking than you do, this minute," he said, laughing at her. "Why do you put your flour for a cream sauce into the butter and cook it before you add the milk?"

"I don't," she said, astonished. "I heat my milk and mix my flour with a little cold water and . . ."

"Well, you're wrong," he said authoritatively. "That's not the best way. The flour isn't thoroughly cooked. Fat can be heated many degrees hotter than water."

Mattie Farnham felt herself sinking deeper and deeper into a stupid bewilderment. Was it really Lester Knapp with whom she sat discussing recipes? She had come over to sympathize and condole with him. However in the living world had she been switched off to cream sauce? She got up, shook herself and took a step or two around the room.

"Don't go looking to see if the furniture is dusted or the floor polished," said Lester calmly. "We concentrate on the important things in our house and let the non-essentials go."

"I wasn't thinking about *dust!*" she told him,

exasperated (although she had been). And then, struck by a sudden thought, "Where's Stephen?"

"Out in his sandpile."

"Why, I thought he ran away if he was left out of anybody's sight for a minute. I thought you didn't dare let him be by himself for . . ."

"Oh, Stevie's all right," said Lester carelessly; "he's coming along like a house afire."

He wheeled himself to the door, opened it and rolled his chair out on the porch. A blue-denimed little figure rose up from the other end and showed a tousled head, bright dark eyes and a round dirty face with a calm expression. "I got my tunnel fixed," he announced.

"Did you?" asked Lester, with interest. "That can business did work?" To Mattie he explained, "Stephen is fixing up a railway system, and the sand kept falling in on his tunnel. We finally thought of taking the bottom out of an old baking-powder can. That leaves it open at both ends."

"It works dandy," said Stephen. He now added of his own accord, with a casual look at Mrs. Farnham, "Hello, Aunt Mattie."

It was the first time Mrs. Farnham could remember that she had ever had a friendly greeting from Stephen. Eva's conscientious attempts to make him perform the minimum of decent salutations, to come and shake hands and say "How do you do?"

usually ended in a storm of raging stamping re-
fusals.

"Hello, Stephen," she answered, feeling quite
touched by his friendly tone. He looked very quiet
and good-natured, too. Well, of course, all children
do grow out of their naughty ways if you can only
live till then. She had always said that Stephen
would outgrow his. But she had never believed it.
It was a good idea to have a sandpile for him. Children always like them. Of course it brought sand
into the house something terrible. Children never
would wipe their feet. But now that any attempt
at real housekeeping had been given up in poor Eva's
house, a little more or less dirt didn't matter. She
had as a matter of fact (although she had denied it)
noticed that the corners of the room were very dusty.
And those preposterous papers on the floor! What
a ridiculous idea!

No more ridiculous than having the sandpile on
the porch! Whoever heard of such a thing!

"I should think you'd find it hard to keep the
porch clean," she said to Lester.

"We don't," he said bafflingly.

"Why not have it out in the yard?"

"Some of the playthings would get spoiled by the
rain." He advanced this as conclusive.

Stephen had squatted down again to his sand.
She went cautiously towards the wide plank to see

what he was doing, prepared to have him snarl out
one of his hateful catch-words: "Go 'way! Go
'way!" or the one he had acquired lately, the insolent, "Who's doing this anyhow?"

But what she saw was so astonishing to her that
before she could stop to think, she burst out in an
impulsive exclamation of admiration, "Why, Stephen
Knapp, did you do all that your*self?*"

Beyond the board lay a tiny fairy-world of small,
tree-lined, pebble-paved roads, moss-covered hills,
small looking-glass lakes, white pasteboard farm-
houses with green blinds, surrounded by neat white
tooth-pick fences, broad meadows with red-and-
white paper cows and a tiny farm wagon with
minute, plumped-out sacks, driving to the railroad.

A large area of her own simple consciousness was
still sunny with child-heartedness, and it was with
the utmost sincerity of accent that she cried out,
"Why, I'd love to play with that myself!"

Stephen looked proudly up at her and lovingly
down at his creation. "You can if you want to."
He conceded the privilege with lordly generosity.

She got stiffly down on her middle-aged knees, to
be nearer the little world, and clasped her hands
in ecstasy over the "sweet little barn" and the
"darling locomotive." Why, she remembered now
that she herself had given that toy-train to Stephen.
The last time she had noticed it was when, unsur-

prised, she had seen Stephen kicking it down the stairs. Lucky it was made of steel.

"It fits in just great," said Stephen, also remembering who had given it. "I never had any way to play with it before. See, it carries the corn from this farm to the city. I'm going to start in on the city to-morrow, over there in that corner, as soon's I get the track fixed. Mother is going to bring me some little houses from the ten-cent store. Mother brought me the little wagon and horses. She brings me something 'most every night. Those bags are filled with real corn-meal."

"Oh, see the real grade-crossing with the little 'Look out for the engine' sign," cried Mrs. Farnham rapturously.

They had both entirely forgotten Lester. He smiled to himself and wheeled his chair back into the house. Mattie was a fat old darling, that's what she was.

He went on darning the little stocking and murmuring to himself,

> "She wars not with the mystery
> Of time and distance, night and day:
> The bonds of our humanity.
> Her joy is like an instinct joy
> Of kitten, bird, or summer fly.
> She dances, runs without an aim;
> She chatters in her ecstasy."

When Mattie came in, not dancing at all but walk-ing rather rheumatically as though her knees creaked, she closed the door behind her and said in an impressive way, "Lester Knapp, that is a very smart thing for Stephen to do. I don't believe you appreciate it. There's not one five-year-old child in a hundred with the headpiece to do it."

He answered with an impressive manner of his own, "Appreciate it! I'm the fellow who does appreciate it! Stephen Knapp is a very remark-able child, I'd have you to know, Mrs. Farnham. I bet you a nickel he will amount to more than any-body else in this whole town if he only gets the right chance."

As she walked home, Mattie thought how funny it was to hear a man going on like a mother, stand-ing up for the least promising of the children!

But all the same, perhaps there *was* more to Stephen than just his cussedness.

How cheerful Lester had seemed! It must be that his food had set better than usual to-day.

Chapter 15

SATURDAYS were great days for "the Knapp Family, Incorporated." They were together at home all day, and always with a great variety of schemes on hand. In the morning Henry usually relapsed from his eleven-year-old dignity back into younger days and played with Stephen, especially since the sand-pile settlement had been started, and since they had a brood of chickens to care for. Old Mrs. Hennessy came to give the house the weekly, thorough, cellar-to-garret cleaning which Lester had found was the best way to keep Evangeline from spending Sunday with a mop and broom. In the kitchen Helen and her father, foregathering over the cook-book, struggled fervently with cookery more ambitious than that of the usual week-day.

Helen loved these Saturday morning cooking-bees as she called them. She and Father had such a good time together. It was so funny, Father not knowing any more than she did about it all and having to study it out from the book. Lots of times she, even she, was able to give him pointers about things the cook-book didn't tell.

For instance, at the very beginning, that historic

first day, long ago, when they had first cooked together and timorously tried to have scrambled eggs
for lunch, it had been Helen who conquered those
bomb-like raw eggs. Lester had gingerly broken off
the top of one, and was picking the shell carefully
away, when Helen said informingly, "That's not the
way. Mother gives them a crack in the middle on
the edge of the bowl and opens them that way."

"How? Show me," said her father docilely, hand-
ing her another egg. Feeling very important, Helen
took it masterfully and, holding it over the edge of
the bowl, lifted her hand with an imitation of
Mother's decisive gesture. But she did not bring
it down. She shuddered, rolled her eyes at her
father and said miserably, "Suppose I hit it too hard,
and it all spurts out?"

Her father felt no impulse to cry out bitterly on
her imbecile ineptitude. Rather he sympathized
with her panic, "Yes, raw eggs are the dickens!"
he said, understandingly.

Intimidated, they both looked at the smooth, oval
enigma.

"*You* do it," said Helen, with her self-distrusting
impulse to shift responsibility to some one else.

Her father refused with horror to assume it. "Not
on your life!" he cried. "You were the one who'd
seen Mother do it."

"Doesn't the cook-book say how to do it anywhere?" asked Helen, trying to fall back on some one else. "There is a chapter at the end that tells you how to take out ink-stains and what to do for people who have got poisoned, and all sorts of things. Maybe it'll say there."

They laid down the egg to search, but found nothing in the four hundred pages of the big book that told them how to break a raw egg.

"Perhaps you could lay it down on a plate and cut it in two with a knife," suggested Lester.

Even Helen knew better than this. She knew better than that when she was *born,* she thought, suppressing a pitying smile, "Gracious no! You would get the shell all mixed up with the insides," she explained. They stared again at the egg.

To Helen came the knowledge that responsibility must be assumed.

"Somebody's got to," she said grimly. "I'll try again."

She took the egg in her hand and resolutely struck it a small blow on the edge of the bowl. The shell cracked a little.

"That sounds good," said Lester; "give it another whack."

She repeated the blow and, holding the egg up above her head till she could see the under side, reported that there was a perceptible crack and some wetness oozing out.

But that was not enough. She must go on and see it through. How queer not to have somebody tell her what to do and make her do it. "I'm going to try to pull it apart," she announced courageously, feeling like a heroine. She got the tips of her fingers into the tiny crack and pulled, shutting her eyes.

Something happened. A gush of cold sticky stuff over her fingers, a little glass-like tinkle of breaking egg-shell in her hand, and there in the bowl were the contents of the egg, the golden yolk swimming roundly in the transparent white.

"Hurrah! Good for you!" shouted her father admiringly.

But Helen found in her heart a new conscience which made her refuse to accept too easily won praise. "No, that's not right," she said, frowning at the crushed, dripping shell in her hand. "When Mother does it, the stuff comes out nice and clean, with each half of the shell like a little cup."

She closed her eyes, summoned all her will-power and thought back to the times when she had watched Mother cook.

Mother held it so (Helen went through the pantomime), she brought it down with a little quick jerk, *so*, and then . . . "Oh, goody! goody! I know!" she cried, hopping up and down. "*I* know. She turns it over after she's cracked it, with the crack on the

up-side, and then she *pries* it open. Give me another egg."

Well, it certainly was a far cry from those early
fumbling days, wasn't it, to now, when both she and
Father could crack and separate an egg with their
eyes shut and one hand tied behind their backs, so
to speak; when they thought nothing of turning out
in a Saturday morning a batch of bread, two pies,
and enough cookies to last them a week. They
didn't even talk about their cooking much any more,
just decided what they were going to make and went
ahead and made it, visiting together as they worked
like a couple of magpies chattering.

Father often told her poetry as she stepped to and
fro; the kitchen seemed to her just chock-full of
poetry. Father had said so much there the walls
seemed soaked with it. Sometimes in the evening
when she went in just before she went to bed to
get a drink of water or to see that the bread sponge
was all right, it seemed to her, especially if she were
a little sleepy, that she could hear a murmur of
poetry all around her, the way a shell murmurs when
you put it to your ear . . .

"Now all away to Tir na n'Og are many roads that run,"

"Keen as are the arrows
Of that silver sphere."

"Waken, lords and ladies gay!
    To the greenwood haste away!"

"Since brass, nor stone, nor earth, nor boundless sea
    But sad mortality o'ersways their power,
    How with this rage shall beauty hold a plea . . ."

It was not water that Helen Knapp drank out of
the tin dipper hung over the sink. It was ambrosia.

And Father told her stories, too, all kinds, lots of
funny ones that set them into gales of laughter!

And they talked, talked about everything, about
her writing, and what she was reading in school,
and the last book she had got out of the Library,
and once in a great while Father would tell her something about when he went to the State University
and what an exciting time he'd had finding out how
much he loved books and poetry. Helen had never
heard Father speak of those years till now. He
seemed to feel, the way she did, that it was easier
to talk about things you cared awfully about when
you were working together. Helen often wondered
why this was, why she didn't feel so queer and shy
when she was doing something with her hands, but-
tering a cake-tin, or cutting animal-shaped cookies
out of the dough that Father rolled so beautifully
thin. She even found that she could talk to Father
about "things."

By "things" Helen meant all that she had always

before kept to herself, what she had never supposed
you could talk about to anybody—the little poems
that sprang up in your head; what you felt when
the spring days began to dapple the sidewalks
with shadows from the baby leaves; what you felt
when you woke up at night and heard the freight-
trains hooting and groaning to and fro in the yards
—Helen loved living near the railroad—what you
thought about growing up; what you thought about
God; what kind of a husband you would like to
have when you were big; what kind of children you
hoped you'd have. "I'd kind of *like* a little baby
boy with curly yellow hair," she said thoughtfully
one day, as she bent her head over the butter and
sugar she was creaming together.

"Henry was like that when he was little," her
father said reminiscently. "It *was* nice. You were
an awfully nice baby, too, Helen. Of course, being
the first, you made the biggest impression on me.
You had ideas of your very own from the time you
began to creep. You never would go on your hands
and knees like other babies. You always went on
your hands and feet, with your little behinder sticking up in the air like a ship's prow."

Helen laughed over that. She loved to have her
father tell all about when she had been a baby, and
how much he had loved her, and how smart she had
been, and sometimes how funny, as on the day

when she had thought Mrs. Anderson had stayed long enough and had toddled over to her, putting out a fat little hand and saying firmly, "By-by, Mis' Anderson. By-by!"

Gracious! How long ago that seemed to Helen, and how grown-up it made her feel, now that she was such a big girl, thirteen years old, helping to do up the week's baking and all. She felt old and ripe and sure of herself as she listened to those baby-stories and wrung out the dishcloths competently. (She and Father had wrestled with the question of how to hold the dishcloths when you wrung them out, as they had wrestled with the method of breaking an egg, and had slowly worked it out together.)

She came to feel that talking to Father, when they were alone together, was almost like thinking aloud, only better, because there was somebody to help you figure things out when you got yourself all balled up. Before this Helen had spent a great deal of time trying to figure things out by herself, and getting so tangled that she didn't know where she had begun nor how to stop the wild whirl racing around in her head. But now, with Father to hang on to, she could unravel those twisted skeins of thought and wind them into balls where she could get at them.

One day, as she washed the breakfast dishes for

Father to wipe, she noticed how the daffodils Aunt
Mattie had brought were reflected in a wet milk-
pan. It made her think a poem, which she said
over in her head to make sure it was all right, and
then repeated to Father,

> "The shining tin usefulness of the milk-pan
>   Is glorified into beauty
>   By the presence of a flower."

Father listened, looked at the golden reflection in
the pan, said appreciatively, "So it is," and added,
"That's quite a pretty poem, especially the last
phrase."

Helen knew it was pretty. She had secretly a high
opinion of her own talents. Why had she said it
aloud except to make Father think what a remark-
able child she was? She washed the dishes thoughtfully, feeling a gnawing discomfort. It was horrid
of her to have said that just to make Father admire
her. It was showing off. She hated people who
showed off. She decided ascetically to punish herself by owning up to her conceit. "I only told that
poem to you because I thought it would make you
think what a poetic child I am," she confessed con-
tritely. "It wasn't really that I thought so much
about the flower."

She felt better. There now! Father would think
what an honest, sincere child she was!

Oh, dear! Oh, dear! That was showing off too! As bad as the first time! She said hastily, "And I only owned up because I thought it would make you think I'm honest and didn't want to show off!"

This sort of tortuous winding was very familiar to Helen. She frequently got herself into it and never knew how to get out. It always frightened her a little, made her lose her head. She felt startled now. "Why, Father, do you suppose I only said *that*, too, to make you . . ." She lifted her dripping hands out of the dishwater and turned wide, frightened eyes on her father. "Oh, Father, there I go! Do *you* ever get going like that? One idea hitched to another and another and another; and you keep grabbing at them and can't get hold of one tight enough to hold it still?"

Lester laughed ruefully. "*Do* I? Nothing but! I often feel like a dog digging into a woodchuck hole, al*most* grabbing the woodchuck's tail and never quite getting there."

"That's just *it!*" said the little girl fervently.

"I tell you, Helen," said Lester, "that's one of the reasons why it's a pretty good thing for anybody with your kind of mind, or mine, to go to college. If you try, you can find out in college how to get after those thoughts that chase their own tails like that."

"You *can?*" said Helen, astonished that other people knew about them.

"I suppose you think," conjectured Lester, hanging up the potato-masher, "that you're the only person bothered that way. But as a matter of fact, lots and lots of people have been from the beginning of time! You've heard about the Greek philosophers, haven't you? Well, that is really about all they were up to."

There was a pause, while Helen wiped off the top of the kitchen table.

Then she remarked thoughtfully, "I believe I'd *like* to go to college."

It was the first time she had ever thought of it.

Oh, no, it was not always recipes they talked about on Saturday mornings!

And on Saturday nights, as he reached for some book to take to bed with him, Lester's hand not infrequently fell on an old, rubbed, shabby volume which fell open at the passage,

"The thought of our past years in me doth breed
 Perpetual benediction: not indeed
 For that which is most worthy to be blest—
 Delight and liberty, the simple creed
 Of childhood whether busy or at rest,

 .   .   .   .   .

 But for those obstinate questionings
 Of sense and outward things,
 Fallings from us, vanishings;

Blank misgivings of a creature
Moving about in worlds not realīzed,
High instincts, before which our mortal nature
Did tremble like a guilty thing surprised:
But for those first affections,
Those shadowy recollections,
Which, be they what they may,
Are yet the fountain-light of all our day,
Are yet the master-light of all our seeing;
Uphold us—cherish—and have power to make
Our noisy years seem moments in the being
Of the eternal silence: truths that wake,
To perish never:
Which neither listlessness, nor mad endeavor,
Nor man, nor boy,
Nor all that is at enmity with joy,
Can utterly abolish or destroy!"

From here on, Lester always felt a great tide lift
him high. . . .

"Hence, in a season of calm weather,
 Though inland far we be,
 Our souls have sight of that immortal sea
 Which brought us hither,
 Can in a moment travel thither
 And see the children sport upon the shore,
 And hear the mighty waters rolling evermore."

It was to the shouts of those children, to the re-
verberation of those mighty waters that the para-

lyzed accountant often slipped quietly from his narrow, drudging life into the "being of eternal silence."

Chapter 16

ONE of the most embittering elements of Lester's old life had been the absence of any leisure when he could really think—consider things consecutively enough to make any sort of sense out of them. He seemed to himself to live perpetually in the mental attitude of a man with his watch in one hand and a heavy valise in the other running for a train which was already overdue. How much value would the judgment of such a man have?

He had always thought he would like to be able to sit right down quietly to think out a thing or two. Now he certainly had all the sitting down quietly that anybody could want. Well, he liked it as much as he had thought he would. And more! He brought under his consideration one after another of the new elements of his new life, holding them firmly under the lens of his intelligence, focusing on them all his attention, and to his astonished relief saw them one by one yield to his analysis, give up their tortured, baffling aspect of mystery and tragedy, and lie open to his view, open to his hand, open to his forward-looking planning. He had never lived with his family before, he had never seen more of their lives than the inexplicable and tangled loose ends over which they all stumbled wretchedly. Now that for months he had had the opportunity for continuous observation, he perceived that there was nothing so darkly inexplicable, after all, nothing that resisted a patient, resourceful attempt to follow up those loose ends and straighten out some of the knots.

Even in the tragic tangle of Stephen's strange little nature, Lester felt he had begun to find his way. He had found out this much: Stephen had more vitality than all the rest of them put together (except Eva, of course). And when it did not find free outlet it strangled and poisoned him, made him temporarily insane, in the literal sense of the word, like a strong masterful man shut up by an accident deep in a coal-mine, who might fall insanely to work with his bare hands to claw away the obstructing masses of dead, brute matter that kept him from the light of day! That was what Stephen made him think of; that was, so Lester divined, the meaning of the wild, fierce flame in Stephen's eyes which had always so shocked and grieved them. They were of another breed, the kind who would sit down patiently and resignedly to die, not fight till the last minute with bleeding hands.

All but Eva—oh, poor darling Eva! How much

better Lester understood his wife after those few
months of observing her in a life that suited her
than after fourteen years of seeing her grimly and
heroically enduring a life that did not.   Was this
Eva the same as the old one?   This Eva who came
in every evening tired, physically tired as he had
never seen her, but appeased, satisfied, fulfilled, having poured out in work she loved the furious splen-
dor of her vigor.

His heart ached with remorse as he thought of
the life to which he had condemned her.   Why, like
Stephen, she had been buried alive in a shaft deep
under the earth, and she had not even had Stephen's
poor passionate outlet of misdirected fury.   What
she thought was her duty had held her bound fast in
a death-like silence and passivity.   He remembered
the somber, taciturn, self-contained woman who had
sat opposite him, year after year, at the supper-table.
Could that be the same Eva who now, evening after
evening, made them all gay with her accounts of
the humors of her profession; who could take off a
fussy customer so to the life that even Stephen
laughed; who could talk with such inspired anima-
tion of the variations of fashion that even he
listened, deadly as was his hatred for fashion and
all that it stood for!   He had never even suspected
that Eva had this jolly sense of humor!   Could it be
the same Eva who so briskly dealt the cards around

every evening and took up her hand with such interest?

Those evenings of whist had been an inspiration of his, in answer to two questions he had set himself: What could he invent that would keep Eva's mind off the housekeeping in the evenings? And what could he and Eva and the children do together, which they would all really and truly enjoy— what was some natural manner in which to make a civilized contact between the two generations and the widely differing temperaments? It was delightful to him to see how Eva enjoyed it, how she liked to win (just think of her caring to win! How young in nature she remained! She made him feel like Methuselah!). How cheerily and heartily she coached Henry along, how the children admired her skill and luck, and how she enjoyed their admiration.

Heavens! How unhappy she must have been before, like a Titan forced to tend a miniature garden; forced to turn the great flood of that inherited, specialized ability of hers into the tiny shallow channels of the infinitely minute detail of child-care; forced, day after day, hour by hour, minute by minute, with no respite, into a life-and-death closeness of contact with the raw, unfinished personalities of the children, from which her own ripe maturity recoiled in an ever-renewed impatience. Eva always hated anything unfinished! And nothing around her ever stayed unfinished very long. How she put through any job she undertook! She had sat up all one night to finish that sofa she had so wonderfully refurbished.

But you couldn't put through the job of bringing up children. No amount of energy on your part, no, not if you sat up all night every night of your life, could hurry by a single instant the slow unfolding from within of a child's nature. . . .

Eva dropped out of Lester's mind whenever he thought of this, and he was all flooded with the sweet, early-morning light that shone from his daughter's childhood. He always felt like taking off his hat when he thought of Helen.

Sometimes when they were working together and Helen was moved to lift the curtain shyly and let him look at her heart, he held his breath before the revelation of the strange, transparent whiteness of her thoughts. That was the vision before which the greatest of the poets had prostrated themselves. And yet the best that had been done by the greatest of them was only a faint shimmer from the distant shrine. He understood now how Blake, all his life-long, had been shaken when he thought of children, "Thousands of little boys and girls, raising their innocent hands." Through all the leaping, furious, prophetic power of Blake, there ran,

like a sun-flooded stream, this passion of loving rev-
erence for little girls and boys.

And under his quaintly formal rhymed words, how
Wordsworth's deep heart had melted into the same
beatitude, " . . . that I almost received her heart
into my own." "Into my own!" Helen's father
knew now how literally a man could feel that about
a little girl.

And yet this did not mean that he thought Helen
was perfect. No, poor child, with her too flexible
mind, her too sensitive nerves, her lack of power
and courage, Helen needed all the help she could
get if she were not to be totally undone by life. He
knew a thing or two about how ruthless life is to
any one who lacks power and courage! Helen must
learn how to stand up to things and not lie down
and give up. He would find ways to teach her . . .
yes, he knew wincingly what sarcastic people would
ask, "How could he teach her what he had never
learned himself?" But the fact that he had never
learned himself was the very reason for his understanding the dire need for it. Perhaps it might
come from athletics. She must learn to play on a
team, how to take rough, careless, good-natured
knocks, and return them and pass on her way. As
soon as he could get about on crutches, somehow—
perhaps he would go to the physical-training teacher
at school and have a talk about Helen. Perhaps he

could get up an outdoor basket-ball team of the children here on the street. He had plans, all sorts of plans. Above all, Helen must go to college. It wasn't so much, going to college; he had no illusions about it. For a strong personality like Stephen's it might very well not be worth while. But for a bookish, sensitive, complicated nature like Helen's, the more her intelligence was shaped and pointed and sharpened and straightened out, the better. She would need it all to cope with herself. She was not one for whom action, any action provided it were violent enough, would suffice.

Would it for Henry? How about Henry, anyhow? How everybody always left Henry out! That was because there wasn't anything unusual about the nice little boy. He was a nice little boy, and if he grew to his full stature, he would be a nice man, a good citizen, a good husband. No leader of men, but a faithful common soldier—well, perhaps a sergeant—in the great army of humanity.

But he had a right to his own life, didn't he, even if he weren't unusual? You didn't want everybody to be unusual. There were moods in which Lester Knapp took the greatest comfort in Henry's being just like anybody else. So much the better for him! For everybody! There would never be tragedy in his life, no thwarted, futile struggling against an organization of things that did not fit him. At times, too, there was something poignant to Lester about Henry's patient, unrebellious attitude. He never fought to get what he wanted. He stood back, took what others left, and with a touching, unconscious resignation, made the best of it. All the more reason for Henry's father to stand up for him, to think of how to get him more of what he wanted.

He began to plan for Henry now. What would Henry naturally want? Just what any little boy wanted. The recipe was well known: Playmates of his own age, a "gang"; some kind of shack in the woods to play pirate; games, lots and lots of games; a pet of his own; perhaps a job at which he could earn real money of his own to spend on a baseball mitt or a bicycle.

Why, Henry didn't have a single one of those things, not one. And he was eleven years old.

That afternoon when the children came home, he waited till they had unpacked their minds of the school-news, and then asked casually, "Say, Henry, wouldn't you like to have a puppy to bring up? I used to think the world of my dog when I was your age."

A quick startled look passed between Henry and Helen, a look rather wild with the unexpectedness of their father's question. Henry flushed very red and looked down dumbly at his piece of bread and butter.

Helen spoke for him, placatingly, "You see, Father . . . you see . . . Mother never wanted Henry to . . . but . . . well, Henry *has* a puppy, sort of."

Seeing nothing but expectant interest in her father's face, she went on, "Old Mrs. Hennessy's Laura had puppies about six weeks ago, and Mrs. Hennessy said Henry could have one. Henry always did want one, *so*. And Henry"—her accent was increasingly apologetic—"Henry sort of did pick out one for his. It's white with black spots. Awfully cunning. Noontimes Henry runs over from school to the Hennessys' to play with it. Mrs. Hennessy and Laura are weaning the puppies now. He's beginning to lap milk. Oh, Father, haven't they got the darlingest little red tongues! Henry's named him Rex. Mrs. Hennessy said Henry could keep it at her house, because Mother . . . "

A new possibility opened before her like the horizon lifting, "Oh, *Father*, do you suppose she would let Henry have it *now?*"

The "now" referred to the change in Mother which they all noticed, but never mentioned, even in so distant a manner as this "now." It had slipped out in Helen's excitement. Lester took no notice of it.

"Do you s'pose she *would?*" asked Henry, in an agitated voice. He was now quite pale.

"Heavens, what a sensitive little chap he is!" thought Lester. "How worked up he does get over little things." Aloud he said, "Well, she might. Let's ask her this evening."

So they did. She came in rather late and pretty tired. Her feet ached a good deal by nighttime, now it was warm weather, and Helen usually had a good hot bath waiting for her when she came. Mother kissed her and said what a comfort she was before shutting the door of the bathroom. Helen jumped happily downstairs, two steps at a time, to help Father get the supper on.

It was steaming on the table when Mother came down in the pretty, loose, red-silk house-dress which she'd bought at the store at such a bargain—for *nothing,* as she said. She looked relaxed and quiet and said she was starved and so glad they had veal cutlets. It was a joy to watch Mother eat after her day's work.

They never washed the dishes in the evenings now, because, Mother getting her breakfast down-town, it was no matter *how* the kitchen looked in the morning. Henry and Helen piled them on the new wheeled tray which Mr. Willing had so kindly sent up, pushed that into the kitchen and put them to soak, while Father and Mother got Stevie to bed and lighted the little bedside candle, at which Stephen loved to stare himself to sleep.

Then they hurried into the living-room for the evening rubber of whist. Mother's luck was especially good that evening, a fact in which they all took an innocent satisfaction. Mother liked it when her luck was good.

Then, all of a sudden, the opening was there, and Father was taking advantage of it in a masterful way. Mother said something about the two little Willing girls who had been down at the store that day with their dog, and Father put in at once, "By the way, Eva, old Mrs. Hennessy wants to give Henry one of a litter of puppies her dog has. What would you say? It's spring-time. It could be out of doors mostly." (How they admired him for being able to speak so casually. "By the way, Eva . . ." He was wonderful. Under the table Helen's hand squeezed Henry's hard.)

Mrs. Knapp still had before her eyes the picture of the two fashionably dressed children and their fashionably accoutred dog with his studded collar and harness and the bright tan braided leather of his leash. She had never thought of dogs in terms of smartness before. "He'd make a lot of trouble for you," she said, looking over at her husband.

"Oh, I'd manage all right. I like dogs," said Lester carelessly.

"You'd have to promise, Henry, to keep him out of this room. I don't want dog-hairs all over everything." (It was the old formula, but not pronounced with the old conviction. After all she would not be there to see. She was often surprised that she worried so little about the looks of the house nowadays.)

"Oh, I'd never let him in *here*," promised Henry in a strangled voice.

"Well . . . " said his mother. She looked down at the cards in her hand.

There was a silence.

"Who took that last trick?" she asked.

"You did," said her husband (although he had).

They began to play again.

It had been as easy as that.

Lester had quite forgotten about the dog that evening as he pottered around the kitchen over some last tasks. He heard the bathroom door shut and knew that Eva had gone in for her evening toilet. At once afterwards his ear caught the stealthy sound of bare feet on the stairway. He turned his head towards the door and saw Henry come hurrying in on tiptoe.

He opened his lips to make some joking inquiry about whatever it could be that kept Henry up so late, but the expression on the child's face silenced

him. Good heavens! Had he cared so much as that
about owning a dog!

Henry came up to him without a word and leaning
over the wheel of the invalid-chair, put his arms
around his father's neck, leaning his cheek against
his father's shoulder.

"Oh, *Father!*" he said in a whisper, with a long,
tremulous breath. He tightened his arms closer
and closer, as though he could never stop.

Lester patted the little boy's back silently. He
was thinking, "I hope he'll come like this to tell me
when he's in love and has been accepted. I don't
believe he'll be any more stirred up." The child's
body quivered against his breast.

After a time Lester said quietly, "Better get to
bed, old man. You'll take cold, with your bare
feet."

Docilely and silently Henry went back upstairs
to bed.

Chapter 17

OLD Mrs. Anderson, having borne seven children and raised three to maturity (not to speak of having made a business of guiding Mrs. Knapp by neighborly advice through the raising of her three), knew what was brewing with Stephen the moment she stepped into the kitchen. She had been expecting Stephen to have one of his awful tantrums again any day. The only reason he hadn't so far was because poor crippled Mr. Knapp was so weak and so indifferent to what the children did that Stephen was allowed to have his own way about everything. But foolish indulgence wore out after a while and only made things worse in the end. All the regulation signs of an advancing storm were there. She noted them with a kindling eye. Stephen's face was clouded; he gave her a black look and did not answer her "How *do*, Stevie dear?" And as she took a chair, he flung down his top with all his might. A moment later, as he lounged about the kitchen with that insolent swagger of his that always made her blood boil, he gave a savage kick at his blocks.

Now was the time to give Mr. Knapp some good

advice that would save him trouble in the end. She never could stand hunchbacks and cripples and had not liked Mr. Knapp very well even before he was so dreadfully paralyzed; but she felt it her duty to help out in that stricken household. "You'll have trouble with that child to-day, Mr. Knapp," she said wisely; "he's spoiling for a spanking. Anybody with experience can see that by looking at him. My! what a relief 'twill be when he's out of the house and goes to school with the others."

It had been her habit thus to diagnose Stephen to his mother. And as for the remark about the relief it would be to have Stephen go to school, it was threadbare with repetition. She scarcely knew she had said it, so familiar was it. It astonished her to have Mr. Knapp look at her as though she had said something which shocked him. She was nettled at his look and replied to it resentfully by a statement of her oft-repeated philosophy of life, "The only way to manage children, Mr. Knapp, is never to let them get ahead of you. If you watch for the first signs of naughtiness and cut it short"— her gesture indicated how it was to be cut short—"it doesn't go any further."

To illustrate her point she now addressed Stephen's listening, stubborn back in a reproving tone of virtue, "Stephen, you mustn't kick your blocks like that. It's naughty to."

Stephen instantly kicked them harder than ever and continued to present a provocatively rebellious back to the visitor.

Mrs. Anderson turned to his father with the gratified look traditionally ascribed to the Teutonic warlords when they forced Serbia into a corner. She tapped the fingers of one hand rapidly in the palm of the other and waited for the father of the criminal to take action. He continued to draw his needle in and out of the stocking he was darning. His face looked like Stephen's back.

What a disagreeable man Mr. Knapp was! She was not surprised that he had been so disliked by all the sensible people at the store. And how ridiculous for a man to be darning a stocking! He might at least look ashamed of it! Mrs. Anderson disliked him so much at this moment that she felt herself trembling and burning, "Well, Mr. Knapp, you're not going to pass over a wilful disobedience like that, I hope," she said, her voice shaking with anger as much at Stephen's father as at Stephen.

"*I* didn't tell Stephen not to kick his blocks," he said dryly.

Her sense of extravagant rightness in the face of insane wrongness flamed over her so hotly that she could scarcely speak. "Well . . . but . . . but . . . oh, I understand! I under*stand!*" she finally brought out bitterly. "I understand. You think it is all right and perfectly proper for Stephen to kick things around as much as he pleases."

Mr. Knapp stooped to look into the oven where a rice pudding was cooking. How ridiculous for a man to be cooking a rice pudding! "I'm sure I don't know why you think you understand anything about it because I have not told you what my opinion on the subject is," he said, over his shoulder.

Stephen's back became more acutely listening. He did not understand the big words and he could not make out his father's tone, except that, unlike Mother, he did not get mad at Stephen and begin to pick on him whenever Mrs. Anderson had been there a little while.

Mrs. Anderson did not make out Mr. Knapp's tone very well herself, except that it was all part of his intense disagreeableness. A weak poor creature Lester Knapp was, a perfect failure at everything, and without even the poor virtue of knowing it. Besotted in self-conceit into the bargain, though she had never suspected that before. Poor Mrs. Knapp! And those poor children! Her mother's heart ached for them, left in such hands.

Mr. Knapp went on drawing his thread to and fro silently. Little by little, out of the air, Mrs. Anderson drew the information that she had been insulted, though she had not perceived exactly when. She felt rasped to the bone. With dignity, she drew her cape up around her shoulders and prepared to go.

"Take the advice of an old woman who was bringing up children before you were *born*," she said solemnly, her voice shaking with the depth of her feeling. "You'll find out when it is too late that they *must be made to mind!* Everything depends on that. Mrs. Knapp, their poor mother, understood that perfectly."

"Good afternoon," said Mr. Knapp, very distinctly.

The door closed behind her ungently enough, and with its slam Lester Knapp felt himself transported by an invigorating wave of anger such as he had rarely felt in his life, simple, hot, vivifying rage as good as a drink of whiskey. It made him feel twice as alive as usual. "Strange thing, the human mind," he thought rapidly. "When I ran into Mrs. Andersonism in business, it only made me sick, sort of hamstrung me with disgust. Anything they'd put their filthy hands on I'd rather *let* them have than touch them enough to fight them. But when it threatens Stephen. . . . God! I *love* to fight it! I'd enjoy strangling that old harpy with my two hands. She thinks she can bully me by threatening my vanity, does she? She thinks she can get

her damned old hands on my little boy, does she? I
should say it was enough to have killed four of her
own."

He looked over at Stephen's brooding back and
set his stirred and sharpened wits to the problem of
switching Stephen off from the track that was taking him towards one of his explosions. He had discovered that Stephen's salvation at such times was
something hard to do, something Stephen could
struggle with, but not quarrel with. He thought
fast, almost excitedly. Would he think of something first, or would Stephen blow up first?

Stephen turned away from the pile of his toys
and began to wander about the kitchen, casting a
somber eye on the too familiar things. "Alexander,
Alexander, what new world can I get for you?"
asked his father, unleashing his inventiveness and
sending it leaping forward on the trail.

In a moment, "Say, Stephen, how'd you like to
beat up a pretend egg?" he asked.

Stephen glowered at him suspiciously, but with a
spark of unwilling curiosity in his dark eye.

"Like this," said his father. He wheeled himself
to the shelf, took down a tin basin, filled it with
warm water, put a bit of soap into it and began to
whip it to a froth with an egg-beater.

Stephen's face lightened. Ever since he could
remember he had seen his mother playing with that

fascinating toy; ever since he could remember he had put his hand out for it; ever since he could remember his mother had said, "No, no, you'd only make a mess," and had hung it up out of reach.

He had gone too far towards a nervous explosion to be able to say "Oh, goody!" or "Give it to me!" but he held out his hand silently. His father took no notice of his sullen expression and did not offer to show him how it worked.

Stephen set the egg-beater in the water and with perfect confidence began to try to turn the handle. He always had perfect confidence that he could do anything he tried. At once the egg-beater slipped sideways and fell to the floor. Stephen frowned, picked it up and held it tighter with his left hand. But he found that when he put his attention on his left hand to make it hold tight, his right hand refused to make the round-and-round motion he so much admired. He had never before tried to do two different things with his two hands. He took his attention off his left hand and told his right hand to make the circular motion. Instantly the whole thing began to slip. As instantly he flashed his mind back on his left hand and caught the beater before it fell. But at once his right hand, left to itself, stopped turning.

"For him, it's just like trying to pat your head and rub your stomach," reflected Lester.

Stephen was disconcerted by the unexpected difficulty of the undertaking. He stood still a moment in the mental attitude of a man who has caught a runaway pig by the ear and a hind leg and does not dare let go. He breathed hard and frowned at the perverse creature of steel in his hand.

His father felt as the spectators at a prize-fight feel when the second round begins. He prayed violently that nothing might interrupt the rest of the bout. Especially did he pray that the old Anderson imbecile might not come in. If she did, he would just throw the stove-lid at her head. What was he for, if not to protect Stephen from marauding beasts of prey? He himself did not make a motion for fear of distracting Stephen's attention.

The little boy went at it again, but with none of his first jaunty cocksureness, cautiously, slowly, turning the handle a little at a time. He made no progress whatever. The combination of the two dissimilar motions was too much for him. If some one had held the egg-beater still, he could have turned the handle, he knew that. But he would never ask any one to do it. He would do it himself. Himself! He tried again and again without the slightest success and began to put on the black, savage look he had for things that displeased him.

His father followed with sympathy as he toiled forward into the unmapped jungle of his own mind.

How he stuck at it, the little tyke! And how touching was his look of outraged indignation at his own unruly right hand! His father said to himself, half-laughing, half-wistful, "Poor old man! We've all been there! That painful moment when we first realize that our right hands are finite and erring!"

He shook with silent mirth over the sudden, hot-tempered storm which followed in a tropical gust, when Stephen stamped his feet, ground his teeth, and, turning red and purple with rage, tried by main strength to master the utensil. He turned his eyes discreetly down on his darning when Stephen, with a loud "Gol darned old thing!" threw the egg-beater across the kitchen. He felt Stephen suddenly remember that his father was there and glance apprehensively up at him. He chose that moment to stoop again to the oven door and gaze fixedly in at the bland face of the rice pudding.

But he did not see it. He saw Stephen's fiery little nature at grips with itself, and inaudibly he was cheering him on, "Go to it, Stevie! Get your teeth in it! Eat it up!" He was painfully, almost alarmingly interested in the outcome. Would Stephen conquer, or would he give up? Was there real stuff behind that grim stubbornness which had given them such tragic trouble? Or was it just hate-fulness, as the Mrs.-Anderson majority of the world thought it? He held a needle up to the light and threaded it elaborately. But he was really looking at Stephen, standing with his stout legs wide apart, glowering at the prostrate but victorious egg-beater. In spite of his sympathetic sense of the seriousness of the moment Lester's diaphragm fluttered with repressed laughter. Cosmic Stephen in his pink gingham rompers!

He took up another stocking and ran his hand down the leg. Stephen sauntered over towards the beater, casually. He glanced back to see if he need fear any prying surveillance of his private affairs, but his father's gaze was concentrated on the hole in the stocking. Carelessly, as though it were an action performed almost absent-mindedly, Stephen stooped, picked up the beater, and stood holding it, trying experiments with various ways of managing that maddening double action. His clumsiness, his muscular inexpertness with an unfamiliar motion, astounded his father. How far back children had to begin! Why, they did not know how to do *any*thing! Not till they had learned.

This did not seem to him the trite platitude it would have been if somebody else had said it to him. It cast a new light into innumerable corners of their relations with Stephen which had been dark and pestilential. They hadn't begun to be patient

enough, to go slow enough. Stephen was to the egg-
beater, to all of life, as he himself would be, put
suddenly in charge of a complicated modern locomotive.

No, Stephen was not! Painlessly, with the hard-
won magnanimity of a man who has touched bottom
and expects nothing out of life for himself, not even
his own admiration, Lester recognized in Stephen's
frowning, intent look on his problem a power, a
heat, a will-to-conquer, which he had never had. He
had never cared enough about either locomotives
or egg-beaters to put his mind on them like that.
Stephen got that power from his mother. From his
other world of impersonality Stephen's father saw
it and thrilled in admiration as over a ringing line in
a fine poem. If only Stephen could be steered in
life so that that power would be a bright sword in
his hand and not a poison in his heart.

The clock ticked gravely in the silence which followed. For Lester the pause was full of grave,
forward-looking thoughts about Stephen. Presently
the little boy come back purposefully to the basin
of water. He put the beater in, and once more tried
to turn the handle. The perverse thing did all that
perversity could imagine, slipped sideways, stuck,
started too suddenly, twice fell to the floor clatter-
ing. Each time Stephen picked it up patiently and
went back to work. Lester ached with fatigue at

the sight of his perseverance. Heavens! *Nothing*
was worth such an effort as that!

> "Why with such earnest pains dost thou provoke
> The years to bring the inevitable yoke?"

But Stephen did not flinch. He felt he almost
had it. Once he turned the wheel three-quarters of
the way around! His heart leaped up. But after
this it balked continuously. Stephen fetched a long
quavering sigh of discouragement and fatigue. But
he did not stop trying. He could not have stopped.
Something more potent than fatigue held him there.
The tough fibers of his passionate will were tangled
about his effort. He could not stop till he dropped.
He was very near dropping. He scarcely knew
what he was doing, his attention was so tired. But
his hands, his brave, strong little hands kept on
working. His back and legs ached. His shoulders
bowed themselves. But he did not stop.

> "Under the bludgeonings of chance . . ."

murmured Lester to himself.

And then, all at once, it was as though Stephen
had turned a corner. Something rearranged itself
inside his head. Instead of toiling uphill he felt
himself begin to glide down easily. Why, he could
do it! That rebellious right hand of his was sud-

denly tamed. Whir-r-r! went the steel spokes flash-
ing in the white suds. They sang like music in
Stephen's ears! Whir-r-r! He could hardly believe it!

Once in a while it stuck or jerked, but he had only
to take thought—Stephen could feel the thinking
place in his head draw together *hard*—and command
his hand to turn regularly. How it hated to, that
old hand! And how Stephen loved the feeling of
bossing it around!

He turned and turned. The foamy suds frothed
higher and higher! Whir-r-r! The kitchen was full
of the sound.

Stephen threw back his head and, laughing
proudly, looked up at his father. His face was
ruddy and glowing with his effort, with his triumph.
All his fatigue was gone. Whir-r-r!

His father drew a long breath. He felt like
clapping his hands and shouting "Hurrah!" It had
been nip and tuck there for a while. Talk about
the cave-man who had invented the bow and arrow!
If Stephen had been a cave-man he would have invented the telephone. What a stirring spectacle it
had been. He felt as though he had been reading
some Emerson. Only it was lots better than any
Emerson!

"Well, sir," he exclaimed to the child, "I certainly will hate to have you begin going to school!"

The rice pudding was done. He took it out and put some coal on the fire and glanced at the clock. Why, it was almost time to expect the other children in from school. How the afternoon had flown! It was hard to put your mind on anything but the absorbing spectacle of Stephen's advance into life. He must get out the milk and cookies with which he welcomed the others in. They always burst in as soon as possible after four. Sometimes Lester wondered what they had done before, in the old days, in the interval between four and six, when he usually found them waiting for him at the door of the store. Evangeline used to say that they were "playing 'round" with their school-mates.

He had not noticed that Stephen had stopped turning the egg-beater and was now looking up hard into his face, until the little voice asked, "What will you hate to have me going to 'chool for?"

Lester had to think for a moment before he could remember what he had said. Then, "Great Scott, Stevie, why wouldn't I? I'll *miss* you—what do you think? I'll be lonesome without my funny, nice, little boy to keep me company."

He wondered what made Stephen ask such a question. The child usually was quick enough to catch your meaning. He wheeled himself into the pantry and did not see that Stephen, after standing for a moment, turned away and went quietly out of the

room. When he came back and found him gone,
Lester thought that probably he had gone upstairs
to look for another toy.

Stephen felt very queer inside, sort of shaky and
trembly. He had never felt like that before. And
the queerness went all over him so that he couldn't
be sure that he wasn't making up a queer face that
Father would ask him about. The first thing to do
was to get away where nobody would see him. He
turned away, trying to pretend to walk carelessly
and went into the empty dining-room.

But it didn't stop. He could feel it, making him
tremble and shake inside. And yet he didn't feel
sick—oh, no! It was a strange good feeling that
was almost too much for him. It was too big for
him. He was too little to hold it. It seemed to
overflow him, so that he could scarcely breathe, in
a bright, warm, shining flood. And Stephen was
such a little boy! He had never felt anything like
it before. It frightened him and yet he loved it.
He must get off somewhere by himself where he
would be safe—and alone—with the new, strange,
bright, drowning feeling.

Under the stairs—always his refuge—he crept in
on his hands and knees, not noticing the dust which
flew up in his face as he crept. Those corners were
not clean as they had been when Mother kept the

house, but Stephen thought of nothing but that now the quivering was all over him, even his face . . . the way it was when he was going to cry. He and his new feeling crept farther and farther in, as far as he could go. He sat down then, cross-legged, his face turned towards the safe, blind wall. He was safe. He was all alone. It was dark. He said to himself so low that there was no sound, "Father will miss me when I go to school." Then, lower still, "Father likes to have me around."

And suddenly Stephen's eyes overflowed and his cheeks were wet, and hot drops fell down on his dusty hands.

But he was not crying. He knew that. It hurt to cry. And this did not hurt. It helped. The water ran quietly out of his eyes and poured down his cheeks. It was as though something that had ached inside him so long that he had almost forgotten about it were melting and running away. He could feel it hurting less and less as the tears fell on his hands. It was as though he were being emptied of that ache.

The tears fell more and more slowly and stopped. And now nothing hurt Stephen at all. There was no ache anywhere, not even the old one, so old he had almost forgotten about it. Stephen felt weak and empty without it and leaned his head faintly against the dusty dark wall.

He sat there a long time, it seemed to him, till little by little he felt the weakness going out of his legs and the emptiness out of his body. He must go back to Father now, or Father would wonder where he was.

But Father would think he had been crying and would ask him why. How could Father tell the difference if he saw the wet on his cheeks? Stephen would have died rather than try to tell any one what had been happening to him. He did not know at all what had been happening to him. He would rub the wet off his cheeks with his hands. Yes, that would do. Then Father would never know. He scrubbed vigorously at his eyes and his cheeks with his fists, and when he felt that there was no dampness left, he backed out on his hands and knees into the dining-room again. Was it the same room it had been when he had crept in? It didn't seem possible! It looked so different. And Stephen felt so different. Like another Stephen altogether. So light! So washed! So clear! He didn't seem to weigh anything at all, but to float through the air as he walked. Nothing looked to Stephen as it had. The walls and furniture had a sprightly, cheerful expression. He waved his hand to them as he floated out to the kitchen.

Lester had been busy at first getting the four

o'clock lunch ready for the children. He had taken down from the pantry shelf a paper bag of cookies, yes, the boughten kind; they happened to be out of home-made ones. He ought to have been making some instead of hanging fascinated over Stephen's hand-to-hand battle with the universe.

But it was, glory be, no longer such a tragic matter, the sort of food Henry had! It certainly was a special provision of Providence that Henry and Helen were so much stronger than they had been; that just when they fell into his inexpert hands, they had begun to outgrow their delicate health. However could he have managed the care of them if they had been sick so often as when poor Eva had been struggling with the care of them? Wasn't it all a piece of her bad luck to have had them during that trying period and turn them over to him just as her wonderful cooking and nursing had pulled them through. What a splendid nurse she was!

He poured out a glass of milk apiece for the children and looked impatiently at the clock. He loved the moment of their noisy arrival, loved the clatter of their feet on the porch, the bang of the door thrown open. Why were they late to-day?

Oh, yes, he remembered. They were due at a rehearsal of the school-play—Helen's play—the one they had worked out together. What fun it was to have her bring him her little experiments in writing! He began to think that perhaps she might have a little real talent. Of course most of what she set down was merely a copy of what she had read, but every once in a while there was a nugget, something she had really seen or felt. This, for instance, which he had found scrawled across the fly-leaf of her arithmetic—poor Helen and her hated arithmetic!

> "The measured beats of the old clock
>   Bring peace to my heart
>   And quiet to my mind."

That was the real thing, a genuine expression of her own personality. How different from the personality of her mother, to whom the ticking of a clock could scarcely be anything but a trumpet-call to action. Different from her father's personality too. The clock always said to him,

> "But at my back I always hear
>   Time's winged chariot hurrying near. . . ."

Ah, what a second-rater he was! How he always thought of everything in terms of what somebody else had said! In earlier days when he was a boy and still thought he might perhaps amount to something this had been an affliction to him, a secret shame. But now he did not grieve over it. Since he had died and come back to this other life, he took everything and himself, too, more simply, with little concern for the presentability of the rôle he was to play. If, honestly, that was the sort óf nature he had, why rebel against it? The only people who got anywhere by rebelling were rebels to begin with. And he was not. Why wasn't it enough, anyhow, to love the beauties other men had created?

He heard Stephen come back into the kitchen. He had been gone quite a while after that toy.

"Father," said Stephen softly, behind him.

Lester started at the color of the little voice. There was something queer about it.

Cautiously, with his ever-present dread of intruding, he glanced at Stephen not curiously, but with a casual air.

The little boy came up to his chair and stood there, looking up at him with a strange expression of shining-quiet in his eyes. He had evidently been crying hard, for his cheeks were covered with the smeary marks of black where he had wiped off the tears with his dirty hands. But what on earth could he have been crying about? There had not been a sound.

And he did not look like a child who has been crying. He looked . . . he was smiling now . . . he looked like a little golden seraph hovering around the golden gates.

"Father," said Stephen in a small, clear voice. He hesitated, evidently trying to think of something to say, his shining eyes fixed on his father's. Finally he brought out, "Wouldn't you like me to bring you a drink of water?" His smile, as he said this, was dazzling, his voice sweet, sweet with lov-ing-kindness.

"Why, yes, Stevie," said his father over a lump in his throat, "I do believe I am thirsty without realiz-ing it."

Stephen pushed a chair before him to the sink, climbed up on it, took down the dipper and held it under the faucet. The bright water gushed out, spattering over him, over the floor. He caught half the dipper full, turned off the faucet, and carried the dipper awkwardly back to his father, who took a long drink appreciatively.

"Thank you, old man," he said as he handed it back.

Stephen set it back on the table and returned to hover near his father, smiling up at him speechlessly.

Lester felt the room filled with the flutter of airy, unseen wings and ached with his helpless wonder at them. What could have happened? What could have happened? He held his breath for fear of say-ing the wrong thing in his clumsy ignorance. All he dared do was to smile silently back at Stephen.

"Father," said Stephen again, although he evi-

dently had nothing to add to the word, "Father . . ."
He could think of nothing else to say to express the
mysteriously born fullness of his heart.

"Yes, Stevie," said his father, his own heart very
full.

"Father . . . would it hurt your sick legs very
much if I sat in your lap for a while?"

Lester reached out hungrily and pulled the child
up into his arms. "There's just one good thing that
can be said about my sick legs, Stephen," he said,
trying to be whimsical, "they positively cannot be
hurt any more."

Stephen laughed a little, nestled, turned himself,
and then with a long sigh as though he were very,
very tired, with a sudden relaxation of all his warm
little body, was asleep, his round dark head falling
back limply on his father's shoulder.

Lester was almost frightened. Had the child
fainted? Was he sick? But the expression on
Stephen's face was of complete calm. It looked like
a smooth, closed bud, secret and serene, close-
wrapped, all the personality at rest, nothing left but
the tender mask of flesh.

Lester stirred involuntarily a hair's breadth.
Stephen felt the movement and his eyes flew open
wide for an instant. At first they were shallow
and meaningless in a mere physical opening. Then,
before sleep took him wholly, he recognized his

father, and all that made the little boy Stephen shone out of his eyes like a candle leaping up brightly before it goes out. That look was for Lester. Without stirring, in the exquisite smile of his eyes, his lips, all his transfigured little face, Stephen gave himself lovingly to his father.

Long after the burning little spirit had gone elsewhere, leaving the inert, deep-breathing, warm, small body on the paralyzed knees, his father sat there, his lips quivering.

Presently he said to himself, "And I am the man who, three months ago, was so eager to get out of life."

PART FOUR

Chapter 18

WHEN Evangeline read the little note asking her to step into Mr. Willing's office, she thought of course the new things from Hasenheimer's had come, and that Mr. Willing would ask her if she could come back that evening to help unpack and place them. But it was Mrs. Willing's voice which called "Come in!" to her knock, and the moment she opened the door she knew by the expression on Mr. Willing's face that something important was on the way.

Mr. Willing waited till she and his wife had gone through the necessary greetings and then brought it out flatly, "Mrs. Knapp, Miss Flynn has just told us that, because of certain changes in her family affairs, she will be leaving us next month."

He went on talking after this, but Evangeline did not need to hear him. She knew everything that he would say before he said it—all except the salary! That was certainly more than Miss Flynn had ever had! And to begin with! There was only one idea in her head. How soon could she fly to a telephone to tell Lester the good news. She could never wait till she went home that evening. She loved Lester for her certainty that it would make him as happy as she was, that he would not feel jealous or hateful. How *good* Lester was!

She saw on the faces of the two people opposite her a reflection of what must be on her own. They understood what the moment was to her.

And to them too. She felt in their voices as they talked to her a new relationship towards her, a new respect. They needed her as she needed them. She was important to them and their splendid work. It was wonderful to be really useful in a big thing!

"Yes, indeed, Mrs. Willing!" she assented with all her heart, as the younger woman said, "We feel that you can understand our position. It is not just a store to us, you see. It is our Life Work."

This seemed a little flamboyant and feminine to Mr. Willing, who said correctively, "We think it rather a remarkable opportunity, all things considered, for giving good store service. With the support the store would naturally get from the town and the farming region around us, we expect," he coughed, "we hope to double the business before so very many years."

"Oh, more than that!" cried his wife. "Of course this is confidential, Mrs. Knapp. We wouldn't want it to go any further. But since we think of you as in on the ground floor with us . . . If with Mr. Willing's poor old uncle's rusty machinery the store actually paid expenses, there's simply no telling what can be done with a modern organization such as my husband has worked out in his mind. Better wages, lower prices, and what merchandise!"

"My idea of *good* merchandise, Mrs. Knapp," said Mr. Willing seriously, "is that it shall be a liberal education in taste."

Mrs. Willing put in spiritedly, "Give us ten years' time and see if the Saturday evening crowds don't look different in this town. The clothes they wear now must give them an inferiority-complex right down to the marrow of their bones!"

"Give us ten years' time," said Mr. Willing, laughing, "and see if there is a single golden-oak, Morris-chaired 'best room' left in town!"

Evangeline felt dazzled by all that was happening; her promotion; sitting here in such an intimate way with the proprietors of the business; having them talk in this wonderful way of their wonderful conception of what the business really was. It was her conception too. Every word found an echo in her heart, although she had not had the education to express it brilliantly as they did. But she was uneasy at being away from her post so long. What would Miss Flynn think? The exquisite surprise it was to realize that it no longer made any difference what Miss Flynn thought! She felt an inch taller.

Mr. Willing said now, "I've been wanting to have a talk with you about things in general, and now's as good a time as any. We want you to understand the situation in a comprehensive way, in a large way. There are certain elements in the retail dry-goods business which give rise to considerable concern on the part of . . ."

"Off on polysyllables!" thought his wife. She cut in briskly, with the effect of scissors snipping in two a slowly unwinding tape, "It's the mail-order houses and the ten-cent stores we're afraid of. It's frightful how they steal the business of country people away from where it belongs. The first thing that has to be done is to give them our dust. And it can be done by making the store known for such good personal service and such real attention to customers' needs that they'll *enjoy* coming to the store. And once they're inside the doors . . ."

"After all, how even the best of women see things in a little, narrow, concrete way!" thought Mr. Willing. "Nothing big and constructive in their minds." Aloud he said with simplicity and dignity, "I was brought up on a farm myself, Mrs. Knapp, and a very poor farm. And I have a very special feeling about our country customers. I know how few occasions there are in farm life for civilized mingling with our fellow-men, how little brightness and color there is in country life. It is my ambition to make every trip to our store as educative as an afternoon tea-party for the women-folk on a farm. And I want every purchase at our counters to help every fine big farm-boy to shuck off his awkward countrified ways that put him at such a disadvantage beside any measly, little, cock-sure, tenement-house rat!" Experiences of his own past burned in his voice, "We're counting on you, Mrs. Knapp, to train your girls to have just the right manner with country customers. *You* know, cordial, but respectful, friendly, but no soft-soap business."

"I know *just what you mean!*" Evangeline burst out suddenly, with such an earnest conviction that they stopped talking for an instant to enjoy her oneness with them. Yes, she would do. She would do.

"My ideal," said Jerome, "is service. What I want the store to be is a little piece of the modern world *at its best*, set down within reach of all this fine American population around us. I want to select for them the *right things,* the things they never could select for themselves for lack of training. With modern methods such as my wife and I are familiar with, a quicker turn-over with better salespeople, we can raise—not wages—but commissions to keep efficiency up to the notch. And we can lower prices and sell goods that will put our people on a level with big-city people. For I have long felt, Mrs. Knapp, that the alarming American exodus to the cities comes from a nagging sensation of inferiority that would disappear with the possession of really satisfactory merchandise. You see," he said, smiling at her, "that in our small way, we will all be contributing to the highest interests of the country."

"Of course on a sound business basis," put in his wife.

"Oh, of course on a sound business basis," repeated the proprietor of the store.

The three shook hands on it with unanimity.

Chapter 19

WITH her materials and patterns laid out on the dining-room table, Mattie Farnham was trying to cut out a dress for her Margaret, an undertaking which was going jerkily because of the arrival, seriatim, of the children from school. They came in at different times, as suited their different ages and their rank in the hierarchy of grades. Little Jim in the first grade was free at two, Loren in the fourth was turned loose at three, and Margaret and Ellen appeared soon after four. The hour of the arrival varied, but the manner was identical: a clatter of hurried feet on the porch, the bursting open of the door, and the questing yell of "Mother! Mo-o-other!"

Mattie always answered with an "Oo-hoo!" on two notes, adding, "in the di-i-ining-room!" but she never waited for them to come to find her. She always laid down her work and all thought of it and hastened to give the returned wanderer a hug and kiss and run an anxious eye over his aspect to see what had happened to him during his day out in the world.

"Jimmy, you look tired. Did you eat your lunch good? Come on with me and get a piece of bread and butter."

"Say, Mother, Teacher picked me out to say the good-morning greeting to the whole school this morning at Assembly."

"Did she? Which one did you say? Weren't you scared? Say it to me. Let's hear."

A half hour later they would still be in the pantry, Jimmy swinging his legs from his mother's cushiony lap, telling her between mouthfuls about everything that had happened in the long interval since he had seen her last. Mattie listened eagerly, stroking the hair back from the square white forehead, gloating greedily over the changing expressions on the little open, rosy face.

Then Jimmy wanted to know what *she* was doing and trotted back with her to the dining-room and had to have the nature of patterns explained to him, and hung over her as she worked, rumpling up the paper and getting in her way, his tongue and hers flying together.

Somehow it was time for Loren. Wherever had that last hour gone to? The crash of the opening door, the shrill whoop of "Mother! Mo-o-other!" And it all began again, this time with an exciting account of how Teacher gave Morton Cummings the awfulest calling-down you ever heard for copying off

of Sadie Bennett's paper. Both Jimmy and Mother
were spell-bound.

But Margaret's dress did not progress very rapidly. At a quarter of four Mattie still had the
sleeves to cut out, and she'd *have* to put her mind
on them because she hadn't bought enough dimity
and they would have to be pieced under the arm.
"Loren, you and Jimmy run out and play a while,
won't you, that's good boys. Mother's got to get
this done."

"Mercy! Evangeline Knapp would have had that
dress all cut out and basted up . . ."

And then, right out of a clear sky, came the un-
heralded thunderbolt of a new idea—how could
it have come like that! She had not thought of
the Knapps, not once all that day. She had been
wrapped up in her work and in the children; yet
the minute she had thought of Eva's name . . . it
was all there, as though she had been studying over
them for weeks! Everything in her head had
shucked together different, like when you look in
a kaleidoscope and give it a shake, and there's a new
design. Why! Why! One thing after another
came to her . . . how could it be she had never
thought of it before? It was so plain now . . .
why, yes!

The inquiring shout of Margaret and Ellen had
no response. Surprised and aggrieved, they pushed

on hastily in search of their mother and found her dropped into a chair by the dining-room table, her big scissors in her hand, her eyes wide and fixed. She answered them absently, she hardly looked at them, she never noticed that Ellen had lost her hair-ribbon, she interrupted Margaret's account of how Maria Elwell's petticoat had come off by jumping up and saying suddenly as though she didn't even know that Margaret was talking, "See here, girls, I've got to run over to your Uncle Lester's for something. You keep an eye on Jimmy, will you?"

What was the matter with Mother anyhow, Margaret and Ellen asked themselves over their four o'clock pieces of gingerbread. But they were not much worried. There was never very much the matter with Mother.

She hurried so that she was puffing as she went up the porch steps of the Knapp house—and yet when she opened the door she did not know why she had come nor what to say. Henry and Helen were just in also, enjoying cookies and milk and telling their father about the events of the day. The sight of the cookies gave Mattie her cue.

"Do those spice-cookies agree with Henry?" she asked.

"Sure they do," said Lester. "Everything does nowadays! Henry seems to have grown right out of that weak stomach of his. He eats like a wolf,

I tell him. The doctor says they do sometimes outgrow those childish things as they get near their
teens."

"Oh, yes, as they get near their teens," said
Mattie.

A moment later she asked, "Helen, aren't you
fatter than you used to be? Seems as though you
were lots fuller in the face."

"Did you just get around to notice that, Aunt
Mattie?" said Helen, laughing. "You ought to see
me trying to get into a last summer's dress. They
don't come together—my!—there's that much of a
gap." She showed with her hands how wide a gap
it was.

"Helen has put on eight pounds," explained
Lester. "The school nurse says all the children are
gaining like everything, now they serve milk at
recess-time."

"Oh, yes, milk at recess-time," said Aunt Mattie.

Helen and Henry finished their cookies and tore
out to inspect their poultry. The children and
Lester had gone into the chicken-business on a
small scale and were raising some brooder chicks
in a packing-case chicken-house in the back yard.
Stephen was there already, hanging over the low
wire-netting "watching their tail-feathers grow," as
he said.

Lester quoted this as he wheeled himself to the open door where Mattie stood looking out at the children fussing maternally over the little peeping yellow balls. "Honest to goodness, Mattie, their tail and wing feathers do come in so fast you can see them grow." He added, *"I'm* watching feathers grow, too. Stephen is fairly sprouting wings he's so good! It's because he can play out of doors again, I suppose, after the winter. We've had such lovely weather of late."

"Yes, it must be because he can play out of doors again," said Aunt Mattie.

As they turned back into the kitchen, where a batch of bread was ready to be put into the oven, she asked, "Lester, aren't you better of your indigestion lately?"

"Sh!" he warned her whimsically, his finger at his lips. "Don't mention it aloud. I haven't had any in months. But I don't want it spoken about. Leave sleeping dogs lie. The doctor always said it was nervous, you know. I don't know much about the geography of my innards, but I've thought once or twice that maybe that awful shake-up my nervous system got might have sorted things over into the right pile, as far as digestion goes. It's not, however," he said with a sudden grim, black look at his paralyzed legs, "a cure for indigestion that I could recommend."

The tears sprang into Mattie's eyes as she turned her face away, "It's pretty *hard!*"

"I don't pretend it's any picnic. But it's of no consequence of course." He was able to say this with a bare and utter sincerity.

"Look here, Lester!" she broke out. "Why couldn't you—I don't believe but what you could go and be a professor somewhere in a University or a High School. Professors don't have to walk around. And you've always set such store by poetry and books and everything. There can't be anybody who's more . . ."

Lester broke in with a laugh at her absurdity. "Why, you dear old girl, you don't know what you're talking about. I'd make a mess of what they want in a school just as much as at the store. What makes you think colleges want teachers who love literature? They want somebody who can make young people sit still and listen whether they feel like it or not. They want somebody who can 'keep order' in a class room and drill students on dates so they can pass examinations. I couldn't do that! And I'd loathe forcing literature down the throats of boys and girls who didn't want it as I'd loathe selling things to people who didn't need them. I'd be just a dead loss at it the way I always am."

Seeing that she did not follow this, he added concretely, "Besides I could no more get a job with-

out all the right certificates than I could set up shop
as a doctor. Nowadays colleges want you to be a
Ph.D. And there isn't a cross-roads High School
that'd look at a man who had only had three years
in a State University fifteen years ago and had
been making a failure of keeping accounts in a
department store ever since."

Mattie recognized the irrefutable nature of all
this. "Yes, I see," she said sadly.

"Isn't Mattie the ignorant, impractical old in-
fant!" thought Lester.

She got up now, with a long breath, and silently
took herself off.

Although it was long past time to start supper, she
did not go home. She went straight down to Willing's and into the Cloak-and-Suits. Eva was busy
with customers as usual. "Everybody wants Eva
to wait on them," thought Mattie, sitting down heavily. Her eyes were fixed on Evangeline. What a
splendid woman she was, and, now she had some
money to spend on her clothes, what a stylish-look-
ing woman! There wasn't anybody in town could
hold a candle to her. Mattie made these reflections
automatically. These were always the first thoughts
which came to her when she saw Eva.

But to-day, ravaged as she was by this new perception, in which she was so all alone, her mind

dwelt little on style. What she saw to-day was Eva's face, alert, interested, sympathetic, and Eva's eyes, which had always had, so Mattie remembered, "a sort of wild look," now so shining and quiet, looking from the suits she was showing to her customers. They were a couple of women from out in the country, elderly mother and grown-up daughter. Mattie was too far off to hear what was said, but she understood perfectly from the pantomime and from the expression of the three faces, what the situation was. The two women had thrown themselves on Eva's taste to help them make up their minds, and Eva, looking at them intently, was putting herself whole-heartedly in their places so that she could give them her best judgment. How happy she looked!

As she watched, a lump came into Mattie's throat, and she felt her eyes hot and misty. What in time was the *matter* with her? She swallowed hard and looked away and tried to think of something else. But she could not. Lester and Stephen and Henry and Helen . . . and Eva! . . . came and stood before her eyes—her opened eyes.

"My goodness! I mustn't get to crying here in the store!" she thought, alarmed, starting up and going to the window.

When she turned around, Eva's customers had made their decision, a momentous one, judging from the relief on their faces. The three women were

chatting and smiling together, relaxed and cheerful.
Mattie heard Eva say, "I know you'll take the greatest *com*fort in it!" She went with her customers
to the head of the stairs, talking like an old friend.
They shook hands with her, respectfully, cordially.
Then she turned around and came almost running
back towards Mattie. "Mattie, I've got something
to tell you," she said hurriedly, smiling. She looked
around her to make sure no one was near and lowered her voice, "Miss Flynn's niece has died and
leaves four little children and their father wants
Miss Flynn—he hasn't got any relative of his own—
to go and bring the children up and keep house for
him. He's in the greenhouse business at Cleveland.
Plenty of money. And she is going."

Mattie did not understand this. She understood
few things at once. She saw nothing but Eva's curv-
ing, smiling lips and bright shining eyes. She understood them with no difficulty.

"Don't you see?" whispered Eva. "Somebody's
going to be moved up to her place, head of the department. They're going to give me a try at it.
Aren't they good! Mattie! It's three thousand a
year! And a bonus for extra sales! And such fascinating work! I'm wild to get my hands on it and
see what I can do with the salesgirls. Oh, Mattie,
we can begin to lay by a little something every
month for the children's college. Perhaps we can

buy a Ford that Lester can get out in with the children. Oh, *Mattie!*"

At this Mattie disgraced herself and showed once more, as she said apologetically, what an idiot she was by bursting into senseless, hysteric tears and having to be carried off in haste to the toilet-room to cold water and smelling salts.

"I've felt all squimbly this whole afternoon," she explained, blowing her nose. "I don't know what's the matter with me. Old fool, I guess."

"Well, it almost makes me feel like crying myself," said Eva, holding out a glass of water to her. "It's come so soon, so much sooner than I dared to hope. And it will mean so much to Lester and the children. They'd never have had a college education any other way. Why, Mattie, I've kept thinking all day about the hymn, 'God moves in a mysterious way, His . . .'"

"*Don't!*" said Mattie huskily. "You'll get me started again."

"Of course," Eva said now, "it's dreadfully hard for a mother to be separated from her . . ."

Mattie broke in hastily, as if to change the subject, "Eva, how is that eczema of yours lately?"

Mrs. Knapp rolled up a fashionably wide sleeve and showed a clean, white upper-arm. "Dr. Merritt finally found a cure," she said, "a new kind of ointment he heard about in a medical convention. It's worked like a charm. I haven't had a touch of eczema—why, in I don't know when! It took the doctor long enough to get around to it, but he finally did."

It was half-past five when Mrs. Farnham left the store, but still she did not start home. *"Let* them wait for supper!" she thought, desperately. What was supper compared to some other things! She hurried heavily along towards Dr. Merritt's house, hoping to goodness he would be in.

He was, sitting on the porch, reading the evening paper. "Hello, Mrs. Farnham," he said, surprised to see her. "I didn't think I'd ever get any business out of *your* family. Who's broken a leg?"

"We're all right," she told him. "I wanted to ask you about the Knapps. You know I'm sort of related to Mr. Knapp. I've been wondering what you really thought about him . . . whether he'll ever be cured, I mean."

The doctor noticed that her voice trembled as she spoke. What a good-natured creature she was, taking other people's troubles so to heart.

He hesitated. It was not at all his habit to talk about his patients to outsiders, least of all to any such chatter-box as Mrs. Farnham. But he had thought several times lately that, if Lester Knapp were to make any progress, he would need to start a campaign to dry up the gushing spring of family sympathy. He knew all about that sort of campaign from much experience, but he was never resigned to the necessity for it. "Darn families and their sympathy!" he often said impatiently. "They 'poor-Charlie' and 'poor-Mary' more sick people into their graves than we doctors do."

He had long suspected that well-meaning Mrs. Farnham did a good deal of "poor-Lestering" at the Knapps. Maybe this was a chance to head her off, to get her mind started along a new track. Of course he must remember to use the simplest, most elementary language with her. She was really almost an illiterate.

"I'll tell you, Mrs. Farnham, just what I think about the case. As near as I can make out, the effusion of blood within the spinal canal has been safely absorbed, or nearly so. There seems to be no displacement or injury to the spinal bones; there is no wasting away of the muscles as would be the case if the spinal cord were injured. There is, I believe, good reason to hope that the loss of power in his legs is a sequel of organic conditions which have now passed away. The case now needs a psychic treatment rather than a mechanical."

"Organic?" said Mrs. Farnham, faintly. The word made her think of church.

"I mean that in my opinion no physical lesion now

exists in spite of the abnormal sensations which Mr. Knapp still feels. We must try toning up the general health, overcoming the shock to the nervous system. As soon as the weather permits, I shall try heliotherapy."

Mrs. Farnham caught her breath.

"That is, treatment of the affected areas by direct exposure to sunlight. They have done wonderful things in France with that treatment in just this sort of trouble. And of course at any time any sort of sudden nervous stimulus might do the business. You see, Mrs. Farnham, Mr. Knapp's case is now like that of the people who are cured at Lourdes, or by Coué. The very same sort of phenomenon."

"I don't understand very well," said Mattie humbly. "What I wanted to know was . . ." her voice faltered, *do you think you can cure him?*"

"Isn't she the dumb-bell!" thought the doctor.

He went on aloud, hoping she would repeat his words to Mrs. Knapp, "Don't you say anything about it, Mrs. Farnham, especially to Mrs. Knapp. I don't want to crow till we are out of the woods. I wouldn't say anything to you if you were not a relative and a sensible woman. I don't want them to have a breath of it, for fear of disappointment . . ." (How strangely she was looking at

him, her face so white and anxious!)   He brought
it out roundly, "Yes, Mrs. Farnham, just between
us, I really believe I can cure him."

She gave a low cry that was like a wail.   "Oh,
Doctor!" she cried, appalled, staring at him.

What was the matter with the woman, now?   He
stared back at her, blankly, startled, entirely at a
loss.

Another look came into her eyes, an imploring,
imploring look.   She clasped her hands beseechingly.
"Oh, *Doctor!*" she begged him, in a quavering voice.

From her eyes, from her voice, from her beseech-
ing attitude, from her trembling hands, he took in
her meaning—took it in with a tingling shock of
surprise at first.   And then with a deep recognition
of it as something he had known all along.

She saw the expression change in his face, saw
the blank look go out of his eyes, saw the understanding look come in.

It was a long rich interchange of meanings that
took place as they sat staring hard at each other,
the gaunt, middle-aged man no longer merely a
doctor, the dull middle-aged woman, transfigured to
essential wisdom by the divination of her loving
heart.   Profound and human things passed from
one to the other.

Mattie heard some one stirring in the house. "I must go! I must go!" she said groaningly. She limped down the path. Her feet were aching like the toothache with the haste of her expeditions that afternoon.

Half an hour later they had to come out and call the doctor to supper, fairly to shout in his ear he was so sunk in his thoughts, the evening paper lying unread across his knees.

"Mercy me! Didn't you hear the supper bell?" cried his wife. "It's been ringing like anything!"

Chapter 20

ON the evening of the day when Mrs. Knapp was informed that she would be put in Miss Flynn's place Helen and her father celebrated by making an omelette with asparagus tips (Mother's favorite supper dish) and Henry was sent scurrying out to bring back a brick of mixed vanilla and chocolate from Angelotti's Ice-Cream Parlor. They did not play whist that evening. They just sat around and talked it over and admired Mother and heard again and again about the thrice-blessed events in the family of Miss Flynn's niece, which led to her retirement. "Of course it's terribly, terribly sad!" Mother reminded them. "Those poor little children left without their mother! Nothing—*nothing* can ever make up to them for such a loss."

But this decent observation cast no shade over the rejoicings. Miss Flynn was but a remote and disagreeable legend to the children; and she had been a particular *bête-noire* for Lester in the old days. As for her utterly unknown niece—no, Mother could not make that shadowy death cast anything but sunshine into their lives. They went on planning all the more energetically about the

277

things they could do if they could have a Ford and go off to the country together for picnics on Sundays —even Father! They talked about which college Helen would like to attend. They talked about which kind of bicycle Henry liked the best.

The children joined in the talk till nine o'clock, and long after they were in bed with their lights out they could hear the distant murmur of Father's and Mother's voices going on planning, such a friendly, cheerful, easy sort of murmur. Helen could not remember when she had ever heard Father and Mother talk together like that. It was like music in her ears. The last thought she had before she fell asleep was, "I am so happy! I never was so happy!"

Her mother fell asleep on the same thought. Apparently the excitement of it was too much for her, for she woke up suddenly, to hear the clock strike three, and found she could not get to sleep again because at once, in a joyful confusion, her mind was filled with a rush of happy thoughts, "I am to have Miss Flynn's place. Three thousand a year. And a bonus! In a year or so I ought to be making four thousand."

Four thousand dollars! They had never had more than eighteen hundred. Her thoughts vibrated happily between plans of what they could do here at the house and plans of what she would do in the reorganization of the department at the store. For some time, as she lay awake, her mind was as active and concrete and concentrated on her work as ever in the store; she was planning a system of post-card notices to customers when something especially suited to one or another came in:—"Dear Mrs. Russell: Among the new things in the department which have just come in from New York are some smocked, hand-made children's dresses that look exactly like your little Margery . . ." "Dear Miss Pelman: Do you remember the suit you did not buy because of the horizontal trimming on the skirt? Mr. Willing found in New York last week the same suit without that line. I am laying it aside till you can drop in to look at it."

She wondered if she could let her salesgirls send out such cards too. No, it must be done with great discretion—above all must not seem too urgent. People didn't like to feel they were being hunted down.

She stepped about mentally among the innumerable details of her plans with her usual orderly mastery of them, her usual animated interest in them, her usual unquestioning acceptance of them as important. From them she went on to plans for a series of educational talks to her salesgirls about the fabrics and styles and fine points of their merchandise. She wished she could do the same thing for the girls in the Ladies' Waist and Sweater Department. There were some such bright girls there, but so ignorant of their business. They'd pick it up in no time if they had the chance, if she were allowed to . . .

Why! With a tremor all over her, she wondered if some time she might not be not only head of her own department, but superintendent for all that floor. By a flash of prescience she suddenly knew as she lay there alone in the quiet that the road to advancement lay open before her, that she could step along surely and steadily to success and take her dearly loved children with her, working for them with all her might, profoundly thankful to be able to give them what she had always so tragically and impotently wished them to have.

The wideness of this thought, the blackness of the night, the unwonted prone passivity of her energetic body, all wrought upon her to a strange softness of mood. She felt almost like a girl again . . . dreaming.

And that made her think of Lester. He had been in her mind more than usual of late, as she had learned more about the lives of the other women employed in the store. She was one of the older employees and almost at once the younger women had leaned on her, turned to her with confidences, and asked her advice as the women of her church had always done. But these were rougher, rawer lives into which she now looked. That haggard-eyed Mrs. Hemp, in the kitchenware department, what a horrible picture she had drawn of her relations with her husband. "He's going with one of the girls in the collar-factory now, Mrs. Knapp. I wouldn't put up with it a minute if it weren't for the children. That man was unfaithful to me, Mrs. Knapp, six months after we were married, and my first baby on the way. And it's been a new girl for him ever since whenever he got tired of the old one." And Margaret Donahue, she that read novels on the sly, but never would look at a man, what had she said? "They make me sick," she declared briefly with an expression on her young face which Mrs. Knapp would have given a good deal not to have seen. "I'd no more let a man come near me than a toad. I've seen too much of what Papa does to Mama."

And the woman who scrubbed the floors, that evening she had come to beg Mrs. Knapp to let her sleep at the store, under a counter, in the toilet-room, anywhere, so she would not have to go home. "You're a married woman yourself, Mrs. Knapp," she had said. "You know what men are like. Judd is in one of his crazy spells! I'm afraid to go home till he gets over it. Honest I am, Mrs. Knapp. Let me stay here! I don't care where! I'll sit up all night in a chair if you'll only let me stay."

Eva had brought her home and let her sleep on a mattress on the floor in her own room. She had felt an immense horrified pity for her; but she had hated her for that phrase, "You are a married woman, Mrs. Knapp. You know what men are like!" Did she think for a minute that Lester Knapp was that kind of a brute! Couldn't she see by *looking* at him that he was a million times too fine to . . . she hated the woman again to-night as she thought of it, and the thought brought up before her all that Lester had been to her.

No woman could have better reason than she to trust the delicacy, the warm loving-heartedness, the self-control, the innate decency of a man. They had been married for fourteen years, and from the sweet, sweet early days of their young honeymoon when, ignorant and innocent both of them, they had stumbled their way towards each other, she had never known a single instant of this poisonous atmosphere of suspicion and hate and endured violence which these other women apparently took for granted as the inevitable relationship of husband and wife. How good Lester had been to her! She had not appreciated it. She had not really thought of it. It had never occurred to her that he might be anything else.

And how good to the children! Never an impatient word, like most men. He was the best father in the world. Not another man she knew could have endured it to be so shut up with the children. How faithfully he had tried to take her place, now that she could not be in her rightful position with them. What lovely memories the children would have of their father, always! Was it possible he was of the same flesh and blood as Ellen O'Hern's father who never, so Ellen said, passed one of his children without aiming a blow at it.

The overflowing of this affection for Lester which had been slowly rising for weeks; her deep thankfulness for what she would be able to do for the children . . . she found herself trembling in her bed. She felt an impulsive longing to share her emotion with Lester, to put her arms about his neck and let him know that she did not take his loyalty, his gentleness, his faithfulness, his fineness, so coldly for granted as she had seemed. She had been so unhappy about their hideous poverty. That was all. It was abominable to be poor! It brought out the worst in every one. When you were distracted with worry about money, you simply weren't yourself.

Warm and flushed, she sprang out of bed, lighted a candle and went softly downstairs in her slippered feet. Neither Lester nor Stephen woke as she went into the room, and she stood for an instant gazing down at them. Stephen was beautiful and strong, sleeping with both rounded arms flung up over his head. Lester was looking almost like a boy in the abandon of his sleep, like the fine, true-hearted, sensitive boy to whom she had given herself as a girl.

But that boy had been vibrant with life from his head to his heels. And now half of his body lay dead. From the first it had been appalling to Evangeline to see that helpless, frozen immobility. How splendidly he had endured it, without a complaint! But she had seen from his eagerness to-night, as they talked of the possibility of having a Ford, how imprisoned he had felt, how wild with pleasure it made him to think he would be able to get out of these four walls. She would never have been as patient as he! If she had been condemned to that death-in-life of half her body, not able even to turn over in bed without waking up to a nightmare of struggle, her legs like so much stone . . .

Had she made a sound? Had the light of the candle disturbed him a little?

Without waking, Lester drew a long breath, turned over easily in bed, drew up his knees with a natural, flexible motion, threw his arm out over the covers, and dropped off to profound sleep once more.

Everybody at the store was sure, the next day,

that Mrs. Knapp was coming down with some serious malady. She was not only extremely pale and shaken by shivers that ran all over her. It was worse. She had a look of death-like sickness that frightened the girls in her department. They sent for Mr. Willing to come.

When he did, he gave one look at Mrs. Knapp's pinched face and stooped shoulders and ordered her home at once. "You're coming down with the flu, Mrs. Knapp. Everybody's having it. Now it doesn't amount to anything this year if you take it quick. But it's foolishness to try to keep on your feet. You get right home, take some quinine and some aspirin, and give yourself a sweat. You'll be all right. But don't wait a minute."

Without a word, Mrs. Knapp put on her wraps and went out of the store. She did not turn homeward. She dared not go home and face Lester and the children till she had wrestled with those awful questions and had either answered them or been killed by them.

Where could she go to be alone? She decided that she would walk straight ahead of her out into the country. No, that would not do. Everybody knew her. They would comment on it. They would ask her questions. She felt that she would burst into shrieks if any one asked her a question just then.

As she hesitated, she saw over the roofs of the houses the spire of St. Peter's pointing upward, and with a rush her heart turned towards the quiet and solitude of the church. Thank Heaven, it was always kept open.

She hurried down a side-street and, pushing open the heavy door, stumbled forward into the hushed, dusky, empty building. She felt her way to the nearest pew, knelt down and folded her hands as if to pray. She tried with all her might to pray. But could not.

The raging unrest and turmoil in her heart rose up in clashing waves and filled the church with its clamor. It was in vain that she tried to combat it with odds and ends of prayers which came into her mind with the contact of the pew, with the familiar atmosphere of church.

"Almighty and most merciful Father . . ."

Lester was better!

"Oh, God, who art the author of peace and lover of concord, in . . ."

Lester would get well . . . would get well!

"God be merciful to us and bless us and show us the . . ."

And then . . . And then . . .

"No! No! No!" she cried out aloud, passionately, and pressed her trembling hands over her mouth, frightened.

She was a wicked woman. God be merciful to me, a sinner. She had no heart. She did not want her husband to get well. She did not want to go home and live with her children.

But she must. She must! There was no other way. Like a person shut up suddenly in an airless prison, she ran frantically from one locked door to another, beating her hands on them, finding them sullenly strong, not even shaken on their cruel steel hinges as she flung herself against them. If Lester got well, of course he could not stay at home and keep house and take care of the children . . . no able-bodied man ever did that. What would people say? It was out of the question. People would laugh at Lester. They would laugh at her. They would not admire her any more. What would people say if she did not go back at once to the children? She who had always been so devoted to them, she whom people pitied now because she was forced to be separated from them. Every one had heard her say how hard it was for a mother to be separated from her . . .

For one instant, an instant she never forgot, Evangeline knew for the first, the only time in her life, a gust of cold, deadly contempt for herself. It nearly killed her, she who had tried so hard all her life to keep her self-respect, she who had been willing to pay any price so that in her own eyes she might be always in the right. Yes, it nearly killed her.

But it did not reconcile her to the inevitable nor bow her spirit in resignation. Never before had she been asked to pay any such price as this.

She couldn't! She couldn't! She stood stock-still in her prison cell and wrung her hands in revolt. She simply could not. After having known some-thing else, she could not go back to the narrow, sordid round of struggle with intolerable ever-renewed drudgery, to the daily, hourly contact with the children's forgetfulness, carelessness, foolishness . . . to Stephen's horrible tempers . . . with no outlet . . . no future . . . poverty for them all, always.

Poverty! It came down suffocatingly over her head like a smothering blanket thrown and twisted hard by an assailant who had sprung upon her out of the dark. She had thought herself safe from that long, slow starvation. To go back to it, to the raging, helpless narrowness of an income tragically too small, to rise up and lie down with that leaden care, to drag it about all day like a ball and chain . . . she could never endure it now that she knew that it was not in the least inevitable, knew how easy it was to avoid it, knew that if Lester were only willing to care a little more, to try a little harder, to put his mind on it really and truly, to *give his heart to it* as she did. . . .

All her old burning impatience with Lester was there, boiling up in clouds from the cauldron of her heart.

Through those turbid clouds she had a glimpse of a woman, touched and moved, standing by a man's bedside and blessing him silently for his faithfulness, his gentleness, his fineness . . . but those figures were far away, flat and unreal, like something in a made-up picture. They were but an added irritation. She hated the thought of them as a creature in flames would hate the recollection of a running brook.

Poverty . . . isolation, monotony, stagnation, killing depression over never-ending servile tasks . . . *poverty!*

There was no way out. She knew that now. But she could not endure it. She never could endure it again. She would hate Lester. She would kill herself and the children.

She had sunk lower and lower till now she was crouching in a heap, panting, her bent arms over her face as if beaten down by relentless blows which she could no longer even try to parry.

What could she do? Her native energy rose up blindly, staggering, like a courageous fighter who has been knocked out but does not know it. What could she *do?* With a terrible effort, she strove to rise to a higher level than this mere brute suffering.

She tried—yes, she really tried for a moment to think what was the right thing to do. She tried again to pray, to ask God to show her what was the right thing for a good woman to do—but she could not pray.

"Grant, O Lord, I beseech thee . . . pour into our hearts such . . ." No, she could not pray. She could not command her mind to any such coherence as prayer. Whirling snatches of the thoughts which had filled her mind incessantly since the night before were blown across her attention like birds driven before a tornado—"The place for a mother is with her children—" How many times she had heard that—and said it. She was a bad woman to rebel so against it. And it would do her no good to rebel. What else could she do? Around and around the cell she tore, beating her hands on those locked doors. Some one had to stay and keep house and take care of the children and make the home. And if Lester were cured he couldn't. No able-bodied man could do such work, of course. Nobody ever heard of such a thing. Men had to make the living. What would people say? They would laugh. They would make fun of the children. And of Lester. And of her. They would think of course she ought to want to do it. Every one had heard her say how hard it was for a . . . And they couldn't go away to another city, somewhere else,

where no one knew them. Her one chance was here, here!

But all at once with a final roar the tumult swept off and went beating its way into the distance, out of the church and her heart. There was a dead, blank silence about her, through which there came to her a clear, neat, compact thought, "But perhaps Lester will not get well. Perhaps he will not get well."

A deep bodeful hush filled her heart. It was as though she had suddenly gone deaf to all the noises of the world, to everything but that one possibility. She was straighter now, no longer crouched and panting. She was on her knees, her hands clasped, her head decently bent, in the familiar attitude of Sunday morning.

At last she was praying.

A moment later she was running out of the church as though a phantom had risen beside her and laid a skeleton hand on her shoulder . . . she had not been praying that Lester . . . no, it was not *possible* that she had been praying that her husband would not get well!

But soon she walked more quietly, more at her usual pace. After all she had nothing to go on, nothing to be sure of, nothing really to make her think it very likely that Lester would . . .

Chapter 21

ONE of the interests of life for Lester was the uncertainty about who was to be his mental companion for any given day. It seemed to be something over which he had no control. Sometimes he had thought it might be the weather which settled the matter. Not infrequently his first early-morning look at the world told him with which great spirit he was to live that day. A clear, breezy, bird-twittering dawn after rain meant Christina Rossetti's child-poems. A soft gray down-pour of warm rain, varnishing the grass to brilliance and beating down on the earth with a roll of muted drum-notes, always brought Hardy to his mind. Golden sun spilled in floods over the new green of the quivering young leaves meant Shelley. And Browning was for days when the sun rose rich and many-colored out of confused masses of turbid clouds.

But it was not always the weather. Sometimes as he opened his eyes, his chosen comrade for the day was there beside him before he had taken in anything more of the visible world than the white vacancy of the ceiling with those familiar blemishes, which were by this time a part of his brain. He did not always welcome the companion of the day, especially when the unseen spirit but repeated and intensified the color of his own temperament, from which he was so glad to escape by following the trumpets and fanfare of a temperament more brightly, more vividly alive. But he had found it was of little use to try to alter the day's destiny. He could indeed, easily enough, bring to mind mechanically many others of the blessed company of articulate human beings who sang for him what he could never say for himself; but he could hear, really hear in his deep heart's core, nothing but the appointed voice.

So he resigned himself to a brooding, astringent day when he woke up one morning and even before he opened his eyes, heard,

"But 'falling, falling, falling' there's your song,
The cradle song that sings you to the grave."

That was no longer meant for him, Lester reflected, as he struggled with the fatiguing, humiliating problem of getting himself dressed without help. He had spent years in falling, falling, falling,—and, tiring of it, had fallen once for all,—fallen all anybody could fall, so completely that there was no more to say about it. That job was done.

With a straining pull on his arms, he managed to swing and claw himself into his wheel chair, and sat quiet for a moment to get his breath. Whoever would think that dead human legs could be so infernally hard to get from one place to another! They seemed to weigh more than all the rest of his body put together, he thought, as he lifted one with both hands and changed it to an easier position.

He sat panting, losing for an instant his firmly held self-control, succumbing to what was always near the surface, a shamed horror of his mutilated, strengthless body. It came upon him that day with such poisonous violence that he was alarmed and aroused himself to resist.

"The thing to remember," he told himself sternly and contemptuously, "is that it concerns only me, and what concerns me is not of the slightest importance. I'm done for, was really done for, long ago. Nothing that can happen to me matters now." He heard as if it were a wistful voice saying,

"But neither parted roads, nor cent per cent
　May starve quite out the child that lives in us,
　The Child that is the Man, the Mystery."

And he replied bitterly to this, "That's all you know about it! Cent per cent can starve it dead, dead! It turned the trick for me, all right."

"Well, no funeral orations over it anyhow," he

told himself. "If it got starved, that's a sign it deserved to starve, that it didn't have the necessary pep to hustle around and get its food.

"All that can be annihilated must be annihilated
That the children of Jerusalem may be saved from
slavery."

But he knew that he did not really believe this clean, trenchant ruthlessness, and cursed himself out for the sniveling sentimentality which he could not kill.

Then Stephen turned over and opened his eyes. Why, there was Father up and dressed already! He scrambled hastily to his knees, "You didn't lace your shoes, did you?" he cried roughly and threateningly. That was a service to Father which he had taken for his very own. He would have killed Henry or Helen if they had dared to do it.

"No, old man, I didn't lace my shoes," said Father, smiling at him, "for the very good reason that I can't. I couldn't get along without the services of my valet."

Stephen looked relieved, slid out of bed, sat down on the floor and began to pull the laces up. Once he looked up at his father and smiled. He loved to do this for Father.

That evening was the second time in succession that Evangeline went to bed directly after supper. She said she was trying to stave off an attack of influenza with extra sleep and doses of quinine. Lester and the children did not play whist when Mother was not there, neither when she was tired and went to bed early nor when she stayed down in the store evenings, taking stock or working over newly arrived goods with Mr. and Mrs. Willing. Whist was connected with Mother, and although she often told them they need not lose the evenings when she could not be there, and would enjoy playing with dummy for a change, they never got out the cards unless she was with them.

Father usually read aloud to them on such evenings, and they wouldn't have missed that for anything. That evening he read a rhymed funny story about a farmer who got blown away from his barn one winter night, and, with his lantern waving, slid two miles down the mountain before he could stop himself. This was a great favorite of theirs and made them laugh harder every time they heard it.

> "Sometimes he came with arms outspread
> Like wings, revolving in the scene
> Upon his longer axis and
> With no small dignity of mein.

Faster or slower as he chanced,
Sitting or standing as he chose,
According as he feared to risk
His neck, or thought to spare his clothes."

And Helen liked the end, too, that Father always
brought out with a special accent, the way the
farmer didn't give up. As he started silently and
doggedly back the long way around, miles anu miles
in the cold, she walked along beside him, sharing
something of his quiet resistance to Fate. *That* was
the way to do when you'd slid all out of the way
you wanted to go!

Father read another one after that about a bon-
fire, which, although she did not quite understand
it all, always made Helen tremble with excitement.
Henry did not understand any of it and did not try
to. It never bothered him now when he did not
understand the poems Father read to Helen. He
just stopped listening and played with his puppy's
ear, and lost himself in the warm, soft heaviness of
the puppy's little sprawling body on his knees.
Sometimes he put his face lovingly down on the
little dog's head, his heart melting with tenderness.
He needed no poetry out of a book.

"It will have roared first and mixed sparks with stars,
And sweeping round it with a flaming sword,
Made the dim trees stand back in wider circles."

"Oh," cried Helen, loving the sound of the words as Henry loved his puppy, "isn't that just scrumptious!"

> "The breezes were so spent with winter blowing
> They seemed to fail the bluebirds under them
> Short of the perch their languid flight was towards;
> And my flame made a pinnacle to heaven."

"Oh, *Father*," said Helen, wriggling on her chair with delight, "isn't it too lovely!" And then, in a passion of longing, "Oh, I *wish* I could write like that!"

Something in the expression of her father's face struck her. She was only thirteen, but an older intuition from her coming womanhood made her say impulsively, with all her heart, "Father, you love it so . . . why don't *you* . . . didn't you ever try to write poetry, too?"

To her confusion, a slow, deep flush mounted all over her father's face. He looked down at the book in silence.

Helen was as horrified as if she had flung open the door of a secret sanctuary in a temple. She jumped up from the sofa, and not understanding her father, nor herself, nor what she was doing, *"Oh, Father, dear,"* she murmured, her arms around his neck.

Henry and his puppy looked up at them sleepily. "Is it bedtime?" asked Henry.

Helen went to sleep that night, still feeling the great hug Father had given her. She had never felt Father love her so much before.

Downstairs before he went to bed her father, turning over the pages of a book, was reading,

"And nothing to look backward to with pride,
    And nothing to look forward to with hope."

"Come, come!" he said to himself. "Terence, this is stupid stuff, you eat your victuals fast enough. We'll have to call this day one of our failures. I'd better get it over with and start another." His heart was still bleeding to the old wound he had thought healed and forgotten for years, which Helen's sudden question had torn open. Good Heavens, weren't you safe from those old buried griefs until you were actually under the sod?

And yet mingled with the old bitterness was a new sweetness, Helen's sympathy, Helen's understanding. It had never occurred to him before that children could give something as well as take all—the all he was so thankful to give them. Why, he thought wistfully, Helen might be the companion he had never had. He shook his head. No, that would not be fair to her. No dead-hand business! She must find her companions in her own generation. He must be ready to stand aside and let her pass on when the time came. That new sweetness was offered to him only that he might learn to make another renunciation.

He looked about him to see if there was anything to be done for the house before he went to bed. "Shall I close that window over there?" he thought to himself. "No, the night is warm. It will give us more air."

He wheeled himself to the closed door of the dining-room, opened it and perceived that the wind was blowing hard from the other direction, for a strong draught instantly sucked past him between the open window back of him and the open window at the head of Stephen's bed. He felt the gust and saw the long, light curtain curl eddying out towards him over the flicker of Stephen's bedside candle.

It caught in an instant. It flared up like gun-cotton, all over its surface. It came dropping down . . . horribly dropping down towards Stephen's unconscious, upturned face . . . flames on that tender flesh!

Stephen's father found himself standing by the bed, snatching the curtain to one side, crushing out the flames between his hands. His wheel chair still stood by the open door.

The draught between the two open windows now blew out the candle abruptly. In the darkness the door slammed shut with a loud report.

But the room was not dark to Lester. As actually as he had seen and felt the burst of flame from the curtain, he now felt himself flare up in physical ecstasy to be standing on his own feet, to know that he had taken a dozen steps, to know that he was no longer a half-man, a mutilated wreck from whom normal people averted their eyes in what they called pity but what was really contempt and disgust.

He was like a man who has been shut in a cage too low for him to stand, who has crouched and stooped and bowed his shoulders, and who suddenly is set free to rise to his full stature, to throw his arms up over his head. The relief from oppression was as rending as a pain. It was a thousand times more joyful than any joy he had ever known. His self, his ego, savagely, grimly, harshly beaten down as it had been, sprang up with an exultant yell.

The flame of its exultation flared up like gun-cotton, as the curtain had flared.

And died down as quickly, crushed and ground to blackness between giant hands that snatched it to one side as it dropped down towards Stephen's unconscious upturned face . . . flames on that tender flesh . . .

Lester knew nothing but that there was blackness within and without him. He was lying fully dressed across the foot of his bed. His face was buried in the bedclothes, but it was no blacker there than in the room . . . in his heart.

What made it so black? He did not know. He was beyond thought. He was nothing but wild, quivering apprehension, as he had been in the instant when, poised on the icy roof, he had turned to hurl himself down into the void. The terror of that instant was with him again. What fall was before him now?

He went a little insane as he lay there on the bed. He seemed to himself to be falling, as he had fallen so many times during his convalescence, endlessly, endlessly, in a dread that grew worse because now he knew what unutterable anguish awaited him. He shuddered, grasped the blanket and tore at it savagely, wondering madly what it was . . . what it was . . . what it was . . .

He came to himself with a great start that shook him, that shook the bed so that it rattled in the dark silent room.

He sat up and wiped his face that was dripping wet.

Now what? His mind was lucid. He was not falling, he was on his bed, in his room, with Stephen sleeping beside him in the darkness. And he knew now that he could get well.

Well, what was he to do, now that he knew he could get well?

He knew beforehand that there was nothing he could do. Life had once more cast him out from the organization of things.

Could he do any better than before his miserable, poorly done, detested work? Could he hate it any less? No, he would hate it a thousand times more now that he knew that it was not only a collaboration with materialism fatly triumphant, but that it kept him from his real work, vital, living, creative work, work he could do as no one else could, work that meant the salvation of his own children. Could he sit again sunk in that treacherous bog of slavery to possessions, doing his share of beckoning unsuspecting women into it . . . and all the time know that perhaps at that very minute Helen was repressing timidly some sweet shy impulse that would fester in her heart when it might have blossomed into fragrance in the sun? It would drive him mad to see again in Helen's eyes that old stupid, crushed expression of self-distrustful discouragement which he had always thought was the natural expression of her nature.

He thought of Henry, leaping and running with his dog, both of them casting off sparkling rays of youth as they capered. He thought of Henry ghastly white, shrunken, emptied of vitality, as he lay on the bed that last evening of the old life, in the condition which they had all thought was the inevitable one for Henry.

And Eva . . . He gave a deep groan as he thought of Eva—Eva who loved the work he hated, who took it all simple-heartedly at the solemnly preposterous value that the world put on it—to shut that strong-flying falcon into the barnyard again, to watch her rage, and droop, and tear at her own heart and at the children's!

Solemnly, out of the darkness, as though it had been Stephen's voice reciting "The Little Boy Lost" to him, he heard,

> "Father, father, where are you going?
>   Oh, do not walk so fast.
> Speak, father, speak to your little boy
>   Or else I shall be lost."

And there was Stephen . . .

Lester had no words for what the name meant to him now—nothing but a great aching sorrow into which he sank helplessly, letting its black waves close over his head.

Presently he struggled up to the air again and looked about him. There must be some way of escape. Anybody but a weakling would invent some way to save them all. He must leave nothing unthought of, he must start methodically to make the rounds of the possibilities. He must not lose his head in this hysterical way. He must be a man and master circumstances.

Would it be possible for both of them to work, he and Eva? Other parents did sometimes. The idea was that with the extra money you made you hired somebody to take care of the children. If before his accident any one had dreamed of Eva's natural gift for business, he would have thought the plan an excellent one. But it was only since his accident that he had had the faintest conception of what "caring for the children" might mean. Now, now that he had lived with the children, now that he had seen how it took all of his attention to make even a beginning of understanding them, how it took all of his intelligence and love to try to give them what they needed, spiritually and mentally . . . no!

You could perhaps, if you were very lucky—though it was unlikely in the extreme—it was conceivable that by paying a high cash price you might be able to hire a little intelligence, enough intelligence to give them good material care. But you could never hire intelligence sharpened by love. In other words you could not hire a parent. And children without parents were orphans.

Whom could they hire? What kind of a person would it be? He tried to think concretely of the possibilities. Why—he gave a sick, horrified laugh —why, very likely some nice old grandmotherly soul like Mrs. Anderson who, so everybody would say, would be just the right person, because she had had so much experience with children. He clenched his hands in a murderous animal-fury at the thought of Stephen's proud, strong, vital spirit left helpless to the vicious, vindictive meanness of a Mrs. Anderson. And from the outside, coming in late in the afternoon with no first-hand information about what happened during the day, how could he and Eva ever know a Mrs. Anderson from any one else?

Well, perhaps not a Mrs. Anderson. Let him think of the very best that might conceivably be possible. Perhaps a good-natured, young house-worker who would be kind to the children, indulgent, gentle. He thought of the long hours during which he bent his utmost attention on the children to understand them, to see what kind of children they were, to think what they needed most now—not little passing pleasures such as good nature and indulgence would suggest, but real food for what was deepest in them. He thought of how he used his

close hourly contact with them as a means of looking into their minds and hearts; how he used the
work-in-common with them as a scientist conducts
an experiment station to accumulate data as material
for his intelligence to arrange in order, so that his
decisions might be just and far-sighted as well as
loving. He thought how in the blessed mental leisure
which comes with small mechanical tasks he pored
over this data, considered it and reconsidered in
the light of some newer evidence—where was now a
good-natured young hired girl, let her be ever so indulgent and gentle? "You can't *hire* somebody to
be a parent for your children!" he thought again,
passionately. They are born into the world asking
you for bread. If you give them a stone, it were
better for you that that stone were hanged about
your neck and cast into the sea.

Eva had no bread to give them—he saw that in
this Day-of-Judgment hour, and no longer pretended
that he did not. Eva had passionate love and devotion to give them, but neither patience nor understanding. There was no sacrifice in the world which
she would not joyfully make for her children except
to live with them. They had tried that for fourteen
dreadful years and knew what it brought them.
That complacent unquestioned generalization, "The
mother is the natural home-maker"; what a jugger-
naut it had been in their case! How poor Eva,

drugged by the cries of its devotees, had cast herself down under its grinding wheels—and had dragged the children in under with her. It wasn't because Eva had not tried her best. She had nearly killed herself trying. But she had been like a gifted mathematician set to paint a picture.

And he did have bread for them. He did not pretend he had not. He had found that he was in possession of miraculous loaves which grew larger as he dealt them out. For the first time since his untried youth Lester knew a moment of pride in himself, of satisfaction with something he had done. He thought of Henry, normal, sound, growing as a vigorous young sapling grows. He thought of Helen opening into perfumed blossom like a young fruit tree promising a rich harvest; of Stephen, growing as a strong man grows, purposeful, energetic, rejoicing in his strength, and loving, yes, loving. How good Stephen was to him! That melting upward look of protecting devotion when he had laced up his shoes that morning!

> "Father, father, where are you going?
> Oh, do not walk so fast!"

Well, there was the simple, obvious possibility, the natural, right human thing to do . . . he could continue to stay at home and make the home, since a home-maker was needed.

He knew this was impossible. The instant he tried to consider it, he knew it was as impossible as to roll away a mountain from his path with his bare hands. He knew that from the beginning of time everything had been arranged to make that impossible. Every unit in the whole of society would join in making it impossible, from the Ladies' Guild to the children in the public schools. It would be easier for him to commit murder or rob a bank than to give his intelligence where it was most needed, in his own home with his children.

"What is your husband's business, Mrs. Knapp?"

"He hasn't any. He stays at home and keeps house."

"Oh . . ."

He heard that "Oh!" reverberating infernally down every road he tried.

"My Papa is an insurance agent. What does your Papa do for a living, Helen?"

"He doesn't do anything. Mother makes the living. Father stays home with us children."

"Oh, is he sick?"

"No, he's not sick."

"Oh . . ."

He saw Helen, sensitive, defenseless Helen cringing before that gigantic "oh." He knew that soon Henry with his normal reactions would learn to see that "oh" coming, to hide from it, to avoid his playmates because of it. There was no sense to that "oh"; there had been no sense for generations and generations. It was an exclamation that dated from the cave-age, but it still had power to warp the children's lives as much as—yes, almost as much as leaving them to a Mrs. Anderson. They would be ashamed of him. He would lose his influence over them. He would be of no use to them.

Over his head Tradition swung a bludgeon he knew he could not parry. He had always guessed at the presence of that Tradition ruling the world, guessed that it hated him, guessed at its real name. He saw it plain now, grinning sardonically high above all the little chattering pretenses of idealism. He knew now what it decreed: that men are in the world to get possessions, to create material things, to sell them, to buy them, to transport them, above all to stimulate to fever-heat the desire for them in all human beings. It decreed that men are of worth in so far as they achieve that sort of material success, and worthless if they do not.

That was the real meaning of the unctuous talk of "service" in the commercial text-books which Eva read so whole-heartedly. They were intended to fix the human attention altogether on the importance of material things; to make women feel that the difference between linen and cotton is of more importance to them than the fine, difficultly drawn, always-varying line between warm human love and lust; to make men feel that more possessions would enlarge their lives . . . blasphemy! Blasphemy!

He read as little as possible of the trade-journals which Eva left lying around the house, but the other day in kindling a fire with one his eye had been caught by a passage the phrases of which had fixed themselves in that sensitive verbal memory of his and were not to be dislodged:—"Morally, esthetically, emotionally *and* commercially, America is helped, uplifted, advanced by the efforts of you and me to induce individual Americans first to want and then to acquire more of the finer things of life. Take fine jewelry. It makes the purchaser a better person by its appeal to the emotional and esthetic side of his or her nature. . . . Desire for the rich and tasteful adornments obtainable at the jewelry store expresses itself in stronger attempts to acquire the means to purchase. This means advancement for America! Should you not, bearing this wonderful thought in mind, be enthused to broaden your contact with the buying public by increasing your distributing . . . " They wrote that sort of thing by the yard, by the mile! And they were right. That was the real business of life, of course. He had always known it. That was why men who did other things, teachers, or poets, or musicians, or ministers, were so heartily despised by normal people. And as for any man who might try to be a parent . . .

Why, the fanatic feminists were right, after all. Under its greasy camouflage of chivalry, society is really based on a contempt for women's work in the home. The only women who were paid, either in human respect or in money, were women who gave up their traditional job of creating harmony out of human relationships and did something really useful, bought or sold or created material objects. As for any *man's* giving his personality to the woman's work of trying to draw out of children the best there might be in them . . . fiddling foolishness! Leave it to the squaws! He was sure that he was the only man who had ever conceived even the possibility of such a lapse from virile self-respect as to do what all women are supposed to do. He knew well enough that other men would feel for such a conception on his part a stupefaction only equaled by their red-blooded scorn.

At this he caught a passing glimpse far below the surface. He knew that it was not only scorn he would arouse, but suspicion and alarm. For an instant he understood why Tradition was so intolerant of the slightest infraction of the respect due to it, why it was ready to tear him and all his into a thousand pieces rather than permit even one variation from its standard. It was because the variation he had conceived ran counter to the prestige of sacred possessions. Not only was it beneath the dignity of any able-bodied brave to try to show young human beings how to create rich, deep, happy lives without great material possessions, but it was subversive of the whole-hearted worship due to possessions. It was heresy. It must be stopped at all costs. Lester heard the threatening snarl of that unsuspected, unquestioned Tradition, amazed that any one dared so much as to conceive of an attack on it. And he knew that he was not man enough to stand up and resist the bludgeon and the snarl.

He had thought he had experienced all the possible ways in which a man can feel contempt for himself. But there was another depth before him. For—he might as well have the poor merit of being honest about it, and not hide behind Eva and the children—he knew that he could stand that "oh . . ." as little as they, that he would turn feebly sour and bitter under it, as he had before, and blame other people for what was his own lack of endurance.

Let him try to imagine it for an instant—a definite instance. If he were once more an able-bodied man what would he feel to have Harvey Bronson drop in and find him making a bed while Eva sold goods?

Good God! Was he such a miserable cur as to let the thought of Harvey Bronson's sneer stand between him and doing what he knew was best for the children? There they stood, infinitely precious, hungering and thirsting for what he had to give them . . . defenseless but for him. Would he stand back and let the opinion of the Ladies' Guild . . .

Yes, he would.

That was the kind of miserable cur he was. And now he knew it. He wiped the sweat from his face and ground his teeth together to keep them from chattering.

They were chattering like those of a man cast adrift in a boat with only a broken paddle between him and the roaring leap of a cataract. The roaring was louder and louder in his ears as he felt himself helplessly drifting towards the drop. He had not been willing to look at it, had kept his eyes on the shores which he had tried so vainly to reach, struggling pitifully with his poor broken tool.

Now he gave up and, cowering in a heap, waited dumbly for the crashing downfall—he who had fallen so low, was he to fall again, lower still? He who had thought he had kept nothing at all for himself in life, must he give up now his one living treasure, his self-respect? Could it be that he was thinking—he, Lester Knapp!—of shamming a sickness he did not have, of trampling his honor deep into the filth of small, daily lies?

The thought carried him with a rush over the wicked gleaming curve at the edge of the abyss . . . he was falling . . . falling . . .

There was nothing but a formless horror of yelling whirlpools, which sucked him down . . .

Presently it was dawn. A faint gray showed at the windows. The blemishes on the ceiling came into view and stalked grimly to their accustomed stand in his brain. The night was over. Stephen lay sleeping peacefully, the harmless, blackened bits of the burned curtain scattered about his bed.

> "Father, father, where are you going?
> Oh, do not walk so fast.
> Speak, father, speak to . . ."

It was not fast he would be walking. Or at all.

A robin chirped sleepily in the maple. It would soon be day. Lester got up, shuffled over to his wheel chair and sat down in it.

After a time he stooped down and unlaced his shoes. Then he wheeled himself over beside Stephen's bed and waited for the day to come.

Chapter 22

D R. MERRITT had telephoned Mrs. Knapp
that he was going to make some very special
tests of her husband's condition that afternoon, tests
which might be conclusive as to the possibility of
recovery. He had chosen Sunday, he told her, because he wished her to be at home. He tried to
make his voice sound weighty and warning, and he
knew that he had succeeded when, on arriving at
the house, he found Mrs. Farnham there, with a
very sober face, twisting her handkerchief nervously
in her hands.

The two women looked at him in silent anxiety as
he came in. He asked with an impenetrable professional manner to have his patient's chair rolled
into the next room. "It is always better to make
those nerve-reflex tests in perfect quiet," he explained.

Mr. Knapp with no comment rolled his chair back
into the dining-room, and the doctor closed the door.

In a few moments, Helen, very pale, with frightened eyes, came in to join the waiting women. She
found them as pale as she, motionless in their chairs,
her mother's lips trembling. She sat down on a
stool beside Aunt Mattie, who patted her shoulder

and said something in a tremulous whisper which Helen did not catch. From the other room, from behind the closed door, came a low murmur of voices broken by long pauses. There was no other sound except Stephen's shout as he played with Henry's dog in the back yard.

More voices from behind the closed door, very low, very restrained, a mere breath which Helen could catch only by straining her ears. She could not even be sure whether it were the doctor or Father who was talking. Another long silence. Helen's heart pounded and pounded. She wished she could hide her face in Aunt Mattie's lap, but she could not move—not till she knew.

Had she heard the voices again? Yes. No. There was no sound from the next room.

Then, as though the doctor had been standing there all the time, his hand on the knob, the door suddenly opened.

Now that the time had come the doctor found it hard to get the words out. He could not think of any way to begin. The three waiting women looked at him, imploring him silently to end their suspense.

He cleared his throat, sat down, looked in his case for something which he did not find and shut the case with a click. As if this had been a signal, he then said hastily, in an expressionless voice, "Mrs. Knapp, I might as well be frank with you. I do

not think it best to go on with the treatment I have
been trying for your husband. I am convinced from
the result of the tests to-day . . . "

His fingers played nervously with his watch-chain.
"I am convinced, I say, that . . . that it would be
very unwise to continue making an attempt to cure
this local trouble. The nervous system of the human
body, you understand, is so closely interrelated that
when you touch one part you never know what . . .
The thing which we doctors must take into consideration is the total reaction on the patient. That is
the weak point with so many specialists. They consider only the immediate seat of the trouble and
not the sum-total of the effect on the patient. You
often hear them say of an operation that killed the
patient that it was a 'success.' And in the case of
spinal trouble like Mr. Knapp's, of course the
entire nervous system is . . . What I have said
applies of course very especially when it is a case
of . . ."

He saw from the strained, drawn expression on
Mrs. Farnham's face that she did not understand a
word he was saying, and brought out with desperate
bluntness, "The fact is that it would be a waste of
time for me to continue my weekly visits. I now
realize that it would be very dangerous for Mr.
Knapp ever to try to use his legs. Crutches perhaps, later. But he must never be allowed to make
the attempt to go without crutches. It might

be . . . " He drew a long breath and said it. "It might be fatal."

When he finished he looked very grim and disagreeable, and, opening his case once more, began to fumble among the little bottles in it. God! Why did any honest man ever take up the practice of medicine?

Back of him, through the open door, Lester Knapp could be seen in his wheel chair, his head fallen back on the head-rest, his long face white, a resolute expression of suffering in his eyes.

Mrs. Farnham began to cry softly into her handkerchief, her shoulders shaking, the sound of her muffled sobs loud in the hushed room.

Mrs. Knapp had turned very white at the doctor's first words and was silent a long time when he finished. Then she said rather faintly but with her usual firmness, "It is very hard of course for a . . . " She caught herself and began again, "It is very hard, of course, but we must all do the best we can."

Helen tiptoed softly into the kitchen and out on the back porch, closing the kitchen door behind her carefully. Then she took one jump from the porch to the walk and ran furiously out to the chicken-yard where Henry and Stephen were feeding the chickens.

At least Stephen was feeding the chickens. Henry was looking anxiously towards the house, and the moment he saw Helen come out, started back on a run to meet her. As he ran his shadowed face caught light from hers.

"It's all right!" she told him in a loud whisper, as they came together. "The doctor says that Father never can be cured, that he'll always have to go on crutches."

"Oh, *Helen!*" said Henry, catching desperately at her arm. "Are you sure? Are you sure?"

His mouth began to work nervously, and he crooked his arm over his face to hide it.

"What's the matter of you?" asked Stephen, running up alarmed. Helen got down on her knees and put her arm around the little boy. Her voice was trembling as she said, "Stevie, dear, Father's going to stay right with us. He's never going to go away."

Stephen looked at her appalled. His rosy face paled to white. "Was he going to go *away* from us?" he asked, horrified.

"Why, of course, he'd have to, to work, if the doctor could cure him. But the doctor says he can't. He says Father never will . . ."

Stephen had been glaring into her face to make sure he understood. He now pushed her from him roughly and ran at top speed towards the house.

He bounded up on the porch, he burst open the door, the house was filled with the clamor of his passionate, questing call of "Father! *Fa-a-ather!*"